THE BILLIONAIRE'S BEST FRIEND

ELIZABETH MADDREY

1

AUSTIN

"Looking tan, Mr. Campbell."

I waved at Stephen as he hurried past me in the crowded hallway. The first day back to school after Christmas—oh, wait, *winter*—break was always a little extra chaotic. The kids weren't excited to be back. To be honest, neither was I.

"Regretting your life choices?"

I didn't have to turn to know it was Kayla. I laughed and held my index finger and thumb about an inch apart. "Maybe this much."

"You're getting spoiled."

Now I did turn. I shook my head. "I'm not the one who bummed a ride to the Caymans."

"Hey. I didn't say I wasn't also spoiled. I can own that. Happily." She let out a hefty sigh. "I'd kill to be back there with my toes in the sand. The only sounds the lapping waves and a muscular, shirtless waiter asking me if I needed anything."

"I don't seem to recall you doing a whole lot of that when we were there." I forced myself not to dwell on the waiter fantasy. She was a grownup and could paint whatever mental pictures she wanted. It wasn't like I wanted her to fantasize about me. "Weren't you the one determined to make sure we learned how to paddle board?"

"You had fun. Admit it."

I held up my hands. "No question. I'm already thinking we need to make another group trip back at spring break. This time without a detour to Kansas on the way home for a friend's wedding."

Kayla brightened. "Wasn't that the best ever?"

I shrugged. Weddings weren't really my thing. I was a firm believer in the institution of marriage, but I'd never understood the need to get all fancy and then have a party. Not that Scott and Whitney had gone overboard. No, the living room ceremony and lunch at a local restaurant had been good. Nice, even.

"Oh, come on." Kayla punched my arm. "It was romantic and perfect. The two of them are perfect for one another. And Beckett was the cutest ever in his little suit. They're going to make a great family."

"That's true." I was glad my friend had found love. Maybe I was a little jealous, but I was working on it. I certainly didn't envy him having a child dropped in his lap in order to get there. "It definitely all worked out. Are you in for another trip to the Caymans at spring break?"

Kayla's eyebrows lifted. "You're serious? You don't want to go somewhere new?"

"I don't know. I guess we could, but it's a week, you know? I'm already thinking about this summer. Maybe taking a month and hitting up the train in Europe." If I did, it would be the first summer I hadn't taught summer school since becoming a math teacher. The change in plans might not go over so well with my principal. But she'd get over it. Probably.

"No summer school?"

I shook my head.

"Wow." She looked like she was going to say more, but the warning bell rang. "Hold that thought. See you at lunch?"

"You know it." I grinned. Because this year, we actually had lunch and our planning period at the same time, we tended to choose a classroom and hang together for those times. "I'll come to you."

"Works. Later." Kayla hurried down the hall toward the computer lab, and I turned and walked to my classroom door.

A handful of students were already at their desks, chattering with one another. More poured through the door after me, racing to get to their seats before the bell rang. Three stragglers made it in just as I was starting to close the door.

"Skin of your teeth, boys."

"Sorry, Mr. Campbell." Knox ducked his head and aimed for a desk at the back of the room.

I shook my head and went to the front of the class. "Welcome back, everyone. Let's do some algebra!"

Groans greeted my statement and I laughed. "It's not as bad as that, is it? First class after Christmas break, and we're going to spend time solving for X. This is the life, I'm telling you."

I didn't miss the eyerolls or the additional groans, but I grabbed a marker off my desk, uncapped it, and strode to the whiteboard anyway. "We're in chapter fourteen. You'll have some practice exercises to do tonight, and you never know what Friday holds. Maybe a pop quiz?"

The morning passed quickly. My first two classes were algebra one. Most were freshmen, but I had a couple of sophomores who were taking it again. That meant they couldn't get the advanced diploma, but very few of them cared. I had my sole geometry class for third period—I hated that one almost as much as my students. I'd never understood the need for formal proofs or what benefit they added to adult life.

Algebra? I could point that out in life without blinking.

Geometry was harder once you got past the basics. Fourth period was algebra two with trigonometry. And then, finally, lunch.

I was ready to sit down after a quick trip to the bathroom.

With my insulated lunch bag in hand, I knocked on the frame of Kayla's lab door. "Ready?"

Kayla glanced up from where she leaned over a monitor, helping one of our shared students. "One sec. You can go ahead into my office. I'll be right there."

I fought a sigh. She said that, but I knew from past experience she wasn't one to walk away from a student who needed—or wanted—help. It was even odds for her actually joining me and getting something to eat.

I strolled past the rows of computers to the tiny office at the front of the room. It had the benefit of a door, but the prospect of privacy was thwarted by the enormous window looking into the classroom.

It was more than I had, though, and it definitely beat the staff room.

I pulled a chair closer to her desk and unzipped my lunch bag to extract the container of salad I'd put together last night. New year, healthier me. Or something.

I stirred it to get the dressing from the bottom of the container mixed around on the greens, and stabbed a bite. Not bad. Not amazing, but it was better than PB&J for the nine millionth time.

I swiped my phone and opened a browser. I was finishing up a quick perusal of the stock market when Kayla bustled in.

"Sorry. Matt tries, but he isn't an intuitive programmer. He's constantly forgetting to declare his variables."

I nodded. I sort of knew what she was talking about. But I did know Matt. "He's doing well in calc. I could see him going into physics or chemistry. Maybe medicine?"

"I don't think he has the stomach for that. But the other two? That's a thought. I'll see if I can work it into a conversation. He's a junior, right?"

"Yeah."

"If he hasn't taken physics, he could do that next year. Get a taste of it." She sighed and flopped into the chair behind her desk, then bent over to pull open a drawer. She extracted a brown paper bag. She glanced over at my food. "That looks yummy."

"What did you bring?"

"Ham and cheese."

I looked at the hopeful expression on her face then down at my salad. I'd only managed a couple of bites. With a shrug, I pushed it across her desk. "We can trade."

"Seriously?" She beamed and tossed me the sandwich. "You're the best. I don't know why I never have fresh veggies in the fridge."

I snickered. "Maybe because you buy them in a fit of optimism and then forget about them?"

"There's that." She grinned and stabbed up a bite. "This is amazing."

I shook my head and took a bite of the sandwich. It was good. I didn't think either one qualified as amazing, but maybe food you didn't make tasted better. "Glad you like it."

"So. Spring break. I have an idea."

I raised my eyebrows.

"Obviously, you're not someone who reads the bulletin at church. But I do." She forked up more salad. "What if, instead of going to the Caymans again, we volunteered to chaperone the youth on their mission trip to Mexico?"

I put a finger in my ear and wiggled it around. "I'm sorry. I think my ear is broken. You did not just suggest we spend our week off from herding teenagers with other teenagers."

"Come on. It'll be fun."

Kayla's eyes were gleaming, and as much as I didn't want to do this—as much as I knew I was going to say no six hundred different ways—I also knew I was going to end up in Mexico during spring break.

Woo.

2

KAYLA

I dropped my backpack by the door, kicked off my shoes, and headed down the hall to my bedroom. It was past time to get out of my teacher clothes and into something comfier. Leggings and the sweatshirt I borrowed from Austin at the Homecoming football game sounded like just the ticket.

My cats were curled in their beds. Both looked up when I came into the room, but neither moved.

"Hi, Ada. Hi, Charles."

I detoured to their beds, squatted, and gave each of them a thorough rub. "Did you miss me at all?"

They responded with purrs and contented meows.

I straightened and headed to the closet. My apartment was of the budget variety, so it didn't run to walk-in closets or *en suite* bathrooms, but it met my needs. I hung my slacks on a hanger and sniffed my blouse. Wrinkling my nose, I tossed it into the hamper and made a mental note that laundry day needed to be sooner rather than later.

I snagged the sweatshirt off the top of a stack in the egg-crate tower that was my makeshift storage for thicker clothes that didn't fit in my secondhand dresser drawers. I tugged on the shirt and some leggings, and frowned at the cats. "You two are lazy today. Come on, let's get dinner. I have grading to do. Big surprise there, right, guys? But maybe there's something good on TV to keep us company."

I was a sucker for reality competitions. There was something so fun about watching people work hard to showcase their talents and abilities and maybe end up with a chance to live out their dream.

I understood how amazing it was to live a dream.

I was blessed that my dream was pretty simple. Teach computer science. Have good friends. The only thing missing was a husband and family, but I wasn't giving up on that. God had gotten me this far, I fully believed He was going to get me the rest of the way there.

Hopefully with Austin.

I sighed and reached for a can of cat food. "How about we live it up, guys? I'll splurge on the good stuff for you two and maybe go crazy and order myself a pizza."

Popping the top on the food elicited more excitement than coming home had. I wasn't going to take it personally. They were still sulking because I'd left them for the Caymans thing. It didn't matter that I knew Mrs. Peabody from down the hall had spoiled them rotten while I was gone. I'd still left and would have to be punished.

It was like a cat law or something.

I scooped a little dry food into each dish, then split the wet food between them and set the bowls down in their spots. "Enjoy, guys. I think I am ordering that pizza."

My budget would whine. I was trying so hard to stick to the plan that Austin had helped me lay out. If I was careful and strict with my spending, I could save up and, in another year— two at the outside—have enough scraped together for a down payment on a little house. Nothing new and shiny, but I didn't care about that. The little bungalows from the 1950s were adorable.

"One pizza isn't going to change anything," I muttered to myself as I opened the app for my favorite delivery place. "I can always not go out on Saturday night with everyone. That'll offset pizza tonight. Then the budget survives and everyone's happy. Right?"

I hovered my finger over the picture of my usual—a small, loaded deep dish. Ugh. I could cook. But now I wanted pizza. I added the pie to my order and checked out before I could change my mind again.

The cats had finished their food, so I picked up their bowls and set them in the sink. "The pizza won't be here for an hour. Might as well get started on the grading, don't you think?"

Ada meowed loudly. Charles was quieter. But since everyone seemed to be in agreement, I went and grabbed my backpack and set up my work area on the couch.

My phone rang. I frowned at the number. I didn't get a lot of spam calls, thankfully, but I also didn't get people I didn't know calling me. Should I just let it go to voicemail? What if it was about the pizza?

I answered. "Hello?"

"Hi." The man on the other end cleared his throat. "Um. Is this Kayla Jones?"

"That's me." I didn't hear any restaurant noise in the background, so probably not about the pizza. But I also didn't hear the call center murmur. So I'd give him a minute and see what happened.

"Oh, good. Hi. This is Luke Donnelly. From church?"

My eyebrows lifted. Why was the youth pastor calling me? "Hi, Luke. What can I do for you?"

He cleared his throat again. "I happened to see you looking at the display board for the spring break trip to Mexico. I was wondering if you were actually interested or just seeing what was what?"

"I'm not really the demographic." I couldn't help teasing. He sounded so adorably flustered.

"Ha. Right. Um. We need chaperones. I sort of figured that might be why you were looking? Like you might want to work with the youth? Help out?"

Did he ever talk in declarative sentences? "I've been thinking about it, actually. Yeah. I might have a line on a male chaperone for you, too, if I can talk my best friend into it."

"That'd be great. That's...great." He cleared his throat for a third time and I started to wonder if he was fighting a cold. "Maybe—do you think you'd want to get together after church for lunch or something, and I could talk to you about the trip?"

"It happens I like eating, so I'm not opposed. But don't you have an email or something that you send out to people who want to help?"

"Oh. Sure. I can do that, too. But I've actually been trying to figure out a way to get to know you for a couple of weeks. Unless you think that's weird and creepy. In which case, please forget I said anything."

I laughed. But even as I did, I had a mental flash of Austin. And then I remembered his comments at Scott and Whitney's wedding. I was his bestie. He didn't see me as a woman. He definitely didn't see me as someone with potential for more than friendship. Apparently, Luke did. Hanging out, wishing for Austin to clue in, wasn't getting me anywhere. So, what the heck.

"It's not creepy. It's flattering. Lunch works. I'll meet you in the foyer?"

"That sounds good. I have to stack chairs and stuff, so it might be fifteen, maybe twenty minutes after everything's finished."

"Why don't I find my way to the youth room? I've been known to stack chairs."

"You don't have to do that."

I smiled. "No. But I don't mind. And then you finish up faster."

"All right. Thanks. Um. Is there any particular kind of food you'd want to get? I sometimes swing by the diner across the street. It's pretty good."

Nope. No way. That was the diner Austin and the guys always went to. Megan, Whitney, and I had been going there a lot lately as well. "Have you been to La Casita?"

"No. It's Mexican? I love Mexican, but I've yet to find a good place."

Hadn't he been in town close to a year? "It is. It's a little mom-and-pop not too far from church. I can drive, if that makes it easier."

"Okay." He paused. "I guess I'll see you Sunday."

"I guess you will. Bye." I ended the call with a grin and scooped Charles into my arms. "What about that, Chuck? I might have a date. Or, I could be misreading things and he just really wants to make sure I'm willing to be a chaperone."

I frowned. That was possible, but seemed unlikely.

"Nah. I think it's a date." I gave him a brisk rub behind his ears and ignored the pang around my heart. Luke seemed nice enough. He got along well with the youth group kids. The handful of students who also went to our church seemed to like him. So why not?

It wasn't as if Austin was ever going to notice me as anything other than his BFF.

Ugh.

"It's fine. It's good, even. Right, guys?" The cats didn't answer me. They just turned their steady, knowing gazes in my direction.

If I couldn't convince them, how was I going to convince myself?

∽

I HADN'T MADE much progress by the time I hit lunch the next day. In fact, I'd been looking forward to seeing Austin more than usual. Was I just a glutton for punishment?

"Where are your students?" Austin strolled through the door to my office, plopped into a chair, and made himself at home. "You always have at least one hanging out to do extra work. Or get help."

I shrugged. It was true. And I'd had three ask for that very thing, but the low-grade headache brewing at the back of my skull had pushed me into saying I needed to close things down for my break. "Yeah, well. Not today."

Austin's eyebrows lifted. "You okay?"

Great. Now I was being snippy. I was never snippy. I knew everyone considered me overly enthusiastic—those were generally their exact words. I preferred peppy, under most circumstances. "I'm fine."

"You don't sound fine."

I grunted. "Am I not allowed to have a bad day?"

"Sure. It's just unusual. How can I help?"

I closed my eyes. It was exactly the right thing to say. And also exactly wrong. Because it made me love him more—like that was possible—and he was clueless. "I think I have a date after church, and I'm not sure that I should have said yes."

"A date?" He leaned in, eyes glinting with humor. "Do tell."

"Luke Donnelly."

"The youth pastor?"

I didn't think Austin could have sounded more astounded if I'd said Tom Holland. "Is that a problem?"

He frowned. "No. I mean, he doesn't seem like he'd be your type."

"Oh, yeah? What's my type?" This ought to be interesting.

Austin took his time digging into his insulated lunch bag. He finally pulled out a single-serve bag of chips and opened it before speaking. "Not Luke."

I laughed, but it ended as a sigh. I retrieved my lunch from my bottom desk drawer. "So, not a decent-looking guy who loves Jesus and kids enough to dedicate his life to serving both of them?"

"That's not...you're in a mood." Austin crunched a handful of chips. He washed them down with a swig from his water bottle. "If he's what you're looking for, then hey, who am I to stand in your way? It's just not obvious. To me, at least."

I wanted to push. I didn't think dating Luke was crazy. He and I appeared to have a lot in common on the surface. I didn't know him well enough—yet—to say whether or not there was more than that. But it also wasn't wrong to date someone and figure that out. "Obvious isn't always what it's cracked up to be."

"I guess." Austin crumpled up the chip bag. "I guess it's in the water. Scott's married. You're dating the youth pastor. Maybe you have an idea of who I can ask out?"

"You know Anita's desperate for you to date her." I shot him a sharp grin.

Austin shuddered. "You're mean today."

"What's wrong with Anita?" I tried to look innocent, but I couldn't stop laughing. The drama teacher was well suited for her job. She also tended to have five or six boyfriends at a time and took great delight in playing them against each other.

"Pretty sure she's not a believer. We could start there." Austin shook his head. "Other ideas?"

It took everything I had in me not to hit him over the head. Maybe I should have, but my mother's constant harping about women asking men out being unseemly had stuck. Yes, I knew we were in the twenty-first century and those rules didn't necessarily apply anymore. But still. There was a big part of me that wanted Austin to figure it out on his own. I wanted the guy I was with to be there because he wanted to, not because I'd asked about it.

Was that too much to ask?

"Not really, but I'll keep my eyes open. I guess it would help if I knew what you were looking for in a girlfriend." I shot him an innocent smile and batted my eyelashes at him.

"Ugh. Not that." He laughed and took his sandwich out of its baggie. "I don't need syrupy sweet and vapid. I want someone I can be friends with."

"Okay. And attractive?"

"Well, duh." He bit into the sandwich.

I started peeling my orange. "Maybe you should fill me in on exactly what that entails."

I listened as Austin bumbled through nebulous descriptions that could apply to just about any woman in the universe. Maybe it was good that he wasn't super picky, but it didn't help me understand why I couldn't fit the bill.

He wanted someone he could be friends with. Check.

Someone who loved math and nerdy things. Check.

Someone who didn't mind getting outside now and then to do semi-sporty things like hiking or swimming or scuba diving. Check, check, check.

Someone who enjoyed cooking.

Well, okay, no one was perfect.

I held up my hands. "Stop. I get the idea."

"Yeah? Know anyone?"

I let myself drown for a moment in his eyes before slowly shaking my head. "Sorry, no. You've described a cross between Wonder Woman and every single woman on the planet. Heck, I qualify for all but the last one. We both know I don't love to cook."

He snickered. "I guess I need to refine my thoughts better."

My smile was tight as I pretended that his words weren't a barb straight into my heart. "I guess you do."

3

AUSTIN

"Wait. What?" Megan came back into the kitchen, her hands planted on her hips. "Kayla has a date and she didn't call me?"

"Take it up with her. Although, she's second-guessing, so maybe that's why." I shrugged before turning my attention back to the soup I was stirring on the stove. It was my night to cook dinner, and as much as I appreciated that sharing a townhouse with my sister meant I had to cook half as often as I would otherwise, I still wished for someone who wanted to take over the task full time. I could hire a personal chef—money certainly wasn't an issue after the whole stock market thing Scott talked me, and the rest of our group, into. But it seemed so...*billionaire*. I didn't want that.

"I'm going to text her." Megan shot me a narrow-eyed glare. "Don't you talk her out of it. It's about time she started dating someone who appreciated her."

"Has she been dating someone who doesn't?" That was news to me. I frowned. I didn't like it. Kayla and I didn't have secrets from each other. We were BFFs. I told her literally everything. I thought she did the same.

"No." Megan's face shifted into a scowl. "Never mind."

"I don't—wait." Ugh. Megan had disappeared from the kitchen doorway. Probably to go text Kayla. Was I supposed to have kept my mouth shut about the date? Kayla hadn't said anything about that.

In fact, Kayla had been pretty short on details in general when it came to her date with Luke. I frowned and turned off the stove. The soup was ready. The grilled cheese sandwiches were warming in the oven. I'd made them first, because whenever I tried to cook things simultaneously, I burned something.

Megan was tired of burned food.

And she hadn't been excited about my plan for her to take over all the cooking.

"Dinner's ready!" My holler would reach wherever she'd wandered off to. That was one—of many—nice things about living in a townhouse in Old Town. Of course, this was an older one, so the walls were thinner. I should be a little more careful about yelling, but our neighbors had to be used to it by now. And the family on the left had a newborn, so it wasn't as if they had much room to complain when I got to hear all the nursery sounds at two a.m. And four. And six.

I ladled soup into two bowls and pulled out the sandwiches. They were still toasty. I sliced them in half diagonally and arranged them on a plate, before carrying the whole mess over to the kitchen table. I had to go back to get spoons and make myself a glass of seltzer water.

Where was Megan?

Whatever. She could let her food get cold if that's what she wanted. I folded my hands in my lap and bowed my head. Thanking God for the food was easy, but when I'd finished that, it still felt like there was more I needed to say. I just didn't know what that was. Was it Kayla?

I huffed out a quiet, "Amen," and dipped my spoon into the soup.

Megan strolled into the kitchen staring at the phone in her hand. She sat then looked up. "Did you pray?"

I nodded.

She bowed her head and prayed so fast it looked like she was nodding. "You're an idiot. You know that, right?"

"Seriously? You haven't even tasted it yet." I scowled and took another bite of soup. Sure, it wasn't the most amazing thing I'd ever made—I was reasonably sure I'd added too much water. Because of course I could mess up a can of condensed soup. "Maybe I should hire a personal chef. That's a thing, right?"

"Yes, Mr. Moneybags, that's a thing. I can get you a link after dinner." Megan chose a triangle of grilled cheese and dunked it into her soup. "But that's not what I was talking about. At all."

I set my spoon down and crossed my arms. "Okay. Then why? Why am I an idiot this time?"

"Seriously, Austin? Kayla. Has. A. Date."

"Okay?" I was the one who'd told Megan, so I really didn't understand what she was getting at. "I'm not going to help her choose an outfit. We might be best friends, but I draw the line at fashion and feminine hygiene."

"Oh my word. I can't even with you." Megan stood, grabbed a second sandwich triangle, and picked up her soup. "You're hopeless."

I watched my sister flounce out of the kitchen with her food, and sighed. I was never going to understand women.

I stared at the food on the table and my stomach twisted. I wanted a big, juicy hamburger and crisp fries. Not this home-body meal.

I took out my phone and frowned at it. After a moment, I opened the group text with the guys and tapped away. Maybe someone would meet me. Maybe they wouldn't. Either way, not hanging out here was exactly the right call.

I couldn't quite make myself leave everything a disaster, so I spent a few minutes putting away the food and stacking the dishes in the sink. I'd cooked, which made it Megan's turn to clean. So that was enough.

I didn't even tell her I was going out.

Yes, we usually did. But it wasn't a rule or anything. And since she couldn't even with me—I rolled my eyes; what a stupid phrase—then I didn't need to disturb her with my comings and goings.

It wasn't a long drive to the burger joint. Technically, it wasn't in Old Town, but it was close enough that it didn't lose the small-town vibe. The parking lot was practically deserted. Not surprising for a Tuesday, but I also wasn't going to complain about not having to fight for a table.

Since none of the guys had responded, I took a four-top and placed my order.

"Hey, man."

I looked up as Cody dropped into a seat across from me. "Hey."

"You order already?"

"Yeah. Haven't been here long, though." I slid my phone back into my pocket. "I would have waited if I'd known you were coming."

"Yeah, yeah." Cody grinned. "I'd say I'm going to try to do better about that but I also don't want to lie."

I chuckled. "I'm glad you came. How're things in the nonprofit world?"

"Pretty good. You remember Jackson?"

Did I? I'd been to one event that the Ballentine Corporation had put on and Cody had introduced me around, but unless someone sat in my class five days a week, I didn't learn names fast. "Maybe?"

"Jackson Trent. He's my direct boss. Doesn't matter. Anyway, he's talking about taking a sabbatical. I guess he and his wife have friends who are missionaries in Mexico and they might go down for two or three months to help out with a big building project." Cody shrugged. "So I might get to take his job on for the duration."

"Nice. Congrats." I gave him a high five. "Is that instead of or on top of your current workload?"

Cody winced. "On top of. So, yeah. I get it. Still. I'm psyched. Where's Megan?"

My eyebrows lifted. "At home, probably? Or maybe she went to the bookstore. Why?"

"No reason." Cody paused when the server brought me my drink and he placed his order. When the server left, he continued, "I guess I figured she'd be here. Don't you cook on Tuesdays?"

"Yeah. And I did. That's what she's eating. I decided I wasn't in the mood."

Cody studied me. "What's going on?"

"I don't even know. That's what's annoying. Kayla's going on a date with Luke Donnelly on Sunday after church."

"The youth pastor?"

"See? That was my response."

Cody frowned. "I don't see them together at all. She's perky and fun. And he's...well, okay, he's a youth pastor so he's kinda the same. Hm. Maybe it's not so wrong after all."

I clamped my teeth together to keep from objecting. Because it was *absolutely* wrong. I just couldn't explain why. "Anyway, I told Megan. She went off to text Kayla. Then when she came back, she's all angry at me because Kayla has a date."

"Huh."

The server came back with Cody's drink and assured us that the food would be up shortly.

"I didn't feel like hanging out in my house dodging glares, so I came here instead." I took a sip and leaned back in my chair. Hopefully, they weren't going to let my food get cold while they made Cody's. I didn't care if they wanted to hold it in the kitchen until his was ready, but I hoped they kept it hot. "Plus, I made soup and grilled cheese, and I wasn't feeling it."

"You know I only cook when I have to. I'm telling you, signing up for those meal boxes was the best thing I ever did."

"That's still cooking."

Cody waggled a hand from side to side. "I mean, I guess technically. But I don't have to think about it. I follow the directions and then bam, dinner. For like three nights because of leftovers."

I wrinkled my nose. I didn't love leftovers. Cody didn't seem to care, and more power to him, but I wasn't going to sign up for that. "I was kicking around the idea of a personal chef. They could do it in a way that I didn't have the same meal for three days running though, right?"

"Probably." Cody lifted a shoulder. "Ask when you shop around. Are you going to include Megan in that? Or is she on her own?"

"I'll see if she wants in. I don't mind covering it, but she gets snippy when I try to pay for things. I think she's miffed that she wasn't part of our experiment." I shook my head. I'd thought about inviting her to buy in, but I hadn't run it past the guys because I'd known she didn't really have the extra cash lying around. Her job as a social worker paid worse than mine teaching school.

"Is she still planning to transition to the bookstore full time?"

"Last I heard." I stared at Cody for a moment. "You keep asking about Megan. Is there something I should know?"

Cody's cheeks flamed red.

"Ooh. You've got the hots for my sister." I grinned and reached for my soda. "You should totally ask her out."

"I thought guys weren't supposed to be happy when their friend dated their sister."

"Nah, man. That's dumb. Why wouldn't I want a great guy for my sister? Unless there's something about you I don't know." I chuckled. Of the six of us, Cody was definitely the most likely to be an open book.

"Probably not." His smile looked a little queasy. "You really wouldn't mind?"

"Nope. I can't speak for Megan, mind you. I don't understand her. At all. In fact, if you do date her? Good luck." I elaborated for several minutes, until the server arrived with our plates on a tray. We thanked her, and she walked off after telling us to let her know if we needed anything.

"I don't know. Maybe it's better to leave well enough alone. Just be friends like you and Kayla." Cody cut his burger into two pieces and picked one up to take a bite. "Since we're putting it all on the table, would it be weird if I got my own place?"

I dunked a fry in the little metal cup of seasoned mayo that was the burger joint's claim to fame. "It's almost to the point that it's getting weird if you and Noah keep living together in a two bedroom, honestly."

Cody laughed and took a drink. "Right? It's been long enough since we got the money, it's finally starting to feel real. I don't see myself quitting Ballentine—they do good work and I'm proud to be part of it—but I might talk to Mr. Ballentine about not taking a salary anymore. It seems dumb for me to take home money that comes from donors and the foundation when I don't need it."

I liked that idea. If the school system could take my paltry salary and actually do something good with it—something that would directly benefit the students—I'd do the same. But knowing how the bloated bureaucracy in our district worked, they'd absorb it into overhead and give the superintendent another big end-of-year bonus.

"Problem is," Cody paused to take another big bite of his burger. "I don't want to leave Old Town. You guys are all here and the commute into Arlington isn't awful. So do I just get my own apartment in the same complex?"

"You could look at the condos where Tristan lives. Then you'd at least own your place instead of renting. But you wouldn't have to deal with the upkeep like you do in a town-house." I wiped my fingers on a napkin and reached for my phone. "Let's look and see what's available. You know Tristan would love having you in his building."

"Yeah. That's not a bad idea. You think I could convince Noah to move, too?"

I laughed. "Probably. Just do everyone a favor and get your own place."

"Yeah, yeah." Cody shook his head. "We're not tied at the hip, you know. It just worked out that way."

"Sure. I get it. And before all the money, it made sense. The two of you do okay, especially for working at a nonprofit, but if Grandma hadn't given Megan and me her townhouse, I probably would have been looking for a roommate myself." I navigated to the website for Tristan's waterfront condo community and tapped on the listings. "Ooh. The rooftop condo is open."

"No way." Cody gestured for my phone. I turned it around and slid it across the table. "Oh, man. That's nice. Do you think Tristan would care?"

"Ask him." I didn't think he would, but it was always better to ask. "Does Noah know you're considering this?"

Cody nodded. "Our lease is up for renewal at the end of February. We've both been talking about it. Is there another unit open?"

I focused on my food while Cody browsed the website on my phone. I'd made it through half of the burger when he pushed the phone back toward me.

"I'll show Noah when I get back home, then ask Tristan. Maybe I'll put it in the group chat and get everyone's opinion."

I shrugged. "I can't imagine anyone thinking it's a bad idea."

"Me either, but you never know. Someone might have a different perspective." Cody polished off the other half of his burger. "I'm glad you decided to eat out tonight."

"So am I." I grinned. If nothing else, it was much more productive to think about Cody and Noah getting places of their own than whatever was up with Megan. Or the fact that Kayla was going to date the youth pastor. I frowned.

"Luke, huh." Cody's eyes glinted with humor. "You want me to help you beat him up?"

"Kayla can date who she wants. She's a big girl." I stabbed a fry into the mayo then looked up and met Cody's gaze. "But yeah, if he hurts her? I might take you up on that."

4

KAYLA

I pulled open the door to Megan's bookstore, smiling as the bells jingled cheerily overhead.

"Be right with you." Megan's voice called from some-where amongst the bookshelves.

"It's just me." I shrugged out of my coat and wandered toward the cozy seating area. The store was desolate. That was how it was most Fridays. They'd get some walk-in traffic after the dinner hour when people on dates went for a stroll along King Street. Except that it was edging toward freezing out there and the sky was clouded over. The weather people were arguing about whether or not we'd get snow out of those clouds in the early morning hours.

"Hi." Megan, arms full of books, appeared from behind the row of shelves on the far side of the chairs. "Is it snowing yet?"

I laughed. "You know we won't get any."

"Hope springs." She grinned. "Anyway, never say never. Sometimes we get hammered."

She was right. Once every ten years or so we'd get "the storm of the century" and the whole metro area would shut down for a week. Or two.

"I'm not excited about them extending school into July, so let's keep the number of snow days down to whatever they budgeted for in the schedule, all right? I really need summer vacation this year."

"Uh-oh. What's wrong?" Megan slid the stack of books she carried onto the top of a half-height bookshelf and pointed to the chairs. "Sit and spill."

I sat. But I didn't know how to spill. Or what. "I don't know what's wrong with me."

Megan made a sympathetic noise. She started to speak when the bells jingled again.

I turned to look and couldn't stop a smile when I spotted Whitney. "I wasn't expecting you."

"Is that good or bad?" Whitney took off her coat and crossed the store to join us. She flopped into a chair with a dramatic sigh. "Gosh, I love sitting down."

I laughed. "Long day with Beckett?"

"Yeah. He was not having anything that was calm today. We walked. We ran. He rode his bike. We went to the park twice." Whitney shook her head. "Now he's Scott's problem. I got kicked out of the house for poker night."

"Austin mentioned that was on. You okay with it?" I studied Whitney. Marriage looked like it suited her to the ground.

"Yeah. It's fine." She waved a hand. "I'm just glad Beckett insisted on staying to play. Scott said he'd get him to bed on time."

Megan scowled. "I think it's dumb having guys' night when someone's married."

Whitney arched a brow. "And girls' night? Those are dumb, too?"

"Oh, fine. Be rational. You don't live with a moron like I do." Megan pointed at me. "Kayla here was about to spill what's going on in her life."

"Yeah?" Whitney shifted in her seat to look at me. "Let's have it."

I frowned at Megan. "Didn't I just say I didn't know what was wrong?"

"Trouble at school? We might get snow, then you'd get a few days off." Whitney grinned. "That would be good, right?"

I groaned. "Only if it doesn't make us extend the school year. Which is what I told Megan a minute ago."

"Sorry I was late." Whitney crossed her arms.

"No." I groaned and scrubbed my hands over my face. "You're not. I'm just grumpy."

"You're never grumpy." Megan perched on the arm of a chair. "It's annoying. So you really need to tell us what's going on. Is it your date? Are you nervous?"

"Date? Did Austin finally get a clue?" Whitney leaned forward. "Why does no one text me? Maybe we need a group chat like the guys have."

"Ugh. No. I'm having lunch with Luke after church. It might not even be a date. It could be that he's trying to lock in spring break chaperones." I fidgeted, uncomfortable with their scrutiny.

"Luke Donnelly? The youth pastor?"

I laughed at Whitney's incredulity. "Why does everyone react like that? He's a nice guy."

"Well, sure. He's a youth pastor, he has to be nice." Whitney's forehead wrinkled. "But I thought you like Austin."

I shook my head and pointed at Megan. "That's all in her deranged imagination. Austin and I are best friends. That's it. He's very clear on that."

"Well, sure. But just because that's how he thinks doesn't mean you can't try to change his mind." Whitney looked at Megan. "Right? Or is your brother that dumb?"

"I have learned not to underestimate my brother's capacity

for stupidity." Megan sighed. "I'm sure you'll have a lovely lunch with Luke."

"You say that, but it sounds like you mean the exact opposite." I frowned. Should I have said no? Or pushed for an explanation of what he was looking for?

"I'm sorry." Megan reached over and squeezed my hand. "I am. I'll work on being more supportive. I guess I'm still a little surprised."

I raised my eyebrows. "Surprised...that someone is interested in me?"

"No. C'mon, Kayla. Don't be like that." Megan scowled. "You know what I mean."

"I don't think I do." I crossed my arms. I was starting to regret having ever told Megan that I was interested in Austin in a way that went beyond being his BFF. And okay, sure, it was nice to have her on my side. It was nice for her to think the two of us would make a good couple. But Austin was pretty clear about the fact that we were besties—and *only* besties. So what? Was I supposed to pine for him for the rest of my life?

Megan glanced at Whitney.

Whitney cleared her throat. "I imagine it's just that she's wondering why you're giving up on Austin."

"Because he doesn't feel that way about me. And I'm tired of waiting." I shrugged. "I don't expect you to understand."

"I think I do." Whitney shot me a sympathetic smile. "It's not always easy to be the one making a move. Especially when you weren't raised to think that it was super appropriate for women to be the romantic initiator."

"Which is dumb." Megan rolled her eyes. "I think women should be able to go after whoever they want."

"No question. If you're comfortable with that. If you're not, then there shouldn't be pressure suggesting that you have to." Whitney pointed at Megan. "Right?"

"Oh, fine. I guess. Yes." She looked at me and huffed out a breath. "I'm sorry. I'm disappointed you're not going to end up my sister."

"I'm going to lunch with Luke. I'm not marrying him." Even as I said the words, I was berating myself. I needed to go out with Luke with an open mind. Not with a mind fixated on Austin and any possibility of getting together with him. That wasn't fair to Luke. Or to me.

"And if he asks you out again?" Megan stood and gathered up her stack of books.

"I guess it depends on how lunch goes. I'm not ruling anything out, okay?" I wished she understood. I wished I was brave enough to give the explanation in clear enough words for her—but I wasn't ready to admit how deep my feelings for Austin ran. Not out loud. Especially not when right now? It seemed ridiculous to have those feelings. "If someone—anyone —wants to ask me out, chances are I'll go. Right now I'm not in a serious, committed relationship. And I'd kind of like that to change."

Megan nodded thoughtfully before wandering to the front window display with her book stack.

I turned to Whitney. "Sorry about the drama."

"Please. I believe you were present for my drama in the fall." She grinned. "And that worked out. Yours will, too. I'll be praying for you."

"Thanks. I need it." I shifted in my seat. "How's married life?"

Whitney's cheeks pinked prettily and she laughed. "Wonderful. Beckett is thriving. He called Scott 'Dad' the other day. I nearly cried. It was a moment."

"Aw." I put my hand over my heart. Beckett was a sweetheart and I was glad he was settling in nicely with the little family Whitney and Scott had created for him. "Is Scott enjoying working for himself now?"

"Eh. Sort of." Whitney wiggled her hand side to side. "It's still an adjustment. And his parents are pressuring him to bring Beckett down to them so Scott and I can go on a more formal honeymoon. Something more than the long weekend we took right after the wedding."

"Why don't you?" If I'd married a billionaire? I probably would put my foot down and demand a month in Europe. Because, come on, money had to have some perks.

Whitney sighed. "Neither of us are sure about leaving Beckett."

"So take him. Take Scott's folks. Then the two of you can get away for a little while here and there but still see Beckett." There were solutions, if she and Scott really wanted to find them. "I'd volunteer if I didn't have to teach."

Whitney chuckled. "Maybe in a little while. It's nice being home and getting our routine established. But spring break, maybe. Or Easter? Down the road. There's time to travel."

"But *honeymoon*." I fluttered my eyelashes at her. "Doesn't that make a difference?"

Whitney gave a sly smile. "Not so far."

I laughed and held up my hands. "Fine. TMI."

She snickered. "You're the one pushing for details."

"Yeah, yeah." I looked over toward the door as the bells jingled again. A group of kids from my high school wandered in, and I fought a groan. That was the biggest problem of the small-town-in-the-burbs vibe of Old Town. There was no escaping my students.

"Want to go hide in the back room?" Whitney lifted one eyebrow and jerked her head toward the back.

"Yeah. Let's do that." I grabbed my coat and ducked down behind the bookshelves, following Whitney to the relative safety of Megan's office.

I was fairly certain my students knew I didn't have a serious relationship with anyone. I heard the under-the-breath comments when kids saw me and Austin together, too. But I just wasn't in the mood to hear them laughing about Ms. Jones in the bookstore on a Friday night.

I wasn't embarrassed to be a nerd, but I didn't need my face rubbed in it either.

NERVES TWISTED in my stomach all through the Sunday morning service. I'd overthought my outfit for so long, I was almost late. And now? I was still overthinking. Was this about chaperoning? Was it more? Both? Neither?

Ugh. It wasn't as though I'd never dated before. I'd had a steady boyfriend all through college. In fact, I'd thought he and I would get engaged senior year and married when we graduated. Turned out he was more interested in my roommate and had been using me to be near her until he could work up the courage to ask her out. So okay, I'd had a *bad* long-term relationship. But still.

I knew how to date.

Megan's elbow jabbed my ribs as she stood with everyone else for the closing song. I dragged my thoughts back to reality and joined them.

When the service was over, Megan grabbed my hand. "You can bail, you know, if you need to."

"I'm fine. I appreciate your concern." I rolled my eyes. "If that's what it is."

"Believe it or not, that's exactly what it is." She slung her arm over my shoulders and squeezed. "You're nervous. I was giving you an out."

"I thought I was hiding it."

She studied me. "Maybe to people who don't know you like

I do."

I'd take it. "All right. I said I'd go help stack chairs."

"Seriously?" Megan started to laugh.

"What? He has to do it. It's part of his job, and he was nervous about making me wait."

"Nothing. It's just very you. Go be helpful. Have a good lunch. And then I expect a full report later this afternoon." Megan poked my shoulder. "I'm serious."

"Noted." I collected my purse and took a deep breath. I didn't mind giving her an update. In fact, I'd go ahead and start a group chat with Whitney so the three of us could talk that way. I just wished I knew what I wanted that update to be.

I made my way through the lingering clumps of people in the worship center and downstairs to the large room the youth used. There were a handful of teens hanging out, helping with the chairs, and joking around.

"Hi, Miss Jones!" Sara, one of my best students, waved and rushed over to me. "Did you grade the programs yet? Will we get them back tomorrow? Did you like the extra that I added?"

I laughed. "I'm not finished grading yet. It's probably going to be Tuesday. I'm sorry. I had an exam in AP that I needed to grade first. It took longer than I expected."

"Oh." Sara's face fell for a moment, then brightened again. "Well, I hope you like my surprise. I have to go. I'll see you tomorrow!"

"I'm sure I will. Bye." I watched her dart off and smiled. Sara reminded me a lot of me as a teenager. Or even more recently, if I was honest. She was fun and bubbly and always cheerful. And those were things I tried to be. I needed to get out of my head and stop this—whatever it was—that was taking those things away.

I crossed the room to where Luke was stacking chairs. "Hi."

He looked up and grinned. "Hi. You don't have to help. It just takes a minute."

I put my purse down against the wall and reached for a chair. "I don't mind. I like to help."

"Okay. Thanks." He grabbed the chair beside mine and the two of us worked in quiet harmony for a few minutes while we gathered the chairs and stacked them against the wall. When we were done, he looked around. "All set."

"Looks like. Why do you have to stack the chairs?" I went over to where I'd stashed my purse and grabbed it. "Isn't this just the youth room?"

He chuckled. "There's a couple of moms groups who meet here during the week. They use this room for games since it's as close to an indoor gym as we have. So moving the chairs makes it easier for them. I guess, technically, we could ask them to stack them and put them back in rows when they were done, but that seems like a lot."

"Makes sense. You ready to eat?"

"I am. I've been excited about a new Mexican place all week." He held the door leading out into the parking lot for me. "You sure you wouldn't rather I drove?"

"If you want, that's fine. I don't actually care either way."

Luke stopped in the parking lot and stuck his hands in his pockets. "I'm trying to decide if this is going to come across as controlling and weird."

I laughed. "It isn't. You drive. It's fine. Which one's you?"

"You're sure you don't mind?" He pointed to a dark blue truck on the far side of the lot.

"I'm sure." In some ways, it was a check in the "pro" column. He'd been the one to ask me out. He wanted to drive. It was certainly a more traditional start to things.

When we reached the truck, Luke opened my door and waited for me to get in, then closed it and rounded the hood.

So far? I'd say things were off to a pretty good start.

5

LUKE

I was so focused on making sure I didn't drive like a lunatic that I didn't manage much good conversation with Kayla on the way to the Mexican restaurant. She didn't seem to mind—at least, not that I could tell—but it still made my palms sweat.

I was bad at dating.

I'd tried, here and there, in high school and again in college. I didn't even bother in seminary. It wasn't that I wouldn't marry a woman with a seminary degree—far from it—I'd just gotten to the point that I realized I was no good at it. And I'd been busy enough then, I didn't have time.

"I'm not sure how I haven't been here. I drive past this shopping center all the time." I pulled into a parking spot and cut the engine.

"I feel like it's easy to miss." Kayla shrugged before pushing open her door. "And there are so many little restaurants like this, I never know which ones are good until someone tells me."

I smiled and opened my door. "True."

We crossed the parking lot. I had to jog the last couple steps to get to the door ahead of her. Was she not used to having guys open doors? Maybe she hated it. What if she was one of those women who looked for the patriarchy in things I considered courtesy? Ugh.

"Two, please." Kayla held up two fingers as she spoke.

The young woman behind the wooden hostess stand collected two menus and two rolled napkins that I assumed held silverware and started toward the mostly empty room full of tables with a whispered, "Follow me."

Kayla was in the process of sitting before I finished debating about trying to hold her chair. So I took the seat opposite her and reached for a menu. "What's good here?"

She tapped the menu that lay in front of her on the table. "I usually get the chicken enchiladas. They have a spicy tomatillo sauce that I like better than the regular ranchero."

I nodded. I wasn't an enchilada fan. The tortillas always seemed to get gummy. Maybe that had something to do with the places where I'd go to eat, but I wasn't going to risk it. For all I knew, Kayla liked gummy tortillas. I scanned the menu for the inevitable three taco combo. There it was. "I think I'll try the number six."

"Which is?"

"Tacos. I'm not super adventurous."

Kayla laughed. "You're a youth pastor. That's probably enough adventure for a lifetime."

I smiled, but it felt forced. Did it look that way? "I like being a youth pastor."

"It wasn't a dig. I'm sorry. I teach high school, so I get it."

Did she, though? It was probably too soon in our relationship to say one way or the other. I barely held back a grunt. Relationship. That was a loaded term. What we had barely qualified as being an acquaintance. Probably better to change the subject. "Do you come here a lot?"

Her eyebrows lifted.

I wanted to shrink into oblivion. It sounded like a pickup line. "That came out weird."

"A little. The answer is: not as much as I'd like to. The friends I usually meet for lunch all like the diner on Sunday afternoons. And now that Scott and Whitney are married, those lunches are turning into a big group thing and..." Kayla trailed off and shrugged. "It's different."

That I got. It was why I didn't have a lot of friends. Everyone paired up and then started wanting to introduce me to someone. Because it was going to be amazing for me. Except the people I'd thought were friends had terrible taste in women when it came to setting me up. Or I was just bad at dating. "Marriage always changes friend groups."

"I don't think it has to." She pursed her lips thoughtfully. "But I guess we'll see."

The server came with a basket of chips and a bowl of salsa. She took our drink orders and then, because Kayla interjected that we were ready, our meal orders as well.

It saved me from arguing the point. And I would have. I could point to a ton of examples in my own life that proved how friendships shifted when people got married. I was, according to my mother, pretty cynical about it.

Silence settled at the table. Was it awkward? Yes. Did I have any idea how to fix it? Not one.

"Why don't you tell me more about the spring break trip to Mexico." Kayla reached for a chip and scooped a generous helping of salsa before chomping into it.

She wasn't a dainty eater. I liked that about her. That and her usual bubbly enthusiasm—though that had been dampened some lately. Maybe because her friend group was changing? I reached for a chip and dipped a corner in the salsa. I didn't love spicy, so I wanted to see how bad it was going to be before committing to a scoop like she had.

I crunched the chip and my eyes watered. Of course we didn't have our drinks yet.

"Are you okay?" Kayla winced and looked around. "Do you want me to see about getting our drinks now?"

I shook my head, holding up a hand. "I'm okay. I'll just avoid the salsa."

I cleared my throat before reaching for another chip and eating it plain. That helped some. "What do you want to know? About Mexico?"

"I don't know. Give me the spiel."

Great. The spiel. I eyed the chips but decided against another. Without salsa, they were just corn chips. And not amazing ones at that. "Okay. Well, we're partnering with Jason and Karin Garcia. They've been medical missionaries in a small community for several years now and are very involved beyond the medicine aspect. They had a flood about eight months ago and rebuilding is slow, so we're going to go down and help. There are some child care opportunities for anyone who doesn't want to swing a hammer, but the focus really is construction."

"What's the spiritual benefit to the kids who participate?"

I blinked. That wasn't a question most people asked. "There are a couple. It's an opportunity for the kids who live here in arguably one of the most affluent areas of the US to see a different, less affluent, way of life. That will, hopefully, encourage gratitude and recognition of the blessings God has given them."

Kayla's expression wasn't encouraging.

The server appeared with our drinks and a mutter about food coming soon. She was gone before I could do much more than say thanks.

"What?"

Kayla frowned. "What what?"

"Judging from your facial expression, I get the feeling you don't agree with my first spiritual takeaway."

She sighed. "It's not that. It's just that there are plenty of opportunities for kids to see and serve the disadvantaged right here. There's an enormous homeless population in downtown DC and several fantastic organizations that could use volunteers. And then you have the low-income families who have homes, but still struggle to scrape by. If the kids aren't grateful for their blessings when they drive past the needs here at home, how is flying to Mexico going to change anything?"

I didn't bother to sigh. It was an objection a few parents had floated as well. And she wasn't wrong, necessarily. "I think we all have snow blindness when it comes to the people and problems we see on a daily basis. Sometimes getting out of our usual routine and location can open our eyes so we *do* see the problems when we return home."

Kayla gave a grudging nod. "All right."

"Beyond that, it gives kids a chance to be the hands and feet of Jesus. These families in Mexico need help rebuilding. And sure, there are people around home who probably need help with construction projects, too, but are the local needs more important somehow than those in Mexico?"

"No. I didn't mean to imply that."

I shrugged. "It wasn't an implication. You basically said it straight out."

Kayla winced. "Do I need to apologize?"

"No, it's fine. You're not alone in feeling this way. I got an earful from the senior pastor about how kids didn't need to go off on tropical vacations in the guise of service. But it's not like we're going to be near the beach or partying. Or even sightseeing. We're literally building houses and other buildings the whole time. We won't see any tourist destinations other than the Mexico City airport. It's not exactly going to be a trip packed with fun." And I'd gotten plenty of lectures in the *other* ear from parents who didn't want to send their kids to Mexico and have them miss out on all the cultural and touring opportunities available. I was beginning to think it was going to be impossible to win.

"Well. I apologize, anyway. It sounds like a good thing to do. How do you know the Garcias?"

It took a moment for me to shift gears. There were other potential areas for spiritual growth that went with the trip, but I guessed she didn't want to hear about them. And that was fine. I was certainly getting tired of justifying my decisions. "You know the big church in Springfield? Grace?"

"Sure. Pastor Brown is a legend."

I laughed. He'd hate that. He'd also argue with anyone who tried to say it when he was nearby. "I grew up there. Jason and Karin have always been supported by the church. There was a time I wasn't sure if God was calling me to overseas ministry instead of the local mission field. Jason went out of his way to talk to me, answer my questions, and pray with me. I've kept in touch."

"That's cool. I don't think I know any missionaries personally."

"I guess it depends on how you define the term."

She cocked her head to the side. "What do you mean?"

I shrugged. "Every believer is a missionary. We're all supposed to live out the Great Commission. That's all a missionary does. You're a missionary to kids at your high school. I'm one to the kids who come to our church and our outreach activities. The believer who works the register at the grocery store is a missionary to the shoppers. Missionaries aren't just people who go live in foreign countries."

"I hadn't thought of it that way."

Kayla might have said more, but the server finally appeared with our food.

"Do you mind if I pray?" I looked up from the plate of steaming tacos in front of me and met Kayla's gaze.

"Of course not." She slid her hand across the table.

I took her fingers and waited a beat. Wasn't there supposed to be electricity? Lightning bolts? Something that went beyond the recognition that yes, I was holding someone's hand? I bowed my head and asked a blessing on the food and our time together, adding a silent plea that I'd get a clue about dating. How to date. *Whom* to date.

Because I really didn't want to waste more time if Kayla wasn't the one. And I had zero idea how to tell if that was the case.

6

KAYLA

I ignored my buzzing phone as I unlocked the door to my apartment. Ada and Charles came running, and their chatty meows lightened the heavy weight that had been pressing down on me since Luke dropped me back at the church parking lot.

"I don't do a lot of dating, guys, but I'm pretty sure that was a disaster by anyone's rubric." I dropped my purse and squatted down to enthusiastically rub the cats. Ada put her two front paws on my knees, so I hooked her into my arms and stood, still rubbing her head. I brushed my cheek across hers and sighed. "At least I got good food out of it. Not that Luke would agree with that, either."

Who couldn't eat salsa? It wasn't as if it had some kind of insanity pepper in it, either. Just onions, garlic, and tomato. Not even jalapeño. I'd asked. Was food compatibility a thing?

Austin loved that Mexican restaurant. In fact, before Scott's nephew had arrived on the scene, the guys used to alternate between the cantina and the deli. When they'd been going to the cantina, I'd invited myself along.

Austin never said no.

I sighed and let Ada jump out of my arms. Maybe he hadn't said it. But maybe he'd wanted to?

I needed to stop thinking about Austin. He'd made it clear we were BFFs. Period. Luke was interested in me, so I was going to see where it went.

Of course, given our first date, maybe he wasn't interested anymore.

My phone started ringing. I groaned and answered.

"Hi, Megan."

"So? How was it? I need details!"

I flopped onto my sofa, my head dropping back so I was staring at the ceiling. "The food was good."

"Uh-oh."

I closed my eyes and tried to summon bright energy. "No. There's no uh-oh. It was a first date. Those are always awkward, right?"

"No. They're not supposed to be, at least."

"Not helping." Because really, if first dates weren't supposed to be a disaster, I was going to have to rethink this whole thing with Luke.

"I don't want to help. You shouldn't be dating Luke."

"Yeah? Who should I be dating?"

"We both know that answer." Megan's sigh turned into a raspberry at the end. "But he's a clueless doofus."

Austin. It was true. That was exactly what he was, and it didn't look to be changing anytime soon. "We're friends. I get not wanting to risk that."

"Really?" Megan made a rude noise. "I didn't realize you were a chicken."

"Hey! Am not." But maybe, deep down, I was. I wasn't going to make a move on Austin and risk him turning tail and running the other direction. I valued his friendship, for one. And for two? I wasn't comfortable being the instigator in a relationship. Call me old fashioned, if you must, I wanted a guy to ask me out. I wanted someone who was interested enough in me to be willing to take a risk.

"Yeah, okay." Sarcasm dripped from Megan's words. "So the food was good. How was the conversation?"

"We talked about the youth trip to Mexico and how he connected with the missionaries there in the first place. That kind of thing."

"I guess that doesn't sound bad. Was there conversation about who you are in there, too? Who he is? That whole getting-to-know-you thing?"

"Yeah. Of course." Not a lot of it, but some. Once we both seemed to recognize that we weren't going to see eye-to-eye about mission trips, we sidestepped.

"And did he ask you out again?"

"No." I bit my lip. "That's a bad sign, right? He was supposed to want to make plans right away?"

Megan grunted. "I don't know. There are those guys out there who have a three-day rule."

"A three-day rule? Like what, they wait three days before they make contact again? I thought those guys were only in sitcoms." I couldn't see Luke falling into that category. He had to know how ridiculous it was, didn't he?

"Sad to say, they are alive and well on the dating apps."

"Wait. Why do you know about guys on dating apps?" This was new. And news. Megan had always been very anti-dating app.

"It was a dare. One of the other social workers said I was only burned out because I didn't have a social life. She made me install it."

"Interesting. And?"

"I've chatted with a few guys." Embarrassment coated Megan's words. "But no actual dates yet. Possibly ever."

"Because?"

Megan groaned. "Because I don't know why they're chatting with me. If they're looking to hook up, they've got the wrong girl. And it's hard to imagine that there are people looking for a serious relationship on a dating app."

"Hey. That's a little harsh. There are a lot of couples who meet on an app and end up happily married for the rest of their lives." I rubbed the back of my neck. "Maybe I should give it a try. We could compare notes."

"No way. Right now, I'm pretty confident that I measure up all right with the other women around here who are using the app. If you sign up? I'm loser leftovers all over again."

I frowned. "Back up. First off, you're not a loser or leftovers. You're an amazing catch and if the guys you meet don't recognize it, that's their problem, not yours."

Megan scoffed. "It is mine, though. Because it still leaves me without a boyfriend."

"Secondly," I went on, raising my voice a little louder because I wasn't about to let my best girlfriend have this level of pity party. "Any guy that looked past you to try to get to me? I'd kick him to the curb. Zero interest. Because he has no taste in women if he's not interested in you. And if I ever made you feel otherwise, I apologize."

"No. It's not you. I'm just...you know what? I don't know what I am."

"Please tell me you're not jealous of my date with Luke. Cause I can mention that you're interested and step out if that's what you need me to do."

"Bleh. No. Luke isn't for me. I also don't think he's for you, but that's because I want you to be my actual sister and marry my boneheaded brother."

I laughed. Her words warmed me. It was good to be loved.

"We don't need marriage to be actual sisters. I already think of you that way. Okay?"

"Yeah, yeah, yeah."

Megan's response made me grin. "Three days, huh?"

"Apparently."

I usually tried to get to church on Wednesdays to help with the youth group. I'd make a point of it, this week. Maybe if I appeared in front of him, Luke would realize it was time to plan a second date. If he didn't call between now and then. "Are we done talking about my date now?"

"I guess."

"Great. Then I can start grilling you about why you haven't followed through on turning in your notice and going full time at the bookstore like you've been planning since before Christmas."

"Maybe I'm not done talking about your date, after all. What did you order?"

"Nope. You said we were done. Come on, Megan. You're miserable. You know how to not be miserable. Why aren't you jumping in with both feet? Or is it that *you're* a chicken?"

"I hate you."

I laughed. "No you don't. You love me. And I love you. I'm also worried that you somehow think a dating app is going to make up for the emotional trauma you're subjecting yourself to daily."

"That seems extreme. It's not emotional trauma. It's just hard. And fulfilling."

Ah. I winced as Charles jumped up and slunk onto my lap, where he immediately began to knead my belly with the tips of his claws. I rubbed his back and nudged him. He stopped. "You're worried the bookstore won't be as fulfilling."

"Maybe. What if it turns out to be just as draining? And instead of being the bright spot I look forward to every week, the bookstore becomes this drudgery that I dread every night before bed? Then what do I do?"

"You're praying about it, right?"

Megan sighed. "Right."

"And?"

"And I have a lot of peace about turning in my resignation. And doing the bookstore fulltime. And Grandma reminded me that the store is mine to do what I want with—and that she knows I'd be happier there."

"So what's stopping you?"

"I'm going to have to fire the daytime staff at the store. None of them work a ton of hours, but I know I can't afford to keep them. I feel bad."

That was fair. School teachers never really had to fire anyone, but I'd given my share of Fs. I never enjoyed that, but it had to be done when the work wasn't right. "I get that. But sometimes you have to do what's right, even when it's hard. What if they're ready to move on to something else but they haven't because they saw how badly you were shaken in December?"

"I guess that's possible. I did hire them as seasonal help." Megan drew in a noisy breath. "All right. I'm putting in my notice tomorrow."

I grinned. "Good for you. Your last day will be...?"

"Um. Hang on, let me put you on speaker." The tone of the call changed. I grimaced. I hated speaker phone. "I have to look at the calendar. I probably shouldn't leave on a Tuesday, right?"

"You can, but it's weird."

"The twenty-seventh is a Friday."

"Do that." It was still two weeks. And Fridays made easier ending days than Tuesdays. "You can let your employees know you won't need them after the twenty-eighth and then start fresh on Monday."

"I can. And I will." Megan's whole tone was brighter. "Thanks."

"You're welcome. I'm going to hold you to it this time." Because this was the second time we'd talked through plans for her to quit and move to the bookstore full time. Megan had used the whole mess with Whitney and her sister to get out of it in December. But now there was no excuse.

If only it was as easy to figure out my own life as it was to organize someone else's.

"Megan said you had a good lunch yesterday."

I raised an eyebrow at Austin's greeting as I closed his classroom door behind me. "Happy Monday to you, too."

Austin shook his head, but offered a grin. "Yeah, yeah. So? You going to be Mrs. Youth Pastor?"

I winced. "Let's not ever call whoever Luke marries that. Okay? That's...awful."

Austin laughed. "You're not wrong. I didn't really think it aloud before I said it. But I also deduce that you're dodging the question."

"Not dodging. We had a good lunch."

"And?"

I dragged a desk closer to his and sat before unpacking my food. "And the trip to Mexico at spring break sounds like it'll be really focused on service and spiritual development."

He cocked his head to the side, and I looked away from his scrutiny. "No beach trips?"

"Not one." I unwrapped my sandwich and took a bite. I wasn't in the mood for ham, but it was what I had. So I'd choke it down.

"You're going to make me volunteer, aren't you?"

I heard the teasing in his voice, but it rubbed me like coarse sandpaper. "No, Austin. I'm not. If you don't want to help out, then you shouldn't. Go on back to the Caymans and spend your break sunning yourself on the beach."

I scowled down at my lunch a moment before sliding it all back into my lunch bag. "I've got some programs to grade. I'm going to skip our little chat today."

"Hey." He stood and followed a few steps behind me.

I ignored him and hurried through his door, out into the hallway. I heard him say my name, but didn't turn.

At the corner, I peeked over my shoulder and got a glimpse of him standing beside his door, hands shoved in his pockets, shoulders slumped.

My heart ached. I ignored that, too.

I wasn't his girlfriend, nagging him into doing things he didn't want to do. I wasn't his conscience. Or his mother. If he didn't want to help out with the youth, that was fine. No one was making him.

I stormed through my classroom door.

The two students working on projects glanced up guiltily.

"What's going on?" I stopped, popped my hands on my hips, and looked between them.

Aidan cleared his throat. "Um. Lucy was having trouble compiling so I offered to take a look. Since you weren't here."

I shifted my gaze to Lucy. "Is that right?"

She hunched her shoulders. "Basically."

"Are you doing it for her, Aidan?"

His cheeks flamed red. "No. No, ma'am. Miss Jones, I wouldn't do that even when she asked."

Lucy hissed at him.

"I mean if. If she asked. I was just—"

"Out. Both of you." I held out my hand. "Give me your thumb drives."

"Oh, but Miss Jones, I'm not done." Lucy's eyes filled. "It doesn't compile and I hadn't even finished the whole program yet."

"Maybe you'll think twice about cheating in the future." I sighed. "You know this will hurt your grade, too. Right, Aidan?"

"Yes, Miss Jones." He opened his mouth as if he was going to add more, then snapped it shut. His shoulders fell.

I felt a little stir of pity. "I understand that you wanted to help. But there are right ways and wrong ways to do that."

Aidan nodded once, dropped his thumb drive in my hand, and took off, his backpack slung over one shoulder.

"This isn't fair." Lucy scowled at me; her thumb drive clenched in her fist. "You said I could have extra time."

"Extra time, yes. Extra help from someone who isn't me? No."

Tears dripped down Lucy's cheeks. "I have to get a good grade on this or my dad's going to think I can't program. And then he won't pay for college because I won't be able to major in computer science."

"Do you even want to major in computer science?" I never would have pegged Lucy as someone who would choose computers as a major, let alone a career.

"No." She sniffled. "But it's the only way Dad will pay. Mom says to go along with it, and I can double-major in something that I actually want to do."

I took a deep breath. "Come into my office, Lucy."

Her eyes widened.

I gestured toward my office then started in that direction. She could either come or not. But if she left without giving me her thumb drive, she was going to have bigger problems than she already did.

I settled behind my desk, pleased to see Lucy standing in the doorway. "Come on in. Have a seat."

Lucy swallowed and perched on the edge of a chair.

"Can I ask why you haven't told your father you don't like computer science?"

She sighed. "I tried. He said I needed to give it more time."

"Which you have. This is your second year learning to program."

Lucy nodded.

"Have you talked to him lately?"

She shook her head. "My brother's going to graduate from MIT in the spring. It's all Dad can talk about. He's so proud. Look at how smart his son is. Won't it be great when he has two computer science graduates."

I lifted my eyebrows. "Are you going to MIT?"

"I applied." Lucy heaved a sigh. "I don't think I'll get in. That's going to be a big enough problem to deal with. Maybe I'll get into Virginia Tech. He won't be as proud, but it's still a good school."

"Where do you want to go?"

"It doesn't matter."

"Yes, Lucy, it does. Don't set yourself up for misery. Going to a college you're not excited about—choosing a major you hate? None of that is a recipe for good mental health." I'd seen enough of it when I was in college to know. I'd seen the burnout and depression in students who were just trying to do what their parents expected with no concern for aptitude or interest.

"They won't listen."

"Would they listen to me?"

A tiny glimmer of hope sparked in her eyes, but it quickly flickered out. "I doubt it."

"Would you like me to try?" It wasn't my favorite kind of parent call to make, but it was still something I considered to be part of my job.

"Do you have to tell them I cheated?"

I shook my head. "Not necessarily. I am going to need you to do a makeup program though. And I'm going to need you to do it after school so I can supervise."

Lucy's shoulders hunched. "Okay."

"You should probably get going so you're not late to your next class. I'll email and set up a time to talk to your parents. You deserve better than this. You're a smart girl, Lucy. And while I wouldn't say computers are your future—they could be, if you wanted it. But since you don't? You need to find something you're passionate about that your parents can get on board with."

"I like math. I'm good at it. Dad just doesn't think there are any jobs for mathematicians other than teaching. He wants me to be able to support myself."

"That's good info. I'll see if I can slip in a word or two about actuaries."

Lucy's eyes lit. "I've read some about that. Working with statistics sounds so cool."

I laughed. It took all kinds. "Let me take a run at your parents and I'll figure out a makeup project."

"Thanks, Miss Jones."

"You're welcome." I smiled at her as she gathered her things and scurried from my office, through the classroom, and out into the hall. I glanced at the clock. I could probably choke down my sandwich before the next class arrived.

I leaned my head back and closed my eyes.

Or I could spend a few minutes praying for the headache forming behind my eyes to go away before it turned into a full-blown migraine.

7

AUSTIN

I pulled out the last chair at the poker table in Scott's living room and sat.

"Hey, man. Glad you could make it." Cody dug into the bowl of nacho chips and crunched at his handful. "We were starting to wonder."

"Cody was starting to wonder. The rest of us figured you'd let us know if you weren't going to make it." Noah jabbed Cody in the ribs with his elbow.

The other guys chuckled.

My face heated. I could take the ribbing, but sometimes it hit a little too close to home. I had almost decided not to come. In fact, I'd sat in my car for a full five minutes before finally giving in and getting out. These were my people. Just because I was becoming increasingly dissatisfied with my life—for no discernible reason I could put my hands on—didn't mean I should shut them out. "Yeah, yeah. Some of us work for a living."

Chuckles turned to laughter. Eventually the absurdity sank in, and I laughed, too.

I held up my hands. "Okay, okay. I'm sorry, all right?"

"Maybe." Scott picked up the deck of cards and started to shuffle. "Depends on if you're going to tell us what's going on."

"That's the thing. I don't know." I took a handful of chips. Rather than gnaw on them straight from my fist like Cody, I selected one and popped it in my mouth. Just because we were a bunch of guys didn't mean we had to act like animals. "I'm just antsy."

Noah and Cody exchanged a knowing look.

I frowned. "What's that look for?"

Cody shook his head. "Think it has anything to do with Kayla dating the youth pastor?"

"What? No. Why would it?" I bristled and ate another chip. "Kayla can do what she wants. We're best friends. I don't own her."

That was a point she'd driven home very clearly this week by her absolute refusal to eat lunch with me. If I stopped by the lab, she was busy with students. If I tried to catch her eye in the hall before class or make conversation in the staff room, she was cordial but inevitably on her way somewhere else to do something much more important than talk to me.

I sighed. "I'm not even sure we're best friends anymore. It's fine."

"What? That's crazy." Tristan flipped up the two cards he'd been dealt and looked at them. "You two are inseparable."

I shrugged. "Were."

"Because she's dating Luke?" Wes frowned. "That doesn't seem like her."

I didn't think we could really say one way or the other. She'd never been serious about a guy in the time that I'd known her. "Maybe. But it's not like she dates a lot."

Scott drew in a breath like he was about to speak, then stopped and shook his head.

"What?" I pointed at him. "Spit it out."

"I have it on good authority that there are reasons for that." Scott stared at his cards and wouldn't look up.

What did that even mean? I looked at my cards and wanted to grimace. In fact, I probably did. The guys all said I had a terrible poker face. Maybe there would be some way to redeem them, but I wasn't optimistic.

"Good authority means Whitney, right?" Tristan glanced at Scott.

Scott beamed. "It does, indeed, mean my wife."

I groaned. "Save us from newlywed goop."

Cody laughed. "Preach."

"Amen." Noah frowned at his two cards. "I'm honestly surprised we get to keep having poker nights."

"I offered to stop." Scott shrugged. "But she likes hanging out at the bookstore with Megan and Kayla."

"Where's Beckett?" Wes glanced around. "I'm used to having a movie on in the background."

"Whit took him along. He likes books and there's that little couch if he wants to sleep. He does pretty well shifting from place to place when he's out, so she figured why not. I didn't argue." Scott dealt three cards in the center of the table.

I pressed my lips together. Those cards weren't going to help me any. "You have learned the importance of the words, 'yes, dear' I see."

"Nah, man. That's dismissive. But I'm not going to argue with her when she has a good suggestion. Unless you all want Beckett here with us. I figured we'd alternate." Scott looked around the table. "Who's in?"

I'm not sure why I bothered betting in the first round. I wasn't going to win. My only excuse was that we put two bucks in the pot to play so it wasn't like I stood to lose much. Given my luck with, well, everything, lately, I'd already kissed those bucks goodbye.

"Is no one going to ask Scott about Kayla's reasons for not dating?" Tristan added another poker chip to the pot.

Darn. I was hoping conversation might find its way to a different topic. I really didn't want to get into it. Sure, I was curious. But I was also hesitant.

"No?" Tristan shook his head. "Well, I'd like to know."

Scott cleared his throat and tossed a pile of poker chips onto the growing pile. "Whitney says—and she adds that Megan agrees, so it's not just a newlywed looking for romance wherever she turns—that Kayla's in love with Austin here."

I was going to laugh, but started choking instead.

Wes banged on my back between my shoulder blades. "You all right there, man?"

I shook my head and stood, grabbing my chair before it could tip. "Be right back."

I got a glimpse of the guys' faces as I strode to the kitchen to get a soda out of the fridge. Why didn't any of them look as surprised as I was?

I popped the top on the Coke and took three long swallows before setting the can on the counter and leaning against the fridge. There was no way. Kayla?

No.

I shook my head. No way.

I carried the soda back out into the living room with me and took my seat.

"So..." Wes's eyebrows lifted. "Not what you thought Scott was going to say, I take it?"

"They're delusional. There's no way Kayla thinks about me that way." I couldn't say I'd never looked at her and wondered. That would be a lie. But I'd gotten over it pretty quickly at the start of our friendship. She never gave me any indication that she thought of me as more than a brother, and I wasn't going to be the guy who ruined a friendship because he misread signals.

Scott, of course, heard what I didn't say. "You think about her that way?"

"Past tense. Way, way past." I was going to stick to that. The casual appreciation of how nice she looked in a lot of the clothes she wore to school wasn't romantic interest. It was just admiring the beauty of one of God's creations. I'd look at her that way if she was my sister. Well. Maybe not my sister. A family friend, then.

"Nope. Not buying it." Cody shook his head to emphasize his words. "You're terrible at poker and your lack of skill isn't helping in this case, either."

The guys laughed.

I felt my shoulders hunch and was incapable of doing anything to prevent it. I knew if I protested, they'd rag on me more. "Are we playing poker here, or what?"

"Oooh. Touchy." Tristan wiggled his eyebrows. "I think we hit close to a nerve."

Scott smiled and dealt the final card.

I sighed and pushed my cards in. "I'm out."

I watched as Cody went on to rake in the pot, and the deck was passed to Tristan to shuffle and deal. Maybe if I wanted the conversation to turn, it was going to be up to me to do it.

I cleared my throat. "Anyone planning a spring break trip?"

"You're the only one of us who still has spring break, man. Although, if you're heading back to the islands, I'm in." Wes flipped up the two cards Tristan had dealt him. "I'm putting in my notice on Monday. Now that everyone is over the shock of Scott leaving, I think I can do it without it being horrible."

"Sorry, man. I know you were ready to go before Christmas." Scott slid his cards closer and peeked at them. "You didn't have to stay just because I left."

Wes snickered. "Yeah, I did. I didn't realize Christopher

could get angry. Stephanie? Sure. But man, Chris has a wicked temper when it gets free."

Scott winced. "Sorry again. I thought they understood."

"Oh, they did. Do. But they weren't happy about it." Wes shrugged and tossed his bet into the center of the table.

Scott nodded and added his own.

"I don't know what I'm doing." I was hesitant to mention Kayla's name, but I knew I needed to explain myself. I sighed and tossed in chips I was sure to lose. "Kayla's going on the youth group trip as a chaperone. She's helping Luke recruit other adults."

"Hey, the beach is the beach. I can do that." Wes watched Tristan deal out the fourth card.

"I'm not sure the beach is in the picture. She said—and I haven't talked to Luke so I only have her words to go by—it's all construction and service. No tourism at all." I considered the four cards on the table and peeked at mine again just to be sure I wasn't hallucinating. Maybe I could actually win this hand.

Tristan laughed. "Good luck getting kids to spend their spring break on that. Every mission trip I went on as a kid had at least one day, sometimes two, where we got to have fun."

I shrugged. That had certainly been my experience, but I couldn't say I objected to any attempts to keep the focus where it needed to be. Not that kids shouldn't have fun serving Jesus. Which maybe was something Luke needed to consider. Were there any plans to keep it from being drudgery?

"So, Kayla roped you in?" Wes shook his head. "Without a chance to dive, I don't think I'm going to be up for it. I realize it sounds terrible, but if I'm leaving Robinson, I'm going to focus my energy on what I need to get my dive shop off the ground."

"You're really doing that?" Noah laughed. "I honestly thought you were joking. You realize we are not near any useful beach, right?"

"Yeah, yeah. There are two other dive shops in the metro area. Both are doing brisk business. I really think we can support another. And I think it'd be a great addition to Old Town." Wes rubbed the back of his neck. "I guess we'll see. It's not like I can't afford to give it a try."

I nodded once. He was right about that. We could all afford a few risks here and there, if we wanted. And it sounded like that was what he wanted. "I'll be a loyal customer. Especially if you're planning dives somewhere easy enough to drive to on the weekends."

Wes grinned at me. "I knew you'd caught the bug."

"I did." I'd been curious about diving for a while. The time we spent in the Caymans over Christmas had given me the opportunity to try it. And I was definitely hooked. It wasn't necessarily a hobby most school teachers could indulge often. But I wasn't a typical school teacher.

"Why are you still teaching?" Tristan flipped over the river— the fifth and final card for us to use in putting together our hands.

I fought a grin. That card just gave me my fourth jack. It was possible someone had a better hand. But it seemed unlikely. "I like it. What else would I do?"

Of all the guys, I was surprised Tristan was the one asking. He seemed content as a lawyer. And okay, sure, he'd left the firm he'd been part of and set up his own shop almost as soon as the money hit our accounts, but he was still doing what he'd done before.

"Dunno. Just asking." Tristan tossed chips on the pile. "All right, let's see 'em."

I flipped my cards over and waited. Cody had a full house and was reaching for the pot. I cleared my throat. "I believe those are mine."

"What?" Cody paused and frowned at me. "No way. You got a fourth in the river? You never have luck like that."

I laughed and scooped up my winnings. "Yeah, well, today's my day, I guess."

Tristan passed the deck to Noah. "Scott's got his consulting thing going. Wes is going to open a dive shop. Noah and Cody are happy at Ballentine because they spend their lives hobnobbing with the rich, famous, and elected seeking to make the world a better place. I opened my own firm. Don't you have any sort of dream beyond math teacher of the year?"

I got a mental flash of myself, spinning and hoisting a little boy into the air as he giggled. But that wasn't a dream money could make happen. "Not really, no."

"You could start your own tutoring operation. Or a school for math nerds. Something that gave you flexibility outside of the school year." Tristan drummed his fingers on the table.

"I like teaching. I like being in the public school, where I feel like I can be a little bit of Jesus's light for the kids. I especially like the school I'm at, because it's not all rich kids who are bored with life and marking time until Daddy buys them a college scholarship. I make a difference where I am. I like it there. I feel like it's where God wants me." I blew out a breath. That last one mattered the most. The guys knew it. I knew it.

Tristan nodded once. "Fair enough. If you go on the spring break thing with the youth, I'll go, too."

I grinned. "Thanks, man."

I'd talk to Kayla about it on Monday. If she'd let me. Surely, if she knew I wanted to volunteer for the mission trip, she'd make some time for me in her schedule. Wouldn't she?

Scott's suggestion that she had feelings for me floated back into my head and lodged there.

Even if it had been true, it couldn't be true now. Could it? She was dating Luke. Well, she'd gone out with him. Once. That didn't make it a significant relationship. Which meant there might still be a chance for me.

If I wanted one.

Did I?

I wasn't brave enough yet to commit either way.

8

KAYLA

"You're back." Megan greeted me with a grin and held open her arms.

I gave her a quick, tight hug before stepping back to look around the bookstore. "You're quiet this morning."

"Saturday morning." Megan shrugged. "We'll get busier when the lunch crowds for the restaurants around here get going. People who didn't make reservations and don't want to sit and wait while their names tick up the list. If the weather's good, at least."

"Supposed to be." It might be nearing the end of January, but in the DC area, that could mean anything from the low sixties and sunny to three feet of snow. My weather app had put it closer to the first one.

Megan cocked her head to the side and studied me. "You're not okay."

I shrugged. "I'm fine."

"Nope. You were subdued last night when we hung out with Whitney and Beckett, and you're bordering on morose this morning. What's going on?"

I laughed. "Morose? What are you reading?"

Megan clutched a paperback to her chest and shook her head. "It doesn't matter. I stand by my word choice."

"You're reading Jane Austen again, aren't you?"

"Even if I am, it's not like that's a crime. Plenty of people enjoy the classics."

I rolled my eyes. "They do. It's a sad truth. And then they start using words like 'morose.' I will admit I am not my usual, what was it you called me? Excessively perky self."

Megan winced. "I never would have said it if I'd known you were going to throw it in my face for the rest of my days."

I fluttered my eyelashes at her. "Maybe you'll learn to think twice before you start pigeonholing people for their personalities."

"Whatever. My point stands: something's wrong."

I sighed and made my way over to the reading-slash-lounging area of the bookstore. I dropped into one of the chairs and shifted so my legs dangled over the arm. "I miss Austin."

Megan pointed at me. "Because you've been avoiding him all week."

"I had to. I've got to break my reliance on him. He acts like I'm a nagging grandma who's going to drag him on a service project whether he wants to come or not." I crossed my arms. I didn't care if he didn't want to go to Mexico. He could do what he wanted with his time and money. He didn't owe me anything.

"Uh-huh. Keep telling yourself that. You're in love with him."

I blew out a breath. She wasn't wrong, but did I have to admit it? He didn't feel the same way, so what was the point? "I can get over it."

"Why would you? He's a great guy. And let me tell you, it's a rare man whose sister is willing to admit that out loud."

My lips twitched. "Well, you're a rare catch yourself."

"See? Austin and I should both be snapped up by someone who adores us. At least my brother, lucky turkey that he is, has someone who meets that definition already in the wings." Megan came and perched on the edge of the chair across from me. "I really don't understand why you won't ask him out."

"Because I shouldn't have to!" I tossed my hands in the air. "Is it really wrong for me to want a guy who wants me enough to risk disappointment and ask me out?"

Megan sighed. "No. Of course it's not wrong. It just might mean my brother is a bigger doofus than I thought."

Maybe I should have sucked it up and realized this was the twenty-first century. Women asked men out all the time. In fact, it kind of seemed like everyone thought I was an idiot because I didn't. Never had. Never planned to. Was this going to be the hill I chose to die on?

I groaned.

"What?"

"I'm being stupid, right? I should just tell Austin how I feel and see what happens." That wasn't quite the same as asking him out. In fact, it was just having a long overdue conversation. Right? "What's the worst thing that could happen?"

Megan met my gaze, eyebrows raised. "Are we playing worst case scenario?"

I squeezed my eyes shut. No. I did not actually want to do that. Because there were a ton of terrible things that could happen. It was already awkward at school because I'd been avoiding him all week. I wasn't going to have the strength to continue avoiding him. I knew that. Accepted it, even. But that didn't mean I had to like it.

So what happened if I poured my heart out at Austin's feet and then he stomped it like a shallow puddle on a rainy day?

Talk about awkward.

I'd have to change schools. Maybe even move out of the area —because even though our county was pretty big, all the teachers knew each other. And math and computer science were too closely related for comfort.

"I don't want to move."

Megan snickered. "I don't know if it's a good thing or super pathetic that I can follow the train of thought that got you there."

"I'm going with good. It's got to be a good thing to have someone who gets me." I blew out a breath. "I can't do it. I can't just tell him how I feel and see what happens."

"So ask him out. That's less pressure than you slugging him in the stomach and telling him you love him."

I could actually picture it going down somewhat like that. Probably with me yelling and calling him an idiot on top of it. "What about Luke? What if I just wait and see how things go there? Wouldn't that be the easiest solution of all of them?"

"Sure. I guess. If you're interested in marrying Luke."

I bit my lip.

"Are you? Can you picture that?" Megan saw too much.

I turned and looked out the window at the handful of people walking past. "It's a little soon to talk marriage when it comes to Luke."

"All right. That's fair. Kissing. Can you imagine kissing Luke?"

I tried. Usually, I had a pretty decent imagination. I pictured Luke, standing close, leaning in...my stomach twisted. I pushed through. Luke's face got blurry before morphing into Austin's.

"That's a long pause." Megan narrowed her eyes as she looked at me. "I'm going to go with no."

"We've only been out once. To lunch. And he doesn't actually like Mexican food, so that taints the whole experience. Maybe I should give it another shot at a place where he would enjoy the food."

Megan nodded. "That's very logical. Has he asked you out again?"

"No." I looked back at my friend. "That's bad, right? It means he knows the date was a disaster?"

"He could be busy?" Megan lifted her shoulders. "There are other possibilities."

"But you don't think they're the reason."

She held up her hands. "I'm not in Luke's head. I don't know how he thinks. I do know, if I asked you out, I wouldn't let the evening end without firming up plans to get together again."

"Aww." I blew her a kiss. "Best friend ever."

"Don't you forget it." She pointed a finger at me.

The bell on the door interrupted my reply, and Megan bounced off her seat and hurried to the front of the store.

I dug my phone out of my pocket. I should be at home grading programs. There were always programs to grade. Ada and Charles had made it clear what they thought of me heading to the bookstore. No one could convey disdain for someone's choices like a cat. But they'd still be happy to see me when I got home. I was onto them.

I had a text from Austin that I hadn't heard chime. I tapped it and my mouth went dry.

HEY. I MISS YOU. ANY CHANCE YOU'RE FREE FOR DINNER TONIGHT?

What was I supposed to do with that?

I knew what I wanted to do. What I wanted to do was jump up and down pumping my fist and squeal. Except of course Megan probably wouldn't appreciate me doing that now that she actually had customers in the store. And also, this could be just another friendly hangout between besties.

As much as I loved spending time with Austin, I couldn't keep doing that to myself. I tapped out a reply and studied it:

WHAT DO YOU HAVE IN MIND?

It wasn't a no. It indicated interest. But maybe—just maybe

—it would let him know that things weren't automatically better between us just because I missed him and he missed me. I shook my head and hit Send. I was asking a lot of six words. Probably too much.

His reply came quickly. *ADA'S? I'VE BEEN CRAVING THEIR SALMON.*

My mouth watered. Their salmon was amazing. Their crab cakes? Heavenly. They were on the spendier side of things though. I'd need to double-check my budget before I could justify the expense. I was scrolling to my banking app when another text popped up from Austin: *MY TREAT.*

That did it. I tried to squash the flicker of hope that bloomed in my chest, but I failed. If this turned out to be another BFFs out on the town thing, I was probably going to cry right there in the restaurant.

Still. I'd get a crab cake out of it. I texted back. *I'M IN. MEET YOU THERE?*

NAH. I'LL PICK YOU UP. SIX?

I swallowed. The flicker of hope brightened and spread. He never picked me up. Well, not never. Rarely. *SOUNDS GOOD. SEE YOU THEN.*

I checked the time on my phone. Ugh. It wasn't even noon yet. What should I wear? I glanced over to where Megan was checking out a couple. I squinted. From their purchases, it looked like they were tourists. I recognized the coffee table book on Old Town Alexandria during colonial times. And was that a walking tour book on top? It was hard to say, but it kind of looked like one of the volumes I flipped through now and then when I was looking for something interesting to do.

I should buy the book rather than treating Megan's bookstore like a library, but it was always nice to have an excuse to drop in. Plus, Megan knew I looked at the thing. It wasn't like she didn't know when my birthday was.

The couple finally left. I pushed out of the chair and hurried over to lean on the cashier's counter. "Big sale?"

She snorted. "No. But it's better than nothing. And those coffee table books aren't cheap. So that's nice."

"If I was going to Ada's tonight, what would you say I should wear?"

Megan's eyes brightened. "Ooh. Luke called? Hm. I might've said you should say no. Act busy. If you train a guy to know they don't have to plan ahead, then they're never going to. Still, it's probably better that you go so you can figure things out. And he might not have a lot of flexibility in his schedule. Hmm."

I fought a smile as Megan rambled. "Are you done?"

She paused, one finger tapping her lips. "Oh! I have it. That green wrap dress. You look hot in that."

"It's sleeveless."

"Right." She huffed out a breath. "Stupid January. Even if it is unseasonably warm today, we're not at sleeveless. Right?"

"Correct." I had no intention of wearing a summer dress. Even if it was clear and sunny today, by six it would be dark and the temperature would be dropping with every passing minute until it hit the projected low of thirty-seven.

"What about that black sweater dress? You could add a scarf at the waist to give it some shape and color."

I nodded slowly. "I have a thick teal belt I just bought. It might be a better choice than a scarf."

"Ooh. You didn't tell me about that one. Definitely. Shoes?"

"Knee boots? I mean, it's a sweater dress. Is there another choice?"

Megan chuckled. "Probably not. It's a good look for sure."

I blew out a breath. "Cool. Thank you. That keeps me from obsessing for the next seven hours."

"Obsessing?" Megan frowned at me. "How did I miss that you were at the obsessing about what to wear level for Luke?"

I raised an eyebrow.

Her mouth dropped open. Her hand shot up to cover it as she started to squeak. "It's not Luke! It's my doofus brother!"

I grinned, nodding. I grabbed her arm and squeezed gently. "Don't freak out yet, okay? It's entirely possible that this is just bestie night on the town."

Megan scowled. "It is, isn't it? Ugh. That would be just like him, too. I oughta—"

"No. Leave him alone. He has to figure it out on his own, not because his sister kicked sense into him." I sighed. I said the words. I mostly meant them. At the same time? I'd really love someone to clue him in. "What if..."

Megan cocked her head to the side. "What?"

"If Luke finds me after church tomorrow and asks me out again, what do I do? It's not like just because Austin and I go out to dinner it means we're a couple now."

"Unless it does." Megan leaned across the counter until our noses almost touched. "Maybe he's finally ready to admit how *he* feels about you. Then you could decide to be a couple and you could tell Luke you are sorry, but you're seeing someone."

I didn't think that was very likely. "Have you met your brother? That's not what this is going to be. Even if it's a step toward more than bestie night out, he's not going to jump like that."

"Then date both of them. A little competition can be a good thing." Megan's grin was sharp. "And honestly, maybe seeing that you've got someone else interested will get Austin to shake a leg."

"It seems dishonest."

She shook her head. "No. No way. You're allowed to date as many guys as you want right up until you agree to be in an exclusive relationship with someone. Don't let anyone tell you otherwise."

"Since when are you a dating expert?"

Megan rolled her eyes. "You don't have to be a dating expert to know that. It's common sense. Now, hopefully my brother is ready to do the smart thing and lock you down. But if not, then I say go out with Luke if he asks. And don't be shy about letting Austin know you're doing it."

I laughed. "Okay, now you just sound like an obnoxious younger sister."

Megan shrugged. "I guess if the shoe fits, I'll wear it."

I checked my phone. Time was not flying, that was sure. "Do you want me to run to the café and get lunch? I could get the cobb salads. Maybe we split a lemon tart at the end?"

"Oh man." Megan closed her eyes. "I can't eat PB&J when I'm offered that. Yeah. Do it."

"All right. And when I'm back? You're telling me the plan for you and the bookstore being full-time."

Megan winced.

I just pointed at her and pushed through the door. There were more people walking up and down King Street. It was still crisp and cool, but the sun was shining and there were no clouds in the sky, so the air would warm eventually. It was a good morning to go out, do some shopping, grab lunch. Maybe go walk by the water.

I turned to look over my shoulder at the Potomac River. It was glistening in the sun. I smiled. This was why I spent more than was reasonable on the rent for my dinky, run-down apartment. Well, that and it was close to the school. I couldn't discount that.

I reached the little café that had the best salads in Old Town and found that the line was already out the door. At least they were quick.

There were three women seated at one of the patio tables, bundled in coats as they ate. They didn't seem to mind. And steam curled off the top of their drinks. I made a mental note to talk to Whitney and Megan about setting up a real girls' night. Or day. Something. Even if I had to take a sick day—I'd deal with sub plans if it meant the three of us got to spend some time when Megan wasn't technically worried about the store and disappearing every few minutes to help a customer.

The line moved quickly, and I was at the counter ordering before I had a chance to get chilled. They worked quickly to assemble the salads. I tried to stand out of the way of the people who wanted to eat inside at the tables crowded together in the tiny space.

"Two cobbs and a lemon tart?" One of the workers called, holding up a brown paper bag.

"That's me." I reached for the bag. "Thanks. Have a good one."

I headed back out into the cool morning and down to the bookstore. There were probably ten people milling around in the stacks. It was a good thing to see.

"Hey. They were busy?"

I nodded at Megan. "Not too bad, though. You're picking up." She grinned.

"I'll take these to the back room?"

"Sure. You don't have to wait."

"Nah. I'm not in a rush. And they're salads. Not like it's bad if they're cold."

Megan laughed.

I went into the little office where Megan kept a computer and half-height fridge. I tucked the food into the fridge and went back out into the main area of the bookstore.

"Hi. Sorry. Do you work here?" A frazzled-looking older man stepped in front of me.

"How can I help?" I didn't work there, but I was around enough that I could probably help him get whatever he needed.

"Do you know where the romance section is? My wife," he said, and held up his hand and pointed to his left ring finger "is desperate. But I just can't..."

He trailed off, and I smothered a chuckle. It was a book, not lingerie. But whatever. Everyone had their limits. "Do you have the title?"

He held out a slip of paper.

I took it from him and grinned. "Your wife has good taste. It's this way."

He cleared his throat. "Do you think I could wait for you here?"

I couldn't stop the chuckle this time. "Sure. I'll be right back."

I wove through the bookshelves to the right place and pulled a copy of the title his wife wanted. I considered a moment before adding a copy of the sequel. If she was desperate for the first one, she'd probably appreciate getting both.

"Oh. Thank you." The man beamed at me when I came back toward him.

"I grabbed the next book in the series as well, in case you wanted to get her extra."

His eyes sparkled. "I'll do that. She'll be in heaven. Thank you."

"My pleasure. Megan, up at the cash register, can get you squared away. Have a good day." I watched him make his way back up to the front.

It was probably another twenty minutes before the store had cleared out enough that Megan came around to find me. "I'm ready to eat. But we should probably hang by the register if you don't mind?"

"Sure. I'll get the food and meet you up there." I went back into the office to grab the takeout bag. Frowning, I made my way up front. How was Megan going to manage on her own? Maybe pushing her to resign from Social Services and go full-time at the bookstore wasn't such a good idea after all.

Megan patted the wooden stool beside her. "Come to the most glamorous eating locale in the store."

I laughed. "It's not so bad. You can see the shelves. Make sure no one needs anything."

"Yeah. True. And hey, no one wonders if the store is deserted and then tries to walk out with six hundred bucks' worth of science fiction." Megan pulled the top off her salad and started to mix it together.

"Are you worried about doing this all on your own?" I stabbed a bite of salad and popped it in my mouth.

"All the time. And I'm terrified that if I don't try it, I'll regret it for the rest of my life." Megan sighed. "I'm doing it. I'm putting in my notice. The part-time workers I had aren't upset at all. They also said if I get to a point where I need some help to let them know. So that was nice."

"I'm proud of you." And I was. It was good to chase a dream. It was why I was a teacher. I knew how that sounded—there were plenty of people who gave me grief about having no ambition. But I didn't think there was anything wrong with doing what you were good at. I was where God wanted me, and that, most of all, was what I cared about.

"Are you worried about dinner tonight?" Megan glanced over at me, eyebrow raised.

"Nah. It's Austin. If nothing else, I know I'll have a good time with someone I enjoy being with." I was going to repeat that to myself as many times as I needed to, because I was definitely going to be a little heartbroken if dinner tonight wasn't because Austin wanted to be more than friends.

I loved being his best friend.

I didn't want to lose that. Almost as much as I wanted so much more.

9

AUSTIN

I brushed a hand down the front of my tie, smoothing it against my torso as I got out of my car in Kayla's parking lot. Should I button my blazer? No, that was probably too much. This wasn't a date. No matter how much I was starting to wish I'd told Kayla it was what I wanted.

Last night, after poker, I hadn't been able to sleep. I was honestly surprised Megan hadn't cornered me this morning to ask me about it. The townhouse we shared creaked. A lot. Especially when someone was up walking around late at night. I'd tried to be quiet, but buildings that were over a hundred years old didn't exactly lend themselves to that. Thankfully, for whatever reason, Megan had quietly downed her coffee before heading out to the bookstore. If she hadn't, I probably would have told her. Even if she couldn't keep a secret. But she had.

So instead, I'd had entirely too much time to think.

Not that I needed any extra thinking time.

I wanted to date Kayla. I also didn't want to ruin our friendship, and I wasn't one hundred percent positive that she was interested in me as more than a friend. So. Step one? Get our friendship back on track.

The fact that she'd agreed to dinner, and hadn't put up a fight when I'd mentioned Ada's and it being my treat, had to be a good sign. Didn't it?

I climbed the stairs to her apartment and knocked at her door. I wished she'd move to a better part of town. Granted, this was probably what she could afford. She didn't have a grandmother like Megan and I did. Well, and now the whole billionaire thing meant I could buy up the whole block and not blink. Point being, this was exactly where I'd be living if I was doing it all on my own paycheck.

The door opened and Kayla beamed. "Hey. I'm almost ready. Come on in."

She wandered off, so I went ahead and stepped into her apartment, careful to shut the door behind myself. She had cats, and Charles was known for trying to run outside if he saw an opportunity.

"There you are." I squatted as Ada strolled into the room, the tip of her tail swishing. She paused, stared at me a moment, then deigned to come over so I could pet her. I found the spot behind her ear that always set her purring, and rubbed. "We're eating at a restaurant named for the same woman you're named after. Did your mom tell you that?"

Ada didn't comment. She seemed content to purr and lean her weight into my scratching.

Charles pranced over. I hadn't seen which direction he came from, but it was obvious he wanted attention, too, given how he butted at my other hand. I laughed and complied.

"There are portraits of your namesake there, too, Charles. But you didn't get naming rights, sorry. It's a cool thing to be one of the founders of computer science, but it doesn't beat out being one of the first *women* in computers. You'll always come behind Ada Lovelace."

Ada gave a quiet mew before adjusting her head. I guess my hand had moved off the perfect spot.

"Have you seen—there they are." Kayla came back into the room, hopping on one foot as she zipped her left boot. "I forgot how much they like you."

I looked up and grinned at her. "What's not to like?"

Kayla snickered. "I need to set out food for them in the kitchen, then we can go. Sorry to be behind schedule."

At the word "food" both cats had deserted me, trotting instead in the direction of the kitchen. I stood and followed. I could delude myself that it wasn't because I wanted another look at Kayla, but I knew the truth.

"You look really good." I shoved my hands in my pockets and leaned against the kitchen doorframe.

Kayla glanced over her shoulder a moment before turning her attention back to the cat food bowls. "Thanks. You cleaned up pretty well yourself."

My tie matched her belt—a blue that teetered on the edge of the color made famous by Tiffany's. It wasn't perfect. That color was probably trademarked. But it was close. I'd bought the tie because it made me think of Kayla. It was good to see I wasn't wrong about her enjoying the color.

"There." Kayla pushed the bag to the back of the counter and quickly washed her hands at the sink. She dried them and headed to the living room, brushing close to me as she went through the door. My senses were overloaded with the fragrance that put me in mind of cherry blossoms and sunshine.

I hadn't slept well last night, and that scent was going to make tonight a challenge, too.

Kayla slipped the gold chain of a small, shiny, black bag over her shoulder. "I'm ready if you are."

I hurried to get to the door so I could hold it open for her.

She chuckled as she stepped through. I pulled it shut behind me. Of course, she still had to lock the deadbolt with her key, so maybe holding it didn't make much sense. But I didn't care. Maybe she'd piece together that this was more—to me at least— than best friends having dinner.

I offered my elbow.

Kayla laughed and poked me in the ribs. "What? Is this prom?"

"Just trying to give you the courtesy you deserve, all dressed up like that." Her rejection stung. Maybe best friends having dinner was the better frame of mind after all.

We made it down the hall to the stairwell and out to my car with very little conversation. I cast around for ideas of what to talk about. Something that would get things back on even footing between us after...whatever it was that happened last week at school.

Maybe, instead of avoiding it, I ought to bring it up?

I clicked the Unlock button on my car's key fob as we approached. I didn't have to hurry to beat her to the handle. Part of me wondered if I ought to just stop. But this habit was one my grandmother had always insisted on, so I opened the door and waited.

"Thanks." Kayla slid into the passenger seat and reached for the door to close it.

I went around to my side. She was already fastening her seat-belt when I climbed behind the wheel. "I'd like to apologize for giving you the impression that I saw you as a nagging wife. I don't. I never could. You don't nag."

Kayla's eyebrows lifted. "I nag a little."

I shook my head.

She lifted a hand with thumb and forefinger a half-inch apart. "About this much. And you're right to call me on it. I shouldn't push on the Mexico thing. I know it's not everyone's idea of how to spend spring break. It's not even what God expects everyone to do. Luke spent a lot of our lunch reminding me that our daily lives are us being missionaries because of the Great Commission. So I really do know better than to go off on you because you're not excited about chaperoning teens on your week off from teens."

My lips twitched and I started the car. "How about we call it bygones? I'll forgive you. You forgive me. And I'll toss in that I'm praying about the Mexico trip, okay?"

"You are? Really?" Kayla bounced in her seat. "It'd be so cool to have you along."

I grinned. It was nice to see a little of the bouncy Kayla back —even if she was going on about the Mexico trip again. I didn't mind—it did sound like a worthwhile thing for the people who ended up going. I just wondered how many students Luke was going to be able to convince to go. Families often took vacations together for spring break. If the kids wanted to go somewhere, it was the beach. There was nothing wrong with either of those things.

The way I saw it? Luke wasn't likely to need a ton of chaperones to volunteer, because he was going to be lucky to get ten kids who wanted to go.

But I kept those thoughts to myself. I could learn. And Kayla was gung-ho about this trip. About Luke, too? That remained to be seen.

For now, I was going to focus on my time with her and not worry about anything else.

It was a short drive to Ada's. I was excited to see a street spot right near the restaurant. I'd been fully prepared to end up in one of the garages with a short walk. But this was practically crossing the street. In better weather, I would have suggested walking from Kayla's, but the warmish temperature of this afternoon was already dipping into decidedly cool.

"Ready?" I shut off the engine and glanced over.

"Yep." Kayla rubbed her hands together. "Crab cake, here I come."

I laughed and pushed open my door. I walked around and met her by the hood of the car and clicked the key fob to lock the doors. There wasn't heavy traffic, so we hurried across without bothering to go up to the corner and the crosswalk. A strong breeze whipped up off the water and sent Kayla's hair blowing around her head like a halo.

Why had I never noticed she was beautiful?

I opened the restaurant door and briefly touched the small of her back as she passed me on her way through.

"Good evening. Welcome to Ada's on the River." The hostess smiled as we approached.

"Hi. Thanks. We have a reservation under Campbell."

She looked down at the reservation book, tapped on one of the lines, and collected menus. "Follow me."

We walked behind her through the tables and their funky, geometrically patterned upholstered chairs. The restaurant wasn't crowded, but it wasn't empty, either. I glanced to the left where glass separated the inside seating from the dockside seating. Maybe Kayla and I could come back in the summer and sit out there. It'd be a lovely place to watch the sun go down.

Romantic.

And I was getting way ahead of myself.

"Your server will be right with you. Have a pleasant meal." The hostess set the leather encased menus at our spots and seemed to fade away.

I waited for Kayla to sit before taking the seat across from her. "I'm glad you were free tonight."

"Me, too." She tossed me a quick grin before flipping open her menu.

I frowned. Maybe I needed to stop overthinking and let the conversation take its natural course. I opened my menu and skimmed the offerings. I'd never hear the end of it if I ordered the burger, no matter how amazing it sounded. So, the salmon. I was a sucker for harissa. I set my menu aside and glanced around while I waited for Kayla to decide.

Naming a restaurant after a mathematician was amusing. How many people knew who Ada Lovelace was? Or Charles Babbage, for that matter? Maybe it was taught in intro to computing classes here or there when teachers spent two seconds on history that got us to today, but who remembered that past the test? My students certainly never did.

I looked across the table at Kayla. "Would Ada and Charles approve?"

"Mine or the originals?"

"Yours, of course."

Kayla set her menu aside and looked around. "I think they would. There's enough fish on the menu to make them happy at least. If they're lucky, I'll bring them each home a bite of crab so they don't feel too left out."

"I'm getting the salmon. I can set a little aside if you want."

"You don't have to do that."

"I know. But I wouldn't want them to suffer."

Kayla snickered. "You know how unlikely that is. But I also won't say no. Because they're spoiled babies." She sighed. "This was a good idea. Thank you."

"My pleasure."

I didn't get a chance to say anything more because our server appeared. He listed the specials, took our drink orders, and seemed a little put out when we declined appetizers and went straight to ordering entrées. Still, he took our menus and left us alone with a promise to be back shortly with drinks.

"What did I miss with you this week?"

Kayla's cheeks pinked. "I didn't tell you about Lucy at all, did I?"

I shook my head. "Lucy Hu?"

"Yeah. When I came back from our lunch a little early," she paused to clear her throat. Was she embarrassed? She didn't need to be. "I found Lucy copying from Aidan MacAllister."

I winced. "He's got a thing for her."

"Does he?"

"Yeah. The signs are there if you know what to look for. They're both in advanced calculus and sometimes I think I see little hearts instead of pupils in his eyes when he looks at her."

Kayla chuckled. "Poor guy. Does Lucy know?"

"I don't know how she'd miss it, but I also don't see her encouraging it."

She furrowed her brow. "Why not?"

"Have you met her parents?"

"I spoke to them on the phone this week."

"Hm. Probably not the same effect. But I guess I'll just say I don't think it would go over well for Lucy to bring home a boy who wasn't Chinese."

"Oh." Kayla's lips stayed in the shape of the O for a moment. Then she nodded. "That makes a few things clearer."

"You said she was copying? As in cheating?"

Kayla shrugged. "Lucy shouldn't be in computers. She hates it, for starters. And while I think she *could* be good at it, if she wanted to, she doesn't. And it shows in her work."

"Dad is pushing it." The server came back with our drinks. I leaned out of the way for her to set them down.

"Got it in one." Kayla paused to sip her water. "I tried to talk to him. Mentioned some great math careers that out-pay software engineering. We'll see how it goes, I guess. But for now, she has a makeup assignment that she has to complete in the lab when I'm present."

"Poor kid."

"What do you mean? She chose to cheat."

I flicked at the hem of the napkin in the middle of my plate, then picked it up and put it in my lap. "I get that. I know a little about family pressure. It's not fun."

"True. And yet."

I held up my hands. "You're right. There's no excuse for cheating. I hope her dad can come around. She's brilliant at math. And she loves it. She gets it—sees the beauty, you know?"

"I do know."

"I forget you love math, too." I shook my head. How did I let that slip my mind? I associated Kayla with the computer lab, I guess, but her passion had always been math.

"Well, you can just stop that, mister."

I chuckled. "Won't let it happen again. Mr. Hu seemed receptive?"

"I think the best I can say is that he didn't seem *un*receptive."

"Well, maybe that's a start. What's the new project for Lucy?"

Kayla sighed. "I don't know yet. I need to get it to her on Monday but I'm not sure what to have her code."

"What if you gave her some freedom? Give her the skills you want to see and let her choose how to demonstrate them." My students always enjoyed when they had more freedom in their projects. That was sometimes harder to figure out how to do with a math project, but I did my best.

"That's a good idea. You're pretty smart sometimes, you know?"

"Only sometimes?"

"Don't push, buster. I said what I said." Kayla smirked at me across the table.

Was it the opening I was looking for? I cleared my throat, but I couldn't get the words out. I wanted to mention that the guys had shown me the error of my ways. Or ask if there was any chance that she felt more than friendship. Instead, I went with,

"Have you thought about what you're going to do for your senior capstone projects?"

Her eyebrows lifted like maybe she'd expected me to say something else, but she went with it. "Not completely. I've got ideas."

"I have a couple as well. I know that two of the seniors— Aidan and Sascha—are going to ask about combining yours and mine. You up for that?"

"Case by case basis." Kayla tapped the stem of her water glass. "For those two? Sure."

"Enough about work. Sorry. Did you do anything fun this morning?"

She gave me an incredulous look. "What do I do every Saturday morning?"

"Grade programs?" Was I supposed to know the answer to that? I didn't have a super predictable Saturday morning routine.

"Bzzt. I was at the bookstore with your sister until around two."

"Oh. Nice." It was. I shouldn't mind that Kayla and Megan were friends, but there was a part of me that wanted to shake my sister and scream that I was friends with Kayla first. She was *my* friend and I didn't want to share. Irrational? Absolutely. Still true.

She cocked her head to the side. "That was unconvincing."

"No. It is. It's good. I'm sure my sister appreciated it. She tell you she's really going to put in her notice this time and give her complete attention to the bookstore?"

"She did. I'm glad. Except then we ate lunch by the cash register, and I started to wonder if she was going to be able to do it all on her own. Sure, we ran the numbers—and I'm pretty sure you ran them too—and they'll work fine. But is she going to be just as stretched and stressed? Or more?"

I shrugged. "Maybe. But she'll be happier. And knowing Megan? She'll make it work. She always does when it matters to her."

"True." Kayla frowned a moment before giving a shrug of her own. "I guess I'll hold off on worrying until we see what's what."

I laughed. That was Kayla to a T. Probably how she stayed so cheerful, all things considered. A thought flitted through my mind and before I took the time to analyze it, I opened my mouth to speak. "Do you think I'm stupid to still be teaching?"

Kayla's eyebrows lifted. "No. I mean, it's kind of funny when I stop and think too hard. You're like a superhero. Math teacher by day, billionaire by night. Except, of course, you don't really live like a billionaire, either."

I sighed. "Is that wrong?"

"Not wrong. Just...strange. I'm going with strange."

"What's strange about it? I love math. I love teaching." I'd kind of thought Kayla, more than anyone else, would understand that. The guys didn't, really. They made noises like they did, but I could see them shaking their heads in disbelief.

"I know that." She reached across the table and touched my hand.

I ignored the sparks that only I seemed to feel.

She pulled her hand back. "But you still drive a beat-up Toyota."

My car was the problem? "I love that car. It gets good gas mileage, fits in any parking spot, and I don't have to worry about it getting broken into or scratched."

Kayla laughed. "All good things. Especially in the school parking lot. But c'mon. You could buy a second car, something fancy and fun, for the weekends."

I blinked. It seemed ridiculous to have a second car just sitting around. "There's only one of me."

"Like I said. Strange."

I scowled and changed the subject to something more neutral. But even as we chatted about other things, my thoughts reeled. Maybe I should be doing more with the money than letting it sit around and grow. I'd bought our townhouse off Grandma. No one but she and I knew that, though. I'd even bought the bookstore—and I sure wasn't telling anyone that. Grandma hadn't wanted to take much for them, but I'd insisted on market value. But still, even with Old Town real estate prices, that was a drop in the bucket. And they were self-serving purchases.

Scott had offered to let us all join the charitable foundation he'd set up. His mom ran it and handled all the disbursements. I was definitely going to do that. My own attempts at keeping up with even a minimum tithe were scattered at best. But maybe I needed to do more.

When the waiter had deposited our food, I looked across the table at Kayla and waited for her to meet my gaze. "I have an idea. But I'm going to need help. You interested?"

Kayla's head tipped to the side. "Probably. Why don't you pray for this food and then tell me all about it?"

10

KAYLA

"No after-church lunch date with Luke today?" Whitney slid onto the bench across from me in the diner booth.

"I think it was a one-time thing." I hoped my shrug was casual. I'd hung around in the foyer longer than usual, waiting to see if Luke was going to come find me. He never did. And sure, there were chairs to stack and all that, but I'd waited past the time it had taken the week before. So...it was entirely possible he'd spotted me and gone out a different door just to avoid talking.

"What'd I miss?" Megan sat beside me and grinned at Whitney. "You're sitting with us?"

"Apparently it's a man-only table over there today." Whitney rolled her eyes, but they were sparkling with laughter. "I don't mind one less meal in charge of a toddler."

"Aw. It's adorable that they've pulled Beckett into their man time." I looked over at the table where Austin and his friends—including Whitney's husband, Scott—sat. "Are they letting him play poker with them?"

Whitney snickered. "They probably would. Scott said a couple of the guys asked where he was this past week."

"Hey. Bookstore time is important, too. Don't let them hog him." Megan unrolled her silverware. "I take his commentary on the kid books very seriously. In fact, I just got a new catalog with some of the upcoming new releases, and I could use input on what to stock."

"You know he'd love to help. Of course, he's just going to point at all of them and name what's on the cover, but he's three. So." Whitney shook her head.

"That's helpful." Megan picked up the menu and then set it down again. "I don't know why I always want to look. I'm not getting something different."

"But you could." I looked at the menu and fought a sigh. I was still full from the enormous crab cake last night. I'd eaten it all while Austin described his very rudimentary plan for an after-school center. I loved the idea. And he had the money to make it happen. But it was going to be a big-time investment. I wasn't sure if my heart could take it.

"What's with you?" Megan's elbow connected with my ribs.

"Are you upset that Luke didn't ask you out again?" Whitney frowned at me from across the table. "I thought you said the first date wasn't great."

"It's not that. It's nothing." I set the menu down. "I'm not super hungry. Maybe I'll try the soup."

Whitney laughed, but broke off when I didn't join in. "You're serious? No one ever gets the soup."

"Maybe it's good and we're all missing out." She wasn't wrong. It had become a bit of a joke between us. No one in our group had ever tried the soup—and we hadn't seen bowls being taken out to other tables, either. "They have broccoli cheddar. How bad can it be?"

Megan winced. "Have you ever tried to make it from a can?"

"Once." Whitney shuddered. "Never again. Even Beckett wouldn't eat it, and he loves broccoli. Which is just wrong. Don't get me started on that."

I chuckled. Beckett's love for broccoli was legendary in the group. "Hey. Be glad he likes a vegetable."

"I know, I know. I'm just so tired of it. And the smell kind of lingers in the house. I swear it's permeating the couch fabric." Whitney looked over as the more-harried-than-usual server stopped at our table.

"Ladies. It's good to see you. The usuals?" She didn't have her order pad out.

I almost felt bad changing it up. I cleared my throat. "I actually wanted a bowl of broccoli cheddar today."

"Just soup?" The server pulled her order pad out of her apron pocket and slipped the pen out from behind her ear.

"I'm sticking with my usual." Megan stacked my menu on top of hers and offered them.

"And you?" She looked at Whitney.

"Cobb salad?"

The server huffed out a little sigh and scribbled on her pad before reaching for the menus. "I'll get your orders right in."

I watched her stride away, her white sneakers squeaking on the linoleum floor. "I feel kind of bad now."

"Right? Oops." Whitney hunched her shoulders.

"A salad, Whit? Really?" Megan crossed her arms. "Why am I the only one eating deliciously unhealthy food today?"

"My stomach has been off the past couple of days." Whitney sighed. "At least a salad still tastes good later."

"On what planet?" I wrinkled my nose. Leftover salad was the worst.

"Mine, I guess." Whitney folded her hands on the table. "But can we go back to where I asked if you were upset about not having another date with Luke, and you deflected?"

"Right?" Megan shifted on the bench beside me so she was kind of facing me. "What's going on?"

"I think it was a one-time thing. I like Mexican food. He doesn't. We're incompatible." I wouldn't actually rule someone out for that, but it appeared Luke would. "Or I made him angry with my questions about the spring break trip. It doesn't matter, anyway."

"Because you're hung up on my clueless brother." Megan glanced over toward the table where all the guys were.

"That doesn't matter, either. We're pals." I paused, following Megan's look over toward the guys. Then I frowned and checked angles. She wasn't looking at her brother. She was looking at Cody? If Austin had a best friend who wasn't me, it'd be Cody. Interesting. I filed that tidbit away to tease her about later when I needed a way to get her to leave me alone.

"Uh-huh." Megan looked back at me and shook her head. "You need to tell him how you feel."

"Yeah, I'll get right on that." I hoped she'd hear the sarcasm dripping. "Especially not now that he's asked me to help him start up a big after-school learning center."

"Yeah?" Megan brightened. "He's really doing it? That's excellent. He's been talking about it, off and on, for years."

He had? I searched my memory. I guess he had. More in the "gee, I wish there was a place where" kind of conversation though. I didn't realize he'd been thinking of starting one. If I was his best friend, shouldn't I have known that?

"Wait. Why would kids at your school need something like that? We're in a fairly high-end area, aren't we? At least based on the housing prices, I figured everyone at your school was from relatively well-off families." Whitney reached for her water.

I shook my head. "We run the spectrum. The districting makes it so we do get kids from middle and upper middle class, for sure, but then we also pull in from down around Landmark."

"Oh. Wow." Whitney's eyebrows knit together. "Who drew the districts?"

I laughed. "Good question. I asked once, when we first started, and got a convoluted answer about increasing diversity and providing equity of opportunity. But I think really what happened was they realized if the districts weren't normal shapes, then they could get away with not building—and staffing—the two more high schools we desperately need on this side of the county."

Megan grunted. "That sounds like the local government for sure."

"Notice goes in tomorrow, right?" It was my turn to jab an elbow.

Megan squirmed away. "Ow. But yes. Tomorrow."

"And you're texting us when it's done. Right?" Whitney pointed at Megan.

"What, you don't believe I'm going to do it?" When neither of us said anything, Megan's shoulders fell. "Fine. Yes. Texting after it's sent."

I rubbed her shoulder. "You know this is the right thing."

"Yeah, I do. But I can't help feeling like I'm letting people down. The people who need me. We're already understaffed and overworked. Who's going to suffer because I decided to chuck it and work in a bookstore?" Megan leaned back to make room for her food to be put in front of her.

I eyed the bowl of thick soup when it was set in front of me. My stomach twisted. Maybe there really was a reason no one got the soup. It was a bright, unnatural orange color with globs of green suspended in it.

"Enjoy, ladies. Let me know if you need anything." The server hurried away.

I dipped my spoon into the bowl, pressing my lips together at the amount of resistance I encountered. Maybe it was a good thing I was still full from dinner last night. "I guess I can see that. I'm not sure I could walk away from teaching. But the big difference, at least in my mind, is that you're not thriving there."

"What do you mean?" Megan poked at the coleslaw on the side of her plate with her fork.

"You feel burdened for these people. You want to help them. But you're not succeeding. Or at least that's what it sounds like to me when you talk. When was the last time you had a win? On anything?" I gave the bowl of soup a little nudge away from me. I was definitely not eating it.

"You're not even going to try it?" Whitney eyed the bowl. "For science, if nothing else?"

I snickered. "Help yourself."

Whitney pressed her lips together, shaking her head vigorously.

"Exactly." I glanced at Megan. "Well?"

"I'm thinking. And maybe the fact that it's taking so long is the answer in and of itself." Megan sighed. "I'm not helping. I'm tilting at windmills."

I rubbed her arm again. She sounded so defeated. "I'm sure there are ways you can still help people. Even working at the bookstore. Maybe you should talk to Austin. I bet there's a way books could factor into his after-school center."

"That's not a bad idea. I'll do that. Am I allowed to know about the center?" Megan's eyebrows lifted. "He didn't swear you to secrecy or anything?"

"Nope. It was just friends chatting over dinner." I couldn't quite keep the frustration out of my voice.

"Sorry." Whitney slid out of her seat, her hand over her mouth, and held up a finger. "Be right back."

I watched her all but run toward the restrooms, then turned to Megan. "Pregnant?"

"That's my guess. Think she has any clue?" Megan picked up her sandwich and took a bite.

"Nope."

"Are we going to suggest it?" Megan looked over toward the guys' table.

I turned my head in the same direction and my gaze locked with Austin's. He lifted an eyebrow and tipped his head toward the bathrooms. I shook my head. He frowned at me. Finally, I had pity on his confusion and mouthed the word, "Tomorrow."

Austin nodded.

"You two are so cute. Why doesn't he get it?"

Megan's words drew my attention back to our own table. "It's okay. We'll figure it out. Probably."

"You have to promise me you'll try. Okay? Because I'm not on board with the whole Luke thing." Megan poked at her food again. "Why did we come out to eat if none of us was actually hungry?"

"Habit. Can we rewind though? What's wrong with Luke?" Because, sure, I'd much rather be with Austin. But if he was determined to keep me in the friend zone, I wasn't going to be a pining spinster for the rest of my days.

"Nothing. There's nothing wrong with him. He's just not my brother."

"Well, you might need to keep a more open mind. Because I don't know how anything is going to work out. With either of them." I was trying to pray about it. That was the advice I knew my mom would give me if I asked. Which was part of why I hadn't asked when she'd called me this morning before church. She was definitely open to the idea of a pastor for a son-in-law. Another teacher did not give her the same warm fuzzies, even though salary-wise, they were probably both about the same. Mom thought teaching was a fine profession for a woman. Not so much for a man. Arguing with her about it was pointless.

"I'll try. You know I'm praying for you, right?"

"I do. I appreciate it." I was about to ask her about Cody, but Whitney came back. She was chalky and washed out. "You okay?"

"I don't know." Whitney scooted back into the booth and pushed her salad away from herself.

"Did you take a pregnancy test yet?"

I gaped at Megan. "Real subtle."

"What? It's kind of obvious."

Whitney visibly swallowed. "But we're not trying for a baby. In fact, we're doubling up on actively *not* trying. We haven't even been married a full month."

"So take a test. If it's not that, then you have the flu without any of the usual symptoms."

I shot Megan a look. There was no need to be so harsh. I reached across the table to touch Whitney's hand. "Would it be so bad?"

She closed her eyes. "I don't know. We haven't talked about kids beyond agreeing that we'd want more. What if he's angry?"

"Scott's not going to be angry." I could say that with confidence. "Surprised, sure. But he loves you. And hey, you've got that extra bedroom in the townhouse, so it's all good."

Whitney's lips twitched at my attempt at humor. "You mean Scott's office?"

"Yeah, well. Babies don't need their own room right away anyway. And if it's a boy, he could always share with Beckett. I read somewhere about how growing up sharing a room, even if it's not necessary, helps build empathy and—"

"Resentment?" Megan interrupted me.

"What's wrong with you?" I scowled at Megan.

"I'm sorry." She lifted her hands and closed her eyes. "I'm jealous, okay? Whitney has Scott. You've got two guys vying for your attention. And I have a bookstore. And the beginning of a headache. I think I'm going to head home. I'm sorry. Congrats, Whit. Kayla's right, Scott will be thrilled once he gets over his shock."

Megan dug into her purse and dropped a twenty on the table. "I'll talk to you guys tomorrow."

"We clearly need to figure out what that was." Whitney watched Megan hurry from the diner. "Do you have any idea?"

Should I mention the three times I caught Megan staring at Cody? It wasn't like she'd been shooting him longing, dreamy looks. She'd just been watching him. "Maybe? You ever get the feeling she's interested in Cody?"

"Cody?" Whitney's face was the picture of puzzlement as she glanced over toward where the guys were eating, then back. "Our Cody?"

"Yeah."

"No. But it's something to keep in mind. Huh." Whitney glanced over again.

"So. Are you going to get a pregnancy test?"

Whitney managed a weak laugh. "Mom gave me one as a wedding gift. I guess I'll dig it out when I get home."

11

LUKE

I flopped onto my couch and reached for the TV remote. Monthly lunches with the senior pastor were an interesting idea in theory, but man. I hated them. If it was just me and Pastor Chaz, it might be fine. Probably would be. But of course his wife had to be there. And she spent the whole time looking for places to slide in subtle—and not-so-subtle—questions about my dating life.

Because apparently an unmarried youth pastor was a problem for her.

I turned on the TV and stared at the menu of streaming options. My landlord had said it would be fine if I wanted to use his cable, but right now that wasn't another expense I wanted to add. I wasn't sure what I'd want to watch that I couldn't stream anyway. I didn't care much about professional sports, and most games I cared about, I could find a way to watch.

Mostly, I just wanted some noise in the background to drown out the sounds of the family living their happy life upstairs.

I navigated to a knife forging show and hit Play on the next episode.

I watched for a few minutes before digging my phone out of

my pocket and staring at it. I should call Kayla. Ask her out again. Maybe be a little clearer about the purpose of the outing and the choice of restaurants.

Except really, what was the point?

Would texting be easier?

Mom and Dad would say it was a copout. On the other hand, Mom and Dad had met on a message board and fallen in love over email before they ever met, so it wasn't like they could really diss texting as a means to getting to know someone. They were all in if I wanted to take another stab at a dating app.

I scoffed.

My one attempt at that had basically labeled me an eternal loser. How many people went through the questionnaire and got told they were unmatchable? There couldn't be many. Not when the app in question prided itself on all the successful, happy couples they'd brought together.

So, no. No more apps for me.

I thumbed open my phone and tapped Kayla's contact before I could talk myself out of it. Again.

"Hello?"

"Hi, Kayla. It's Luke."

"Hey. How are you?"

I fought a groan. This was dumb. The whole thing. Except I'd really like to get everyone off my back. "Good. Ish. It was my turn for lunch with the pastor today. He rotates through the staff each week."

"Ah. That's nice of him."

"I guess. I don't get a ton of homecooked meals, so that part is definitely good." Not that the pastor's wife was an impressive cook, but the food wasn't bad. The roast was tender, the potatoes weren't gluey. And I always brought home a container full of leftovers that would last for at least two meals. I cleared my throat. "I was wondering if you might be free for dinner tomorrow. I realize it's a school night."

She laughed. "I have been known to go out on school nights."

"So is that a yes?" Did that sound desperate? I definitely wasn't trying to do that.

"Yes. When and where? I have a computer club meeting after school, so I should probably meet you."

I winced as one of the guys on the TV screen burned himself with hot metal. Was it wrong to have her meet me? "Do you like Italian? There's a good place in Old Town. Mia's, I think it's called?"

"Sure, I know it. That sounds good. What time?"

"Five?"

"I can do that."

There was a long pause. Was I supposed to say more? "How has your day been?"

"Pretty typical Sunday. Church and lunch at the diner. Now I'm hanging out with my cats. I have a little grading I could do, but I try not to work on Sundays when I don't have to. I have a new book I picked up yesterday that I was thinking of starting. I'll probably call my parents later."

"That sounds like a nice day. I didn't realize you have cats." I liked cats. I liked dogs better, but cats were okay. I couldn't have either since the family whose basement I rented had serious allergies and they couldn't risk it. I didn't really have time to care for a pet anyway.

"Yep. Ada and Charles. They're my babies." She laughed, and I imagined she was talking to them as much as to me.

"Are they any special kind? Breed? I don't actually know a lot about cats."

"Nope. I got them from a rescue when they were kittens. Ada is a tortoiseshell. Charles is a tuxedo. Both are shorthaired."

"Nice." I didn't actually know what that meant, but I could look it up later. "It's nice that you have two so they can keep each other company when you're at school."

"That's why I went ahead and took them both. They were already pretty bonded to one another from their time at the shelter, even though they weren't from the same litter. So far, it's definitely working out. For all of us. You don't have a pet?"

"Nah. I wouldn't mind a dog at some point, but right now I'm living in a basement apartment, and it's not really feasible."

"I'm sorry."

"It's okay. I don't really have time right now, either. The pastor's pushing me to go back for my master's degree. He says when I grow out of youth ministry it'll be a good thing to have already handled. Make me a better senior pastor candidate." I reached for the remote and paused the show. I wasn't really following it, and it was getting to the interesting part.

"Is that what you're hoping for down the road? Your own church?"

Was it? My head dropped back on the sofa and I stared at the popcorn ceiling. "I don't know. Maybe? Right now, I like working with the youth. I guess it's not something I can do forever, though. At least, I've never met a fifty-year-old youth pastor, you know? Everyone seems to see it as a steppingstone."

"Hm. I guess that's true. I haven't done a lot of thinking about it, if I'm honest."

I chuckled. "Why would you?"

"You've got time to figure it out, though. Do you want to go back to school?"

"Not really." I cringed. She was too easy to talk to.

"Then why are you thinking about it?"

I could give her all the reasons the pastor continued to bring up. I had the time now, when I was single and unencumbered with a wife and family. The church would let me do the work during the day as long as it didn't interfere with handling my job. It was a good thing to have on my résumé. Blah blah. In the end, it boiled down to the same reason I was trying to figure out if there was relationship potential with Kayla. "It seems like I'm expected to do it."

"And do you always do what you think people expect of you?"

"I guess I try to. Is that bad?"

"Not necessarily. But—and I'll admit it seems weird to be the one saying this to you—when you're a pastor, I feel like it's more important to pray about it and do what God wants. Not anyone else."

I closed my eyes. She wasn't wrong. "It's not always that easy."

"I get it." Sympathy laced her words. "I'll pray for you to have clarity."

"Thanks. Is there...is there something I can pray for you?" Was it overstepping to ask? We weren't really even friends yet. It felt like I was pushing for intimacy she might not be ready for.

"Oh. Uh."

"You don't have to share. Only if you're comfortable." *Way to go, Luke. Make things awkward.*

"I guess you could pray about a project I'm working on—I'm not sure exactly which direction to go with it."

I wanted to ask for more details. Maybe there would be a way for me to offer advice or help out in addition to praying. But I also wasn't going to. Not after how hesitant she was to share anything in the first place. "All right. Will do."

She cleared her throat. "I should let you go. I'll see you tomorrow at five."

"Yeah. Of course. Looking forward to it."

Kayla made a noise that could have been agreement before the call ended.

I tossed my phone on the cushion beside me and unpaused the TV. I didn't know much about forging, but given that stilted conversation, I probably knew more about it than I did women.

MONDAYS WERE my second day off. Pastors had to flex their weekends a bit, since Sundays were, obviously, workdays. I spent my morning tidying up the apartment and going for a long run. I liked to drive over to one of the parking lots for the Mount Vernon trail and then run beside the Potomac down to the end of the trail at Washington's house, then come back. It was about fifteen miles round trip, and I could do it in just over two hours.

Every now and then, I toyed with trying for the Marine Corps Marathon. Or any marathon, really, but the Marine Corps made sense since it was right here. I'd done a handful of halfs, and liked them well enough. But I didn't know if I had the full twenty-six miles in me.

I'd never tried.

On work days, I kept my runs to five miles. I had a couple of nice routes to choose from and liked to vary from day to day.

But I looked forward to Mondays and the time spent with my feet slapping the trail along the river. It was my best praying time.

Today I'd been distracted. I tried to funnel the thoughts into actual prayer, but couldn't quite pull it off. Still, when I got back to my car, sweaty, lungs burning, and that warm pull in my muscles that told me I'd gotten a good workout, my head was clearer. More settled.

I was going to let the pastor know I didn't plan to apply to grad school.

My stomach clenched. I didn't like the idea that I'd be letting him down, somehow. Disappointing him. But I just didn't feel called to do that. Right now, I didn't feel any call to a senior pastor position, either.

I liked working with the youth. I liked knowing I was helping to shape the next generation of the Church. And hopefully I was giving them the tools that would help them stand firm and hold fast to their faith when they went off to college and out into the world as adults.

And Kayla?

Well, we'd already agreed to dinner. Beyond that, I didn't know. I liked the idea of having a girlfriend—or a wife. People would stop asking about it then. Stop implying that I was some sort of creeper for wanting to help with the youth as a young, single guy.

I popped the trunk and dug in my duffel for a towel. I scrubbed it over my head and neck before tossing it back in the trunk and shutting it.

My phone rang as I slid behind the wheel.

I fought a groan when I saw Pastor Chaz's number, but I tapped to accept the call. "Hi, Chaz."

"Luke. I'm glad I caught you. How are you?"

"Good. Just finished up my long run. Yourself?" I didn't bother starting the car. I'd likely need to look something up or take notes or any variety of things it would be better not to do when driving. The pastor didn't call to chit chat. "What can I do for you?"

"I've had a call from one of the parents expressing concern about the Mexico trip."

My heart sank. I'd sent all the kids home with a detailed brochure about the trip yesterday. "That didn't take long."

The pastor gave a short laugh. "I know. And I know I approved everything before we even reached this stage, but I told her I'd talk to you and see if there any room for change."

"What's her concern?" I imagined it was one of two things. The cost, which I couldn't really do anything about. We were flying to Mexico. That was never going to be inexpensive, but I'd managed to wrangle a decent deal if we were able to get enough people to commit to going. Or it was the fact that we weren't doing any sightseeing.

"The schedule." Pastor Chavez paused to clear his throat. "She expressed concern that the kids would be traveling to another country and missing out on all the opportunities to actually experience that country while they were there."

I tried counting to ten. It didn't help much. "How is helping out citizens of that country not experiencing the country again?"

"Luke." The pastor's voice carried a warning. "Is there any way to take either the first or last day and change it into something touristy?"

My kneejerk response was no. That wasn't why I wanted to take the kids on this trip. If they wanted to go see the Mexican beaches, they should talk their parents into a family trip. "Not really."

"Why not?"

I took a deep breath and let it out slowly. "For starters, it would increase the cost. Right now, our transportation costs once we land are minimal. We don't have to pay for lodging, either, as we'll be rolling out sleeping bags in the church right there in the village. The village, which isn't anywhere near the beach. I'm assuming it's the beaches that she thinks her child needs to see?"

There was a pause. "She did mention the beach. Or the ruins."

"Right. Well, we aren't going to be near either of those. Best case? We could spend a day in Mexico City. But that would necessitate a hotel. And probably more chaperones than I was planning on, because I don't think we'd do as well in the city trying to get around as a huge group. We'd need to split into teams of four or five, each with an adult." I shook my head. The logistics sounded horrible. "And I'm not sure what there is to see there in the first place. I'm sure there are museums or something, but I don't think the kids are going to be jumping for joy about that as an option."

Pastor Chaz chuckled. "You're probably right. All right. I'll call her back and try to explain."

"Did she say why she didn't call me?" That stung. I wasn't exactly new. I'd been the youth pastor for a little over a year now. Was there going to be a point when the parents would accept that I was the one in charge?

"Not really. Would you like me to ask her?"

What would the pastor say if I said yes? It was tempting.

He sighed. "You're upset."

"No. It's fine. I appreciate you touching base with me." I could hear the stiffness in my voice, but I couldn't do anything about it.

"I'm sorry, Luke. I should have told her to call you. Would you like her contact information? You can call her back?"

I scoffed. "No. At this point, it's clear she'd rather hear from you. I'm sure if I tried to reach out, she'd just call you to confirm that I had the authority to answer the way I did."

"I don't think it's that bad." The pastor's voice was full of concern. "Do you really feel that way?"

"I do. I keep waiting for the parents to accept me and get excited about the program. But everyone keeps going back to you or reminding me of how Kyle did things."

"Kyle was here a long time. Ten years."

"I know. Believe me. But he and his family moved to Texas so he could start a church, and you all hired me to replace him. Not to be him with a different name." It drove me crazy that no one seemed to understand—or support—my desire to do things my own way.

"You have to—"

"Give it time. I know. You keep telling me." I probably shouldn't have cut him off, but I was tired of being told the same thing over and over. "Maybe the spring break trip is a bad idea. It's not too late to cancel it."

"Is that really what you want to do? Because of one question?"

I frowned. It was the first question, but I was pretty sure it wasn't going to be the last. "I guess we can wait and see how high that number gets before next week."

"I have confidence in you, Luke. I think the trip's a great idea. It's new and not like anything we've ever done before. And there's a lot of good potential for the kids to get their hands dirty and learn what it can mean to serve others. All the things you told me when you first proposed the trip. They still ring true. Don't let one mother derail that."

"How many should it take?" I shook my head. "Sorry. I appreciate you calling to check and I appreciate you getting back to the parent. And passing along the same message to the rest of them who call. Will you do me a favor, though?"

"Sure."

"Keep a count." Maybe them calling Pastor Chaz was a good thing. Maybe it would help him see how little the parents were doing when it came to accepting me as the youth pastor. I'd been hired and approved by the congregation after a search committee and multiple interviews and visits. But maybe they'd only agreed to hire me because I was the candidate the committee put forward. Maybe they'd be better off with someone else.

Maybe I'd be better off someplace else.

"All right. I can do that. Will you tell me why?"

"Because I don't think you realize how resistant people are to change."

"Kyle's gone."

"I know that. You know that. I'm not sure the parents have accepted it." I sighed. "I'd like it if you proved me wrong."

"I guess we'll see. I'm praying for you."

"Thanks."

I ended the call and dropped my phone on the passenger seat. I'd go home. Shower. Grab some lunch. And then I guessed I'd spend a little time on the computer trying to decide if there was anything in Mexico City that was worth rearranging the whole trip to try to get to see.

At least that might keep me from spending the rest of the day anxious about my second date with Kayla.

12

AUSTIN

"That smells good." I breathed in again and tried to place the tangy, tomatoey scent that filled Kayla's office. "Is it lasagna?"

"Yeah." Kayla's cheeks pinked. "Leftovers from Mia's."

"Nice. When'd you go?" I sat and unzipped the top of the little insulated cooler I'd brought my lunch in today. Nothing as tasty as Mia's, but the cheesy rice and hamburger mixture was a staple meal when it was my turn to cook.

"Last night." She paused and cleared her throat. "With Luke."

"Oh." I looked down at my food and frowned. How was I supposed to handle that? I'd taken her out on Saturday and apparently botched the attempt to explain how I felt about her so badly that she'd agreed to go out with the youth pastor again. Maybe it'd been set up before? "I'm surprised you didn't mention that when we were talking about our week on Saturday."

"He called Sunday afternoon." She set down her fork. "If it's weird, I don't have to talk about it."

"No. Of course not. It's fine. How was it?" I really didn't want to hear about her date. Except…maybe I did. Maybe there'd be an inside scoop—some insight into how to win her heart that I was missing. I pried the lid off the container holding my food and scooped a bite.

"Okay." She shrugged and picked her fork back up. "He doesn't seem happy with his job."

"That's too bad. What makes you say that?"

Kayla ate for a minute. I recognized the line in her forehead as an indication that she was organizing her thoughts before she spoke. She poked at her lasagna. "He spent a lot of time talking about it. I guess the parents still compare him to Kyle and get upset when he tries to do things that aren't the way they used to get done."

"Luke's been here more than a year. That seems odd."

She laughed. "Come on. How long did it take before parents stopped asking you why you let kids use calculators in some of your classes?"

I grinned. "Still waiting on that. All right, that's fair. Change is hard, I guess, all around. You don't think he'll leave, do you?"

"Nah." Kayla took a bite. She chewed, swallowed, and reached for her water bottle. "I didn't get that impression. But the whole Mexico trip may get canceled."

"What? No way."

She tipped her head to the side. "Like you care."

"Hey. I was planning to volunteer. You talked me into it." Especially if she was going to keep going on dates with Luke. I wasn't letting her go to Mexico with him for a week. Not when I could tag along and be part of the trip.

"Yeah?" She brightened. "That's great. Well, maybe it is. If the trip's on."

"What's the problem?"

Kayla shook her head. "Parents complaining about there not being any touring."

"Which is not the point of the trip." I sighed. I could feel Luke's pain. Parents were my least favorite part of being a teacher. "Poor guy."

I could have bitten my tongue. I did *not* want to feel bad for Luke. At the same time, I understood his frustration. "Hopefully he'll be able to work it out."

"Yeah." Kayla looked in her lunch bag and pulled out a baggie of cucumber slices. "Have you done any more thinking about the after-school center?"

"Thinking, yes. I'm not sure what the first step is. How do I get the ideas out of here"—I tapped my head—"and translate them into a functional thing?"

"Pfft. Please. It's a word problem. Think of it that way, and let's break it down into parts. At least we know money isn't an issue, Mr. Billionaire." She opened a drawer in her desk and pulled out a notepad, then reached across her desk for a pen.

I rolled my eyes. She didn't tease me about the money very often. I appreciated that. I'd worked hard—all of us had—to keep it semi-quiet. So far, it seemed we'd been successful.

"What, now?" I scooped another bite of my lunch and studied her face. "Wouldn't it be easier to do after school? You could come over and we could work on it. I'm making dinner again tonight. It won't be fancy, but I won't poison you."

She laughed. "There's an invitation."

My face burned. "I could order in."

"I was teasing. I've eaten your cooking before. It's good. Why don't we start now and still plan to do more this afternoon? Does that work?"

"Yeah. That sounds good." I made a mental note to text Megan quickly before my next class and let her know. It was one of our agreements that we tried to keep the other informed when we were having company. Of course, Megan should still be at the bookstore, so it wouldn't matter, but a heads up was never wrong. It was almost too bad she couldn't join us. Sometimes she had good ideas. I'd have to pick her brain about the center.

Maybe helping with this would get her mind off how obnoxious her supervisor was being about the fact that Megan had handed in her resignation.

"All right. So it's multiple parts, right? We have the whole building situation."

"What's the building situation?" I frowned and watched her write the word "building" in big, block letters.

"You need one."

I laughed. "Oh. That situation."

"Yeah. That one." She tapped her pen on the notepad. "Maybe we need to outline what you need from the space so we know what we're dealing with."

"We could do that. Or I could point out that the church building across the street is for sale."

"The church..." Kayla tipped her head to the side. "When did that happen?"

"Not sure. I just noticed a sign when I drove past this morning on my way in. I already put a call in to the listing agent. I'd like to at least look at it. It seems ideal."

"It seems ideal, because it is ideal." She grinned and scribbled under the heading on her notepad. "Okay, so that's handled."

"Whoa." I held up a hand. "It's maybe handled. We need to look at it. It could be terrible. Maybe it's falling apart. Maybe the reason they're moving isn't that they outgrew the space, but because it's cheaper than fixing up what's there."

She frowned. "Even so, it's not like we couldn't knock everything down and build what you needed there."

Everything in me warmed when she used the word "we." I liked having her on my side. Working with me. Like we were a team. A unit. "Maybe. But even if the building is good, I need to talk to Tristan about how terrible getting the zoning changed would be. At least, I assume I'd have to get that changed. I don't know a whole lot about it."

Kayla nodded and made a note. "That should be easy enough to look up, though, right? Or like you said, maybe Tristan can just tell you."

"Right. Still, if the real estate agent gets back to me, would you go look with me?"

"Of course. You know my schedule pretty well."

I lifted my eyebrows. I wasn't sure that was the case. "Not if you're having pop-up dates these days."

"Oh, please." She shook her head. "Fine. If Luke calls and asks me out again, I'll let you know. Deal?"

"Deal." It was good. I definitely wanted to know if she was setting up more dates with Luke. Ugh. Or did I? Was there any chance for me to convince her that our friendship should shift into something else? "Great. That's settled then. What's next, after the building situation?"

Kayla crunched a circle of cucumber and tapped her pen on the edge of the pad. "Programming, I guess. After-school center has a lot of scope."

I sighed. This was the problem I was having. It was why I hadn't been doing much other than continuing to think about the fact that I wanted to do it. Taking these first steps ended up being overwhelming. "I don't know."

"Why don't you tell me what you're thinking?"

My heart lifted at the compassion evident in her expression. "So the problem is I have too many ideas. I know I want tutoring. There are so many kids who struggle simply because they don't have the help and one-on-one attention they need. I can't make anyone take advantage of it, but I can at least do what I can to remove the obstacles."

"Like cost."

"Exactly."

"I get that, too. Kids who say they need help but can't afford it. What subjects?"

I spread my hands. "All of them?"

Kayla chuckled. "Go big or go home, huh?"

"Yeah? I was thinking we could possibly pay the teachers—or students who were doing well but were looking for an outside job—to provide the tutoring. That way we have a little more say in the qualifications. It's not a volunteer situation where you just have to be happy for what you get, you know?"

Her eyebrows lifted and she held my gaze. "You're not worried about underwriting that? I mean, footing the startup costs, sure. I can see that. And ongoing overhead, again, yeah. But the staff? On an ongoing basis?"

"What else am I going to do with all this money? I want to be smart about it, obviously, but it's not like I'm not getting wealthier with every passing day. Interest, investments, all of that. I have to do better about spending it. And I want to make a difference. Why not combine the two?" I reached around and squeezed the back of my neck. "Do you think this is a terrible idea?"

"No." Kayla shook her head. "No. I think it's a fantastic one. But it's going to be a bigger project than I think I realized."

I managed a laugh. "This is the problem I keep having."

"We'll figure it out. We solve problems for a living, after all."

I grinned. There was that "we" again. The "we" I was starting to realize I wanted to be a permanent part of my life.

I was about to speak when a knock on the door had me turning.

Kayla leaned to see around me. "Hey, Lucy. What can I do for you?"

"Hi." Lucy shifted nervously from one foot to the other. "Do you have a minute? I wanted to talk to you about this makeup project."

"Sure. Come on in." Kayla shot me an apologetic glance.

I gathered my lunch and stood. "I'll catch you later, Kayla."

I edged past Lucy and headed back to my classroom.

The rest of the day passed like a normal school day. Basically, that meant there was drama, a few tears, too much coffee, and not enough time to run to the bathroom. I loved it.

There was probably something wrong with me.

When the final bell rang and my advanced calculus students packed up their bags, I heaved a relieved sigh right along with them and slid my phone out of my desk drawer. There were three texts. Hopefully, one was from the real estate agent.

I didn't know how quickly commercial property sold, but that space was certainly in the right location. If the building worked at all—or if demolition was a possibility—it really was ideal.

I gave a mental fist pump when the first message was, indeed, the listing agent. I skimmed her text and checked the time before answering in the affirmative. I could make it over there in thirty minutes. This afternoon was blissfully meeting and club free. I wasn't sure about Kayla, but if she couldn't join me, it wasn't the end of the world.

"Mr. Campbell?"

I looked up and quickly put my phone into my pocket. "Trevor. What's up?"

Trevor thrust a file folder at me. "Would you be willing to write me a recommendation?"

I took the folder and flipped it open. I grinned and looked up at him. "You're applying for the MIT summer program?"

He swallowed audibly. "Yeah. You said you thought I could do it. My mom...she's not sure. And even if I get in, I have to get one of the scholarships if I'm going to be able to go. But I want to try."

"You get in? I'll cover the cost."

"Oh. No. Mr. Campbell, I can't ask that."

"You didn't ask. I offered." I tipped my head to the side. "And I'll expect you to be willing to talk to my classes next year about the program."

Trevor gave me a lopsided smile. "I can do that."

"When's the deadline?"

"Um. Next week?" Trevor winced. "I spent a lot of time second-guessing. They only have five scholarships. The competition for those has to be amazing. And I mean, my mom does okay. Probably better than a lot of other people. I think we could probably swing it without aid if Mom was willing to scrounge, you know?"

I wasn't so sure. I'd talked to Trevor's mom a few times. She was working two jobs to keep a roof over their heads. Maybe Trevor didn't know that. I wasn't going to be the one to clue him in. "I'm glad you decided to go for it. Do I give it back to you or send it in directly?"

"There's instructions for submitting it in there. I've already got everything else turned in. I just need three recommendations."

"Who are you choosing for the other two?"

He wiped his palms on his jeans. "I thought I might ask Miss Jones. I've got a pretty solid B plus in her class right now, and I think I can get it up to an A before the end of the term. And then maybe Mrs. Winston."

"Nice. I'll do mine tonight. Tomorrow at the latest. You'll keep me posted?"

He nodded vigorously. "I will. Thanks, Mr. Campbell."

"My pleasure." Trevor darted back into the hall and I checked the time on my phone. I'd planned to swing by Kayla's room in person to ask, but Trevor had eaten up that time. I shot off a text inviting her to meet me there for a walkthrough and then quickly gathered the piles of work to take home and grade.

Between walking through the building across the street and Kayla coming for dinner to talk about the program, it was going to be a late night getting the grading done.

Not that I'd been sleeping all that well since Kayla had started dating Luke. At least tonight I'd be up doing something productive instead of tossing and turning.

13

KAYLA

I dropped my bag by the front door and kicked off my shoes then moved out of the way as Austin came behind me. He set his own things down and gave a heavy sigh.

"What's wrong?" I turned so I could study him. He looked tired. More tired than I'd seen him in a long time. How come I hadn't noticed it at school? Probably the fluorescent lights. They made everyone look so awful, I was used to discounting it.

"I don't know. Let me get started on dinner." Austin headed toward the kitchen.

I followed, trying to figure out where to begin. Getting him to open up wasn't hard. Not usually. It was a matter of nudging in just the right spot. "Can I help with the food?"

Austin was staring into the fridge. He closed the door and turned around. "Let's just order in."

"Okay." I didn't really want takeout, but I also wasn't going to push for a homecooked meal when he was clearly grumpy. I could get a salad or something. "What are you in the mood for?"

"I don't know. Do you have a preference?"

Ugh. I thought through the various options that wouldn't have excessive delivery fees. "What about the deli?"

He wrinkled his nose.

"Or not." I managed a tight smile. "Pizza? Chinese? Walk into town and see what strikes you?"

Austin pulled out a chair at the kitchen table and sat. His shoulders slumped. "I was really hoping it would be this amazing, perfect space. You know?"

I pulled out the chair opposite him. "I get that. But it wasn't awful."

"It was close."

I snickered. He wasn't wrong. The current owners were clearly moving because maintaining the building had gotten to be too hard, so they were just walking away. There was *a lot* of work that needed to be done. "Look at it this way, you can get it exactly the way you want it."

"Yeah, I guess."

Everything about him looked so dejected that my heart broke a little bit. I stood up and went around the table so I could wrap him in a hug from behind. I rested my chin on his shoulder. "What are the options? You can buy this place and, worst case, knock down the buildings and start from the ground up. Or you can keep looking. What matters more? Move-in ready or location?"

Austin reached up, and his hand closed gently around my forearm. He twisted his head so our noses practically touched.

My gaze locked with his and for a moment, time stood still.

"Hey guys, what are we having...oops. Sorry." Megan made a show of stomping out into the hallway.

I straightened and cleared my throat. I looked around the kitchen. Anything was better than risking making eye contact with Austin again. Not after that. Whatever that was. Should I make up some excuse and leave?

That was what I wanted to do.

Well. Not entirely.

What I wanted to do was throw myself into his arms and finish what it had seemed like we were on the cusp of starting.

But that was a bad idea. Terrible. Absolutely rotten.

I risked a glance at Austin and felt my lips twitch. He was scowling into the hallway.

Maybe, just maybe, it wasn't too late after all.

I crossed the kitchen and tugged open the fridge. "Wow."

Austin chuckled. "You see why I'm thinking takeout?"

"I'm pretty sure Old Mother Hubbard had more food than this. How does this happen?" I wasn't a huge fan of the grocery store, but I never let it get down to ketchup, a bottle of ranch that was basically empty, and olives that looked like they were past their prime.

"It's Megan's turn."

"It's my turn for what?"

I closed the fridge and lifted my eyebrows. "Groceries?"

"Oh. Right. I was supposed to do that last week. Is it bad?" Megan crossed the kitchen and opened the fridge back up. "Oops."

I let out a breath. At least she hadn't come barreling back in here waggling her eyebrows and making a big deal of the thing —whatever it was—with Austin that she'd interrupted. That was good. It was nothing.

Megan's elbow dug into my ribs and she leaned close to whisper, "I'm gonna need details."

Or...it had been too much to hope that she'd let it go. I gave a slight shake of my head. There weren't any details. And I sure wasn't discussing it now, with Austin in the room.

Megan rolled her eyes. "What are we ordering? Or, I guess since it's my fault there aren't groceries, I could go pick something up."

"Who's watching the bookstore?" Austin tipped back on the rear legs of his chair.

Megan brightened. "You remember Mrs. Madison? She used to work with Grandma some. She came by last week and said if I ever wanted a few hours off in the evening, she'd hang out and hold down the fort for ten percent off her purchase. I talked to Grandma, she said I'd be dumb not to jump on it. So I did."

"Nice. You know, I'd work a night here or there for a discount, too." I could grade papers anywhere. And discounts at a bookstore were always a good thing.

"Yeah, but if I'm taking time off, it's because I want to hang out with you. So that doesn't work." Megan shrugged. "But I'll keep it in mind."

"For when you get a hot date?" I fluttered my eyelashes at her.

She snickered. "Sure. Cause that's going to happen."

"Food? Dinner? Anyone else remember that conversation?" Austin tipped forward and rested his elbows on the table. "Since Meg offered, I say she goes and picks up Thai."

"Ooh. Brilliant."

"Aw, come on. That's not even in Old Town." Megan crossed her arms. "You're taking advantage."

"Whatever. You offered. And it's not that far." Austin pointed at her. "I'll call in the order. But you should get going so you're there when it's ready."

"Yeah, yeah. Get me pad Thai. And a spring roll. Do you think they can do the mangoes and sticky rice to go? If they can, get that." Megan turned and headed toward the front door.

"Bossy, isn't she?" I chuckled and sat. "Although she's not wrong about the dessert."

"It's true. You getting your usual?" He looked up from his phone, eyebrows raised.

"Please."

He grinned and tapped his phone. The other end rang several times before a harried voice picked up. Austin placed the order quickly, shooting me a thumbs-up when they were able to do the sticky rice. That would make Megan—and the rest of us, honestly—happy.

He ended the call and set down his phone, then looked up and held my gaze. I'd counted four of the heartbeats that roared in my ears before he spoke.

"Location. That's what matters most, right?"

I squashed the seed of disappointment in my heart. Of course he wasn't going to bring up anything else. What was there to say?

I swallowed. "I think so. The kids can cross at the corner and be at the center in what, five minutes? It's easy. Even the ones who drive wouldn't necessarily have to move their cars."

His fingers drummed on the table top. "I don't think it's worth trying to salvage the existing buildings. Even if we fixed them up, they aren't exactly what we need. You're right about starting fresh. Then we can make sure everything is exactly what we want."

There was a tiny part of me that wondered if he was talking about more than the youth center. It was probably wishful thinking. I didn't want to tear down our whole friendship just to try building something else—something more—in its place though, did I?

"I don't think we'll end up with exactly the same thing as was there before—but I think what we get will be better. Longer lasting." Austin leaned forward. He took my hand—electricity sizzled up my arm—and his gaze locked with mine. "I'm willing to give it a shot if you are. If that's what you want."

My mouth was so dry I could only nod.

His lips curved and he reached across the table to take my hand. "To be clear. You're agreeing that we should try dating, right? And also that I should buy the property, knock down what's there, and get the youth center built to meet our needs?"

I laughed and squeezed his hand. "Yes. To all of the above."

"What about Luke?"

I frowned. "What about him?"

"Well." Austin cleared his throat, his expression earnest. "I'd just as soon you weren't also dating someone else if we're dating."

That was fair. Of course, there was just one big misconception. "Luke and I aren't dating. We never were."

"You went out with him. Twice. On dates. That's dating."

"No, it's not. It's going out on two dates. And honestly, they barely qualify as dates." Why was I being prickly about this? I didn't want to date Luke. I wanted to date Austin. But something about his tone rankled deep in my soul. "Am I allowed to have dinner with friends still, or do I have to run that by you first?"

Austin held up his hands. "By all means, keep having dinner with your friends."

He'd put air quotes around the word "friends" and I wanted to scream. "It seems to me that I was having dinner with you, my best friend, while I was also having dinner with Luke. Was I two-timing him?"

Austin growled. "We hadn't officially defined any sort of relationship at that point. So no. But now that we have, I'd like to believe that you aren't going to keep playing the field. We've been friends for more than five years and I've barely seen you date anyone and now you're determined to keep two guys on a string?"

"On a string?" I spluttered. I wasn't trying to keep anyone on a string. "And if I haven't dated much in the last five years it's because I was in love with you and waiting for you to get it through your thick skull!"

"Oh yeah? You have a weird way of showing it." Austin banged the table. "You could have just said something."

"You could've noticed." I crossed my arms, seething.

Austin looked away.

"Exactly." I pointed at him, restraining—just barely—the temptation to poke him in the chest. "When push comes to shove, you'd rather keep quiet and hope someone else takes the initiative. We wouldn't even be friends if I hadn't approached you. But I wasn't going to drag you kicking and screaming to the altar. Still won't."

"That's hideously unfair."

"Tell me about it."

Austin was the most infuriating man I'd ever known. He was also the smartest and kindest, but right now, I couldn't focus on those things. I loved him. As a friend, for sure, but also more. At least that was what it seemed like. Maybe I was wrong. "I'm dragging you into this youth center, too. Aren't I?"

"What? No." He looked at me, startled. "And I don't see what that has to do with anything."

"I'm just looking at the big picture. If I hadn't made a move, we wouldn't be friends. If I hadn't pushed, you wouldn't be doing more than thinking about the youth center. Did I do something that pushed you to asking me to be your girlfriend?" I studied him as his gaze slid away from mine. My heart sank. "I did, didn't I? It was going out with Luke. You just don't want someone else playing with your best friend."

"Kayla. That's not the case. Maybe you dating Luke was the wakeup call I needed, but it doesn't change the fact that I want to be with you."

"Doesn't it?" My mouth was dry. Rather than keep sitting at the table wishing desperately for water, I got up and moved across the kitchen to get some. I was as at home here as I was in my own apartment. Because Austin was my best friend and his sister was close behind. I was basically their third sibling.

I got down a glass and filled it from the dispenser in the

fridge door. I didn't go back to the table, but took a long, cold drink and then topped off the glass.

"Maybe we're taking things too fast." I felt sick. It had to be the cold water on an empty stomach, didn't it? I sat back down across from Austin and put my glass on the table, clenching both hands around the cool cylinder.

"I don't understand." A hint of panic flared in his eyes and he reached across the table for my hand.

I shifted out of reach. "I want to marry a man who believes I'm worth pursuing. Not someone who loves me because we get along and I'm convenient."

"That's not—"

"I know you think that." I cut him off. If he started talking, chances were high that I'd lose my nerve. And this was too important. "But I'm not sure it's true. I've always been around and ready for whatever trickle of time you were willing to give me. And when I started to get tired of that, I shifted things and spent more time with Megan. And you know what? You didn't seem to care. You adjusted your stride and things went on just fine. Until it looked like I was moving on with Luke."

"Kayla..." His voice was strained and quiet.

I shook my head. "So here's the deal. I'll go out with you, when you ask. And I'll go out with Luke, if he asks. I'll help you with the youth center. I'll help him with the Mexico trip—or whatever the alternative ends up being for spring break if that falls through. And we'll see what happens."

"What do you mean 'see what happens'? I don't like this."

I managed a slight smile. "I'm not keen on it myself, but I think it's probably best. I need to know if you really love me. Or if you just don't want someone else to have the chance."

The front door slammed, saving me from having to listen to Austin's reply. He could be persuasive, when he wanted to be. This might be one of those situations.

"I think that's a new record." Megan set the paper bag of takeout food on the table beside me and headed to the sink. "I must've hit a special pocket in the traffic, because I got there and back in about five minutes under my previous best time. What are you two doing?"

I absolutely didn't want to talk about that with Megan. Not yet. Maybe not ever. I met Austin's gaze for a moment and caught his subtle head shake. At least we were on the same page there.

"I'm going to open a youth center." Austin leaned back in his chair. "Kayla's going to help me with all the details."

"Yeah?" Megan finished washing her hands and reached for the kitchen towel that hung on the handle of the oven. "That's great. You can tell me all about it while we eat. I might have some ideas, you know."

"Counting on it." Austin stood and started opening the bag of food. "Are we eating out of the containers or do we need plates?"

"Plates. Geesh, Aus, we're not savages." Megan shook her head as she opened the cabinet where they kept their plates. "I also declined plastic forks, because we have metal ones here. And those always work better."

The casual sibling banter soothed my nerves and I started to relax. I should probably offer to help, somehow, but they honestly had it under control. And I wasn't positive my legs would hold me yet. Ultimatums weren't my typical style. Austin knew that. But this was too important to just slide into.

I wanted to spend the rest of my life with someone who was going to fight for me. Someone who wanted to be there, even when it was hard.

I honestly believed Austin was that man. God and I had had a lot of conversations on the topic, and He'd never yet made it seem like I was wrong. But I might've missed it.

Maybe Luke asking me out was a wakeup call for both Austin and me.

Megan handed me a plate and fork then sat beside me. "Have you started looking for property yet?"

"Actually…" His glistening eyes latched onto mine. "I think I already found it." Looking away, continued speaking, "I'll have to tear everything down that's there, but I hope when it's finished it's going to end up being the right choice."

My throat closed at Austin's words. They didn't sound nearly as hopeful and optimistic as they had earlier this evening.

What if, in this quest to find a husband who loved me enough to pursue me, I ended up losing my best friend?

14

AUSTIN

"Thanks for going with me, man." Cody fastened his seatbelt and looked over at me as I slid behind the wheel of my car.

"I've always liked looking at real estate. Although I think the whole gang is in shock that you and Noah are going to stop living together. I was honestly starting to wonder if the two of you were going to be like those twins who married twins and then all lived in the same house together until the end of time." I grinned as Cody punched my arm. "Hey. Don't hit the driver."

"You weren't moving yet." Cody shook his head. "And it's comments like that that pushed us over the edge. In today's world, you have to know how that sounds. Two single guys living together?"

I laughed. "I think there are still people out there who can accept that platonic roommates are a thing."

"You'd be surprised. People need to be less fixated on the sex lives of everyone around them."

"That'd be nice, wouldn't it?" I turned out of the diner parking lot. "Remind me where we're heading?"

"Toward the river, near Jones Point."

"Fancy." I wiggled my eyebrows. Old Town proper didn't have a lot of housing that couldn't be considered fancy. Megan and I were blessed that our grandmother had purchased her historic townhome before the prices were as outrageous as they were today. The annoying thing was that there wasn't a lot of middle ground. It was either ritzy or low income. At least if you wanted to stay in Old Town. And if you wanted affordable? South or west were the best options. And these days, even those were tricky.

Not that any of us had to worry about affordability. But at the same time, none of us wanted to spend mega money on a home just because we could.

Cody shrugged. "I guess, yeah. But why not, right? And I'll have a better river view—and access—than Scott."

I laughed. "Bragging rights. Now I get it."

"Only if the house is good, but yeah." Cody grinned. "Someone has to beat him at something. First, he has this great idea and we all get rich. Then he lands himself an amazing wife complete with built-in kid. I mean, what's next?"

"Well, when you put it that way." I grinned. None of us were actually competitive. At the same time? "If nothing else, we can alternate poker night locations."

"You could always volunteer to host, you know. You and Megan have that nice townhouse right in the middle of Old Town. When was it built?"

"Eighteen eighty. And yeah, I should. We used to all share. Since Beckett's got a mom and a dad now, we ought to get back to that." Would that work, though? Scott and Whitney alternated Fridays when it came to who was in charge of Beckett. When Scott had him, being at their house made it a lot easier once bedtime rolled around. "Although maybe that doesn't work with getting him to bed and all that. What do I know? I'm not a parent."

Cody glanced over at me. "And you want to be?"

"I don't know. Eventually, yeah. And I guess it's starting to feel like eventually is creeping up on me. I'm not getting any younger."

"Turn here."

I followed Cody's directions and parked beside a pale yellow, four-story end unit. "Where's the front door?"

"On the end." Cody pointed. "I like that it's not all in a row with the others."

I got out of the car. I kind of liked that, too. Not that I didn't love the place Grandma had given us. Cody wasn't wrong, we were right in the middle of everything. And while the building was old, it had been well maintained and upgraded over the years, so we didn't have to worry about the plumbing and elec-trical or anything like that.

"I like the roofline."

I followed Cody around to the front door, my gaze taking in the squared-off roof. "That's one of those funny French words, right?"

"Mansard. Yeah." Cody shrugged. "It's nice, though. I'm not sure if the window at the very top is decorative or if there's an actual attic space."

So maybe only three stories. Which was still plenty. "You couldn't tell from the listing online?"

"I didn't pay a lot of attention. It was in the right area and the price was something I was willing to pay. I figured it was better to just come look at it, and the agent said he'd meet us here at two." Cody twisted his watch around to check the time. "So he should be here any minute."

"Parking is gonna be a pain." I looked around. There was

some street parking, but nothing looked assigned, and it was likely to fill up quickly in the evenings when everyone got home. We'd been lucky to get the spot we had.

"There's a two-car garage." Cody started toward the other side of the townhouse.

I followed. Where had they stuck a garage? From the front it didn't seem possible. But sure enough, as we rounded the corner, we ended up in an alleyway type setup between the townhouse rows. All the garages opened onto this street.

"All right, I take it back."

Cody chuckled. "Looks like maybe the agent is inside. The door's up and there's a car there. Let me text him and see. I don't want to accidentally walk in on the owners."

"Good plan." I tucked my hands in my pockets and looked at the rows of decks that stretched out as far as I could see. Why anyone would want to sit outside and stare at the back of someone else's townhouse was beyond me. Our townhouse had a little walled garden space behind it. The flagstone patio was something Grandma had added, and so when Megan or I wanted to spend time outside, we had a little bit of privacy.

Of course, we didn't have a garage. Just permit street parking. And sometimes it was a pain to get close to the house, although there were unwritten agreements between all the neighbors on our street to use the spots closest to our own doors. It worked. Mostly. Some folks had more cars than seemed reasonable, and so there were occasional issues.

"Yeah, that's him. He said to come on in that way and we'd start at the bottom and work our way up. I guess there's a family room on the ground level, too."

"Nice." That was more than Scott had. "Is this bigger than Scott's then?"

"Guess so." Cody paused to take in the other side of the

garage before pushing open the door leading into the house. "Hello?"

"Hi. Cody, right? I'm Greg." The man extended his hand, grinning and showing off glaringly white teeth. "You brought a friend?"

"Yeah, this is Austin."

I waited, but that appeared to be the only intro I was getting. I shook Greg's hand. "Nice to meet you."

"Are you in the market, too?" Greg was reaching into the breast pocket of his button down.

"I have a house over on North Royal."

"Yeah? Nice. If you ever want to sell, let me know. I love listing those beautiful historic places." Greg held out a card.

I took it and slid it into my pocket. I had no intention of ever selling Grandma's townhouse, but it wasn't as if I could guarantee the future. Maybe there'd come a time when it made sense to leave the area.

"Do you want me to give you a tour, or would you rather just look around?" Greg flashed that gleaming grin again.

Cody glanced at me then back at Greg. "It's okay if we just look?"

"Of course. I'll hang out in the kitchen—one floor up—if you have questions." Greg started toward the stairs. "Take your time."

"He's a little intense." Cody muttered when Greg had disappeared from view.

"Yeah, well, he's gotta hustle for a living. This is a nice family area. Wet bar and fire place. It's gas?" I moved closer to inspect the fire, nodding as I found the switch that would turn the logs off and on. "Is there a bathroom down here, too?"

Cody wandered to the other side of the room and peeked through a doorway. "Yeah. Over here there's a half bath."

That was nice. Saved people from having to run up and down stairs all the time. "Ready to head up?"

"Yeah." Cody started up the stairs. "From what I remember about the listing, the main floor is an eat-in kitchen and an open plan living-dining room. The kitchen opens onto the deck we saw in the back."

"And the front door?" I reached the top of the stairs and looked around. There was, in fact, an open plan living and dining room. It was nicely staged so you could get a picture of what it might be like to live here.

"Yeah." Cody pointed to the front door. It was separated, sort of, from the living area by a change in flooring.

"Do you have enough furniture to fill a place like this?"

Cody laughed. "No. But that's an easy fix, too. I'll just hire Scott's decorators and tell them to go at it."

That was reasonable. "Maybe you should get Megan to help you. She's got a pretty good eye and knows what you like. She did our place."

Cody shot me a startled look. "Megan?"

"Yeah. My sister. Megan. Who decorated the place where I live. Unless you hate that, in which case I wish you'd said something. I've always thought it was good."

"No. It's great." Cody frowned at me before stalking into the kitchen.

I wasn't sure what I'd said wrong, but I also wasn't going to explore it. Cody could hire Scott's decorators if he wanted. It wasn't like he couldn't afford them. I just remembered how much fun Megan had sprucing up our place when Grandma first let us move in. In fact, maybe I ought to ask her if she wanted to change anything up.

Because I could afford for her to do that, if she wanted, and I certainly didn't care as long as she didn't paint the whole thing pink.

"The kitchen is huge." Cody poked his head out into the living room. "You've gotta come see it."

I crossed the living room and stepped onto the marble floor, my eyebrows lifting. "You're not kidding. Scott's going to have kitchen envy."

Cody snickered. "He really is. This is the size of his living room. There's seating at the island and space for an actual table."

"The fact that you have an island is impressive."

Greg grinned at us from the glass-topped table where he was sitting. "The floors are heated as well."

I started to laugh. "You're joking? I didn't know people really did that."

"No joke. Radiant heat. It's great in the winter—you can go barefoot and not have any trouble." Greg's smile was tight.

"Hear that, Cody?" I closed the distance between us so I could elbow him in the side. "You can be barefoot in the kitchen and your toesies will stay toasty."

"You're such an idiot." Cody shook his head. "Let's go up."

"The next floor is the owner's suite. The floor above that has two additional bedrooms and a sitting area." Greg set his cell phone down on the table. "Let me know if you have questions."

I followed Cody as he breezed through looking at the rest of the house. There were touches that bordered on ridiculous as far as I was concerned. Cody didn't disagree. At the same time, it wasn't like it was bad to have a three-sided gas fire that separated the bedroom portion of the owner's suite from a large sitting area. Or the his and hers walk-in closets that could easily be bedrooms on their own.

Upstairs, the rooms were smaller but no less luxurious. And the bathroom that joined them was more than ample for any guests.

Cody sank onto one of the arm chairs in the top floor sitting area. "What do you think?"

"It's nice." I perched on the edge of the sofa and looked around. "It's a lot of room."

He blew out a breath. "Too much? I don't have to get a house. I could get a condo on the water like Tristan. Maybe that's the smarter choice."

I watched Cody reach around and massage his neck. Something in his expression made it clear he didn't want a condo like Tristan. "You want a house, though, right?"

"I mean, yeah. I like the idea of having a place to bring a wife and start a family. You're not the only one who feels like 'eventually' is creeping up on you faster than you realized." Cody frowned. "Although maybe I should wait until I have someone before buying. What if she hates it?"

"I don't know anyone who could hate this place. Unless she's completely anti-townhouse. But then she's probably not going to be the right woman for you. You're as rooted in Old Town as the rest of us. It's not like you want to move out to the suburbs and get a mini-mansion on one and a half acres, right?"

Cody grimaced. "No. I don't want to spend fifteen or twenty hours commuting each week just so I can dedicate my weekends to lawn mowing."

"To be fair, you can hire a landscaping company to handle the mowing." I grinned. "But I get your point. And it makes mine. You're not going to marry someone who doesn't love living here. Or at least is willing to. So if you like this place, I'd say you should buy it."

"Do you think Megan would like it?"

My eyebrows lifted, and I waited until Cody met my gaze. "Is there something I should know about you and my sister?"

He shook his head. "Not yet. Maybe not ever. I don't think

she thinks about me like that at all. But I wouldn't mind it if she did. Would you?"

I had to fight to keep my jaw from dropping. "I can't say I've ever given it any thought."

"Maybe you could. And let me know what you come up with." Cody stood and started back toward the stairs. "I'm gonna go talk to Greg about making an offer on this place."

I watched Cody leave but couldn't quite get my legs to follow. Cody and Megan? It wasn't a pairing I would ever have made. Although there was no reason not to. Cody was great. Megan deserved someone great.

Except when I tried to picture my baby sister with a husband and kids, I couldn't quite get there.

I sighed and sagged back into the couch. Why did relationships have to be so complicated? First this mess with Kayla that had been going on for close to two weeks. And now Cody and Megan?

There was part of me—a big part—that wanted to rewind to the start of the year and do it over.

Although...at the start of the year, I'd been Kayla's best friend and I hadn't even realized how badly I wanted it to become more. Would I really go back to that?

In church this morning, they'd reminded everyone about the Valentine's Day banquet put on by the youth as a fundraiser. It was this Saturday—Valentine's Day was next Tuesday—was it too late to ask Kayla to go with me?

I squashed the thought that Luke had probably already beaten me there. I wouldn't know if I didn't ask.

I pulled out my phone before I could sit and obsess about it, and tapped out a text.

I REALIZE THIS IS LAST MINUTE, AND ALSO A TEXT WHICH IS PROBABLY MORE NEGATIVE POINTS, BUT I WAS HOPING YOU'D GO TO THE VALENTINE'S DAY BANQUET AT CHURCH WITH ME ON SATURDAY.

I frowned at the message, my finger hovering over the arrow that would send it. Then I quickly added on a final thought.

NOT AS FRIENDS.

There. I hit Send.

Now the ball was in her court.

I really hoped she'd say yes.

15

KAYLA

"I can't believe Cody's looking at townhouses." Megan was slouched on my sofa with her feet up on my coffee table. Ada had draped herself across Megan's stomach and was purring contentedly.

"Why not? You had to realize he and Noah wouldn't live in an apartment together forever." I looked around my own apartment. I'd love to have the funds to just go look at property in Old Town by the river and buy it. But that wasn't happening any time soon. Not on a teacher's salary.

No, if I wanted to own a place, I'd have to head south. Probably into Prince William County at that. Or Stafford. Then I'd be stuck on the road for hours every day. I suppressed a shudder. No, thank you. I'd deal with renting.

"I guess." Megan shrugged and switched from scratching behind Ada's ears to gently rubbing from head to tail. The tip of Ada's tail flicked and her purring quieted, but it didn't stop. "Did Whitney text you?"

"She did. It's so sad."

Megan nodded. "Right? One positive pregnancy test and then her symptoms went away and like five days later her period starts. The doctor wouldn't even call it a miscarriage. Just a 'chemical pregnancy,' like there wasn't a baby there at all."

"She seems to be doing okay?" I didn't talk to Whitney as much as Megan seemed to, so I wasn't actually sure. But I hadn't gotten the impression from her texts that she was in deep mourning.

"She's conflicted. She really wasn't ready for a baby yet, but she was also starting to get excited. I imagine the two of them will start talking about moving up their baby timeline now."

"More than likely. That'll be fun. I like babies when I can give them back."

Megan grinned and looked around. "Where's Charles?"

I chuckled. Charles, for whatever reason, was not a big fan of Megan. "He's probably in the bedroom. You know he gets freaked out when you're here."

"Unfair. Ada loves me. Don't you, baby?" Megan leaned down and nuzzled the top of Ada's head.

"She does. Take the win. You know how cats are." I was going to add something about not looking for unconditional love from any animal that wasn't a dog, when my phone buzzed. I grabbed it from the coffee table and opened my texts.

My eyebrows lifted as I read Austin's words. I did not, as yet, have a date for the Valentine's Day banquet. I honestly hadn't been planning to go. Spaghetti and garlic bread made by grudging teenagers wasn't really my jam. And also? A date with Austin directly under Luke's nose seemed overly complicated.

I set my phone down on the coffee table, prepared to ignore it until I could figure out how I was feeling.

"Anything important?" Megan was watching me.

I wanted to blow it off and tell her no. But I wasn't going to lie to her. And maybe she'd have some insight. I hadn't actually told her about the conversation Austin and I had while she was out getting Thai food. It had been easy enough to avoid over the last two weeks.

Or maybe it hadn't.

Maybe that was why she'd pushed so hard about hanging out this afternoon after church.

"You better start talking. Something's up, and I'm not letting you off the hook until you spill." Megan shifted, eliciting an annoyed noise from Ada. Megan quickly resumed scratching behind the cat's ears. "Sorry, baby. Your mom is being silly."

I groaned. "Fine. You know what? Fine. Maybe you can explain the whole situation to me, and I can figure out exactly what's going on."

"Ooh. A situation? I love those. They're so often juicy." Megan tapped her toe against my leg. "Don't skimp on details."

I couldn't help but laugh at the teasing tone. "There are no details. Yet. Maybe never."

"Because?"

"You have to promise me you're going to listen as my friend, not Austin's sister."

"Uh-oh." Megan's hand stilled, and Ada meowed imperiously. "All right. I'll do my best. No name calling though, okay? He's my brother. Even if he's a bonehead."

"You can name call? That doesn't seem fair." I pressed my fingers to my eyes and collected my thoughts. "Okay. You know I've been out with Luke twice."

"Right. I also cleverly notice you're not calling them dates."

"Who's telling this story?" I glared at her. "But also, no, I'm not. I don't think they qualify as such. We're just getting to know each other."

"Which normal people call dates. But okay. Go on." Megan sent me a saccharine grin.

"That apparently made your brother, the aforementioned bonehead, jealous. So when he and I went to dinner, he wanted it to qualify as a date, but I didn't know that, because we go to dinner all the time. Then the whole youth center thing started, and we were talking about that and the property across the street being an ideal location, except what's built there already isn't what's needed, so it's better to tear it all down and start over, and there was this whole undercurrent where I knew he was talking about more than the buildings."

"Mmm. I love a good, tense undercurrent." Megan leaned forward. "Were lips involved?"

"No. Stop." I paused as the idea of kissing Austin wormed its way into my head. Mmm. How would that be? It would have to be amazing.

"I don't believe you." Megan's voice was a sing-song.

I yanked myself back to reality, tucking that little fantasy away for later. "Tough. There has been no kissing. Yet."

"Ooh. Yay!" Megan clapped her hands, startling Ada enough that she leapt off Megan's lap and dashed out of the room.

I laughed.

Megan looked stricken.

"Don't worry. She'll come back."

"She better." Megan folded her hands in her lap. "So. No kissing yet, but you two are a couple?"

"Also not yet?" I imagined my smile was more of a wince, because Megan looked furious.

"What are you doing? This is my brother. The man you've been in love with for at least two years that I know of."

"Wait. I never said—"

"Please. What am I, stupid?"

I pinched the bridge of my nose. "I guess it probably seems dumb to you. But hear me out, okay? I'm tired of doing all the heavy lifting. And I explained it to him. We're friends because I sought him out. He's finally doing more than just *thinking* about the youth center because I pushed him."

"And you don't want to be a couple because you dragged him kicking and screaming." Megan sighed. "I guess I get that. So where does that leave things?"

"I told him I'm open to dating him. But that I'm also not going to commit to exclusivity."

"What? That's dumb." Megan shook her head. "Austin's not built like that. If he thinks you want someone else, he's going to step out of the way. He's a gentleman."

I bit my lip. I'd had a sneaking suspicion that was a possibility. But that didn't make it wrong for me to want a man who was willing to pursue me. Maybe it meant Austin and I were fundamentally incompatible.

The thought made my stomach twist.

I didn't want another man. I wanted Austin.

"So the text was..."

Leave it to Megan not to let well enough alone. "Austin asking me to the Valentine's banquet on Saturday."

"Talk about waiting for the last minute." Megan shook her head. "I return to my previous bonehead comment. Are you going to go?"

"I don't know. Are we at the Valentine's date stage of things? Isn't that for established couples?"

Megan grunted. "Maybe you two are so perfect for each other because you're *also* a bonehead. Are you or are you not in love with my brother?"

"I don't—"

"Bzzt. Answer the question. Yes or no."

I sighed. "Yes."

"Are you in love with or in any other way interested in Luke?"

I probably wouldn't get away with qualifying that answer, either. I could see being friends with Luke. We had a few things in common. Even if he had terrible taste in food. Well, it wasn't all bad. Mia's had been fantastic, as usual. But I didn't know how anyone went long periods of time without eating something spicy. "Maybe?"

"I'm calling that a no."

I laughed. "Really? Maybe means no now?"

"In this case it does. Come on, maybe you and Luke end up being friends, but if there was chemistry between the two of you, I would have heard about it by now."

That was probably true.

"Look. I know you've been trying to play off your interest in my brother. I remember decorating the bookstore at Halloween, even if you don't."

"Oh, I remember. If you recall, I'd already told you I could hear you talking about me. So yeah, I caught your little, 'if you love him so much why don't you marry him' thing. As well as the rest of your commentary to Whitney." And fine, it had been the kick in the pants I'd needed to share my feelings with Megan. Right now? The jury was out about whether or not that had been a good idea.

Megan's cheeks blazed red. "I'm not apologizing."

"Fine. I didn't ask you to."

"The point, however, is that this has been going on a long time. And yes, fine, my boneheaded brother only came to his senses because Luke came on the scene, but doesn't he at least get *some* credit for not just walking away and moping forever?" Megan wiggled her fingers and made a kissy noise.

I turned to see what she was looking at and smothered a chuckle. Ada had poked her head out from under the credenza that held my TV and was eyeing us suspiciously.

"Pssh pssh. Come here, Ada." Megan leaned forward, beckoning to the cat.

I wanted to tell her that was the opposite of how to get Ada to come, but I would've been proven wrong before the words were fully out of my mouth, because Ada slunk across the floor and leapt into Megan's lap.

"There's my girl." Megan rubbed Ada's head and shot me a triumphant look.

"That's what I want, too. You see?" I nodded at Ada. "Why is it okay for her to need someone to chase but it's not okay for me?"

"Well, we can start with the fact that she's a cat." Megan blew a wisp of hair out of her face. "Do you really want someone who isn't going to take no for an answer and just keeps after you, wearing you down, until you finally cave?"

"No. Of course not. I just...ugh. You don't understand." Maybe I was inconsistent, but I believed there was a middle ground here. One where I didn't have to be the one making it clear I was interested before a guy took a chance on asking me out.

"I do understand." Megan reached over and touched my leg. "But you love Austin. He's not an alpha male caveman. He's a math teacher."

"Hey. He's still very manly. I don't expect you to notice, because you're his sister and that would be ick, but he's built. And hot."

Megan grinned. "I believe the word I'm searching for is, in fact, ick. But I'm glad you're noticing these things. Or making them up. Either one is fine. It proves my point."

"Oh? You had a point?"

She shot me a glare. "Go to the banquet with my brother. Okay? Maybe you'll get a Valentine kiss out of it."

I pushed that little fantasy right back out of my mind. I shouldn't be kissing anyone until I was committed to an exclusive relationship with them. It was one thing to insist on being able to date whoever asked. But I wasn't going to be getting physical with anyone until there was more to it than casual dating.

"Those are long thoughts." Megan tipped her head to the side. "Do you not want to go out with Austin after all?"

I shook my head. "I do. I'm just not sure how much it's going to bother Luke to have us right there under his nose."

"Feels like that's his problem. It's not like he asked you."

I sighed. No. He hadn't. And I'd kind of expected that he would, since this was a fundraiser for the trip I'd agreed to help with. Although, it was looking like the trip might not happen, so maybe that was part of it. "You're right."

Megan tipped her head toward my cell phone. "Are you going to let him know? Put him out of his misery? You know he's sitting there waiting for you to say yes."

Honestly? I wasn't sure about that. And there was a small, probably mean part of me, that wanted him to wait and wonder.

"Hey. This is my brother and your best friend." Megan shot me an arch look. "Don't be coy."

"Yeah, yeah. You're right." I grabbed my phone and opened Austin's text.

I'D LIKE THAT A LOT. THANKS FOR ASKING ME.

I hit Send and set the phone back on the table. "Happy now?"

"Yeah. You?"

I had a real, official date with Austin coming up. Little butterflies danced in my stomach. Not as friends. I smiled slightly. He'd tacked that on to be sure I knew what he was asking. Because I'd made such a big deal out of things two weeks ago.

He could say we weren't going as friends, but I knew we were. We'd always be friends. But now I could open the door and hope our friendship expanded to more.

16

LUKE

This was a terrible idea. Why had I let myself get pushed into chairing the Valentine's banquet? Sure, the youth group could use a fundraiser, but I'd been investigating things we could sell—donuts and candy had been high on my list—and those would have been so much less awkward than this.

I tugged at the knot in my tie and looked out over the fellowship hall.

It looked like something had vomited pink and red everywhere.

"What do you think? Isn't it gorgeous?" The pastor's wife patted my arm. "I think the women outdid themselves this year."

"It's definitely something special." I clamped my mouth shut. I couldn't take back the words—wouldn't even if I could—but she had to have heard my tone. And that tone was not happy.

"What's wrong, Luke? This'll get the youth program probably close to two thousand dollars. Surely you can put that to good use?" She tipped her head to the side. "It's better than selling donuts no one wants."

"What's wrong with donuts?" I'd emailed the parents and

asked about various things they'd be interested in buying and selling. Everyone loved donuts. Especially since one of the famous chains had a fundraising program. Sure, they wouldn't be as fresh as timing a visit to the shop when the "Hot" light was on, but they were still delicious.

She wrinkled her nose. "So bad for you."

"And spaghetti is healthy?"

She stiffened and sniffed. "I didn't realize the menu didn't meet with your approval."

"I'm sure it'll be fine. The couples coming will probably love it." Because who didn't love overcooked noodles covered in jarred pasta sauce and frozen garlic bread? Oh, that's right, everyone.

"When will your date get here? I'm surprised you didn't ask Kayla to come and help set up."

"I didn't ask anyone to come as my date." I'd been second-guessing that decision, too. But I wasn't going to be able to concentrate on someone else while this was going on. Not while I was supposed to ensure the service was organized and the short musical program happened like it was scheduled.

"Oh, Luke." The pastor's wife shook her head. "How are you going to find a wife if you don't take someone out for Valentine's Day? What must Kayla think?"

At least I didn't have to answer because Pastor Chaz showed up and slid his arm around his wife's waist. He kissed the top of her head. "It looks lovely, hon."

"Luke doesn't think so. Do you?"

I wanted to squirm under the weight of her glare and his lifted eyebrows. "I didn't say that. I said it was something special."

The pastor's lips twitched. "See? That's a fine compliment. Why don't you go check on the kitchen, honey, before we hand everything off to Luke and prepare to enjoy ourselves."

"Oh, all right. I'll see you at our table." She shot me a narrow-eyed look before heading off.

"You need to work on your tact, son."

I bristled. "I have said before that I didn't want to be in charge of this. I think it's dumb and borders on inappropriate for a youth group fundraiser."

"Your objections are noted." Pastor Chaz sighed. "And they're not completely off base. Fact is, usually women's ministry runs this. But with you being determined to hare off to Mexico at spring break, we thought this would be a good way to help."

Everything about the pastor's words hit me wrong. I turned to frown at him. "You know what? Let's make everyone happy and cancel the spring break trip. It's clear I don't have your support. You haven't backed me up with the parents, and they want it to be some kind of church sponsored beach week with an hour of Bible study in the morning so we can pretend the kids are learning about Jesus before they go off to flaunt their bodies in front of one another and try to sneak away from the chaperones to give their hormones free rein."

"Now, Luke. That's not what I want—"

"But it's what the parents want. Except maybe not the hormone part, but they're not thinking it through if they don't think that's what's going to happen without organized activities." I shook my head. This wasn't the time or the place to get into it. And I was perilously close to saying something irrevocable. Something that sounded a lot like, "I quit."

"It's possible. And maybe I should have been more forceful, but we've never done a spring break mission trip."

I heard what he didn't add on. Everyone was happy with how things had always been done, and there was no need for me to try and change things.

Pastor Chaz patted my shoulder, clearly unaware of the fact that I was seething. "When will Kayla get here? I hope the two of you will consider sitting at our table. I'd like to get to know her better."

I clenched my jaw. "I didn't invite a date. I'm going to be too busy making sure things run smoothly."

The pastor shook his head. "I don't understand. I'm sure I saw her name on one of the place cards when they were printing."

I blinked. I'd delegated that whole business to his wife. She'd had significant opinions about how they ought to be done, and I hadn't wanted to spend any time fighting about it. They were place cards. People would pick them up off the table when they checked in and then put them at their spot. It wasn't entirely impossible that she'd decided to come alone in order to support the youth.

"You didn't know." Pastor Chaz shook his head again. "I hate that you let her get away. She's going to make someone a good spouse someday. I'll just go check in with my wife."

I took a moment and let the knowledge wash over me that, yet again, I'd let down the pastor. I wasn't cut out for this job. I certainly wasn't cut out for this church.

With a sigh, I pushed away all thoughts except what needed to happen next to make this event a success, and turned to go check in with the teens who had volunteered to run the check-in table.

"You two look nice. I appreciate you dressing up for this."

"Sure thing, Pastor Luke." Marci beamed at me and brushed at her skirt.

"Mom was glad I'd have a chance to wear this dress again." Carrie rolled her eyes. "She bought it for me to wear to homecoming but she was super annoyed about it."

"You both look nice. You know what to do?" He glanced down at the lists that sat on the table in front of each girl. "Mark off people as they arrive. If they haven't paid yet, we take cash and checks. There's some change, but not a lot, in the lock box there."

"We've got it, Pastor Luke." Marci grinned. "After they check in, they grab their place cards and find a spot at a table. Easy."

"All right. Any problems, let me know. We have an extra table set up, so we can take five walk-in couples." I didn't think we'd need them, but I also didn't think it was a problem to set up one more table. It had taken what, two more minutes?

"We've got it." Exasperation leaked through Carrie's voice. "When is your date coming?"

Ugh. What was with everyone? Although I shouldn't be surprised. Carrie's parents were friends with the pastor and his wife, so it made sense that there'd been talk. I forced a smile. "Too busy for a date tonight."

Marci's eyes got wide and she gasped. "But Pastor Luke, it's *Valentine's.*"

"Technically, that's on Tuesday." I watched the girls exchange a smirk and wanted to sigh. They were going to tell everyone I was planning a date for Tuesday. Which was fine. Let them. In fact, maybe I'd talk to Kayla about it tonight. I checked my watch. Nearly go time. "All right. Thanks again, ladies."

I heard voices carrying down the hallway. Sounded like our first couples were on their way. I hurried back to the fellowship hall to switch on the music. Strains of romantic piano music drifted out over the set tables. The pastor had given me the CD and insisted on using it. I guess the artists—there were two pianos—came to our church, though they'd been on tour a lot and I didn't think I'd met them.

I didn't often get a chance to sit in on one of the services because of youth obligations.

"Oh, great, you've got the Carters' CD playing." Pastor Chaz appeared at my elbow with a grin. "I'm told they'll be here tonight. I'll make a point of introducing you. Nick is around more than Louisiana, but they both tour and we're always happy when they can provide music when they're in town."

"They sound great. I'm sorry I haven't caught them since I've been here."

The pastor gave me a long look. "You don't get to Sunday morning service every week, do you?"

I shook my head.

He sighed. "We ought to see what we can do to fix that. We knew it was a problem—Kyle often mentioned it. We just haven't found a way to fix it."

Ah yes, Kyle. My predecessor who could do no wrong. I wondered if he knew that. At this point, they could fix it for my replacement. Wait. Was I really thinking that? Oh boy, I was.

"You okay, son? It's going to be fine. Not much they can mess up in the kitchen, it's one reason we stick to spaghetti for these things." Pastor Chaz's voice held a hint of censure. Of course, his wife had filled him in on our initial interaction.

I offered a tight smile. "I'm sure it'll be great."

"That's the spirit. I'm going to go grab my seat, but if you need anything, let me know, and I'll do what I can."

I watched Pastor Chaz join his wife at a table. He kissed her and held her chair out for her. She blushed prettily. He looked like he was in heaven. Most of the couples that were slowly filtering in and taking their places did. And I...didn't care. There was no longing in my heart for that. Just a quiet sense of subtle obligation.

I spotted Kayla on the far side of the room. She looked nice —pretty, even—maybe I'd go over and...oh. She was holding hands with her date.

I followed the arm up and my eyebrows lifted. That was Asher? Aidan? No. She'd talked about him a little—he was her best friend. Austin. That was it. And I guessed they were moving past the best friends portion of the program.

Now I did sigh.

It wasn't that I suddenly felt that longing for a wife and family—I didn't. But Kayla had been easy enough to talk to, and I was reasonably convinced that if she and I continued going out here and there that everyone—particularly Pastor Chaz—would leave me alone about settling down.

Which left me where?

I caught Pastor Chaz giving me an odd look and realized it was time to get the show on the road, as it were. They'd set up a microphone at the front of the room, and I headed over to it.

"Good evening, ladies and gentlemen. Thanks so much for coming out to our fundraising dinner for the youth. Hopefully you'll have a fun evening with your valentine. Let's pray."

I bowed my head a moment before saying a short blessing over the evening and the food. It seemed inadequate to me, but I always felt that way when I had to pray out loud. Which just started me questioning my decision to be a youth pastor all over again.

God? What are You doing here?

I ended the prayer and smiled. "Enjoy your evening."

I spotted an empty seat at a table near the back. I aimed myself in that direction, trying to avoid making eye contact with anyone. I didn't want to get sucked into conversation and have to explain, again, that I didn't have a date.

"Is it okay if I sit here?" I rested my hand on the back of a chair.

"Pastor Luke, of course." The woman was one of the youth group mothers, and I should have known her name. But I didn't.

"Thanks." I pulled out the chair and sat.

"Will your date be late?"

I offered a tight smile. "I wasn't sure it would be appropriate, since I'm in charge. In fact, I should probably pop into the kitchen and check on things. Excuse me."

I tucked the chair back in after I stood and headed to the kitchen. I saw Kayla wave, but acted like I didn't. I didn't want to have her cheerily introduce me to her date and then have to make conversation with the guy who had just complicated my life more than I wanted to admit.

17

KAYLA

"I'll be right back, okay? I just want to pop into the youth room real fast." I reached for Austin's hand and squeezed it. It had been nice to spend last night together at the Valentine's banquet. Even nicer to come to church together this morning. "Don't be that way."

"I'm not being any way." Austin squeezed my hand. "Want me to tag along?"

I sighed. "Really? You think that's a good idea? Talk about rubbing salt in the wound. No. Just wait here, okay?"

"I was kidding. I'll wait." Austin leaned back against the wall in the church foyer.

I watched him for a moment, nodded, and headed toward the youth room. It was long enough past the end of service, that it should just be Luke stacking chairs. Hopefully there wouldn't be any of the kids still hanging around.

I peeked in and let out a breath. Luke was alone, stacking chairs just like I'd figured. I cleared my throat.

Luke dropped the chair he was carrying onto the stack and turned. I couldn't decide what emotion flickered over his face before he schooled his expression. "Hi."

"Hi, Luke. I feel like I owe you an explanation."

He shook his head. "You don't. I didn't ask you to the banquet because I knew I'd be busy, and it didn't seem fair to expect you to sit alone for a lot of the night. It was certainly reasonable for you to go with someone who did ask."

I studied him before nodding. "Did you want to ask me?"

Luke's mouth opened, then snapped shut. He wouldn't meet my gaze. "I don't know how to answer that."

"It seems easy. To me, at least." I tucked my hands in the pockets of the skirt I'd decided on at the last minute this morning when I was getting ready for church. Normally I went with jeans, like everyone else, but after last night with Austin, I'd wanted something a little fancier.

"It should be. I absolutely agree that you're right. And I guess I ought to apologize to you for the fact that it isn't."

"I don't want an apology, Luke. But I wouldn't mind an explanation." Why was I pushing? It wasn't that I wanted to date him —things with Austin and I were finally moving in the direction that I wanted them to go. The direction that I really felt God wanted them to go. At the same time, there was a part of me that wondered if explaining to me might help Luke understand for himself.

He sighed and ran a hand through his hair. "Just before Christmas, Pastor Chaz pulled me aside and said some of the parents had reservations about a young, unmarried youth pastor. The implication—though he didn't say it out loud—was that my job was hanging in the balance. I was encouraged to start working on finding someone with whom I could settle down and start a family."

"Ouch."

He lifted a shoulder. "Something like that. There were other conversations that followed and your name came up—probably because I'd mentioned that you'd asked about the mission trip.

One thing led to another and it seemed like I should just ask you out and see what happened. I really am sorry."

"It's okay. I don't think I would have done differently in your shoes. I enjoyed getting to know you. I think we could be friends."

His lips twisted. "Friends. I'd be okay with that. I don't really want more. And I'm guessing based on last night, you don't either."

I shook my head. "I'm sorry."

"Don't be. I realized last night, in a moment of clarity, that I'm not sure I want marriage. Certainly not right now. Maybe not ever. And I'm not sure what that means in terms of my job here. Or as a youth pastor at all. But I'm going to trust God to make that clear."

I smiled. "That's always the best plan. I'll pray for you, Luke. And if you ever want to hang out, you'd be more than welcome in our group. We're not all couples."

"I appreciate that. I'll keep it in mind."

I was pretty sure that was a "no," but that was also okay. "So. Spring break trip?"

He shook his head. "I'm sending out the official cancelation notice tomorrow. It's not worth trying to shoehorn mission work in between a Mexican vacation."

I winced. "I'm sorry. Does that leave your missionary friends in the lurch?"

"Maybe a little. I think, since we won't be having an official youth group activity, I'm going to head down. Jason has always been a bit of a mentor—even if I can't get all the repairs they need done, I could use the time with him." Luke shoved his hands into his pockets. "And the time away."

My heart hurt for him, but I didn't see a way to help other than prayer. So I'd just do that. "Okay. Well, I'm still game to try and help with the youth when you need someone."

"I appreciate it."

I closed the distance between us and wrapped my arms around him in a quick, tight hug. When I stepped back, I smiled. "Hang in there."

"Yeah. And congratulations on the thing with...Austin, right?"

I laughed. "Thanks. And yeah. Austin. He's actually waiting, so I should go. Take care, Luke."

He just smiled.

There was nothing else to say, so I just turned and made my way back to the foyer. Austin was still leaning against the wall, right where I had left him. My heart sped up. It always did when I saw him, but this time, instead of trying to squash the feeling, I let it come.

"Everything okay?" Austin pushed off the wall and held out his hand.

I slipped my fingers into his. "Yeah. Turns out, he wasn't feeling it either."

"All's well that ends well, then?"

"Something like that, yeah." I quashed the tendril of guilt that was trying to linger. It was unfounded and unnecessary. It wasn't as though Luke was heartbroken. Not about me, at least. Maybe about his job—or career path long term—but I couldn't do anything about that. "Are we eating at the diner with the rest of the gang?"

"Do you want to?" Austin opened the foyer door and held it for me. "I'm fine with that. Or we could go somewhere just us. We haven't done Mexican in a while."

I brightened. "Yeah?"

"Yeah. Do you mind driving? Megan and I came together, and I told her to take the car. I thought that'd probably be okay."

Everything in me warmed when he smiled at me. "I don't mind that at all."

It didn't take long to get to the restaurant. I squashed the tiny feeling of déjà vu. Not that Austin and I hadn't ever come here together before I'd brought Luke.

"Two?"

Austin nodded at the hostess and gestured for me to go ahead of him when she started toward a table. He put his hand in the small of my back and I wanted to arch into it like a cat. It probably wouldn't be seemly. And I didn't want to scare him off. This change in our relationship was new enough, that was a definite possibility.

"Your server will be right with you." The hostess set menus on the table and disappeared.

I slid into the booth on one side and reached for a menu.

Austin hesitated, then slid into the seat opposite me. "Has it changed?"

"Has what changed?" I peeked over the menu.

"The food? You have like three things you get here, if it hasn't changed."

I laughed and put the menu down. "I could branch out. You don't know for sure that I won't try something new. Look at us. Didn't I just last night agree to be in an exclusive relationship with you?"

He grinned and reached for my hand. "You did. And if that was the opening for you to realize the joy of fajitas instead of an enchilada and taco combo, then I'm for it."

I wrinkled my nose. "I don't think I'm taking risks that big. And honestly, fajitas are just laziness on the part of the restaurant. Here's all your food separated out. Go ahead and put it together into a soft taco. Or, if you're not dumb, order the soft tacos to begin with and make them do the work for you."

Austin shook his head. "You're missing out. There's something about that sizzling plate. And you can't get the peppers and onions on a soft taco."

"Ugh. Why would I want to?" I gave a mock shudder. "Darn it. You had to say enchilada and taco combo, didn't you? Now that's what I want."

He snickered. "It's what you were always going to get. But you can blame me now, that's fine. I can take it."

"All right, Mr. Sassy. What are you getting?"

"You have to ask? Chicken fajitas. They're amazing and you get to put them together so you have a perfect bite every time. Not like a soft taco where the ingredients aren't placed just so."

I wanted to roll my eyes, but I'd seen Austin eat fajitas before, and he did, in fact, take the time to minutely spread the pieces out so they were evenly distributed. "Fine. Get DIY soft tacos. I wish they were honest and named them that."

"Anyway." Austin set the menus on the edge of the table and glanced out into the restaurant. "Noah knows an architect. I guess they grew up together. He sent me her contact details and I'm going to reach out about the youth center this afternoon."

"That's quick work. Have you even made an offer on the property yet?" Maybe it didn't matter. The building needs were going to be the same, regardless of where he ended up building. Except, if he did find another location, it might have a building that was functional enough that it was worth modifying instead of demolishing.

"I wanted to go walk through it one more time. The listing agent said I could come by this evening. Want to tag along?"

I did. But I also had a lot of grading I hadn't finished because of the dinner last night. After we left the church, we'd gone walking along the water near home. Past the Torpedo Factory and into Founders Park.

It had been close to midnight when he dropped me off at my apartment.

"Can I say maybe? If I focus, I can probably get my grading

done this afternoon. Then I'd be free to join you. Depending, I guess, on what time you were thinking."

Austin took out his phone. "We hadn't come up with a firm time yet. I don't want it to be too dark though. Maybe five? But you'd still have some time after the walkthrough for more grading. I can't imagine we'd be there more than an hour. And I won't push for dinner."

Was it bad that I was disappointed by that? I chewed my lip but was saved from having to answer immediately by the server finally getting to us. We placed both our drink and food orders and she melted away after dropping a basket of chips and a little bowl of salsa on the table.

"Is it me, or did she seem unprepared for us to be ready to go?"

I shook my head. "It was not you. Maybe she's having a bad day."

"Could be. Doesn't mean I'm excited that she's the one who's supposed to be feeding us. Especially now that I know you need to get in and out with a little more speed than usual."

I sighed. "I'm not trying to rush us."

"I know." He squeezed my hand before reaching for a chip. "I just really want you to come tonight."

"Okay. Five works. And what if you brought your grading—because I know you have some—and afterward I could put together something simple and we could work at my place for a little?" We'd done that before. A lot. Until it had gotten too hard for me and I'd started pulling away and spending time with Megan instead. It seemed like a good time to bring back our homework dates.

He grinned. "Sounds good."

"Can I ask why you want to go see it again? You know you don't want the building. But don't you also already know you want the lot?"

Austin shrugged. "I guess I'm nervous. It's a bunch of money. And the youth center means a lot to me. I want it to be perfect."

"You know it won't be, though, right? There's going to be at least ten things that you get close to perfect but not quite all the way. That's how life works. Sometimes you have to accept good enough."

"Wow. That's...a philosophy." He frowned. "And not one I ever would have imagined you having."

"I can be pragmatic." Just because I tended to be on the cheerful, optimistic side of things didn't mean I couldn't recognize that life rarely turned out the way we wanted it to. Plans or not, things went wrong. "I'm just saying, you have to prepared for things to go badly. Then you adjust and adapt."

"All right. That's true, and I do that. But it sounded like you were saying perfection wasn't possible no matter what."

"Well. I mean let's be real. It isn't. Only Jesus is perfect. The rest of us? We can do the best we can, and do that adjusting and adapting as needed. But it's not a great plan to expect perfection. Out of anything."

"Not even math homework?"

I groaned. "That's completely different. I expect programs that run and so okay, fine, perfection is possible in some cases."

He grinned. "See? So there's a possibility."

"Fine. We'll aim for perfection with the new building." I wasn't sure about the likelihood, but I'd keep my questions to myself. He was nervous, and I wasn't used to seeing Austin that way.

"That's the spirit."

"So this architect. Noah grew up with her?" I didn't know Noah as well as some of the other guys in the group. I was Austin's friend. That was literally how they'd described me. Austin's friend, Kayla. Or more recently, Megan and Austin's friend, Kayla. But never really part of the group.

Which was fine. I wasn't looking to horn in on the group. Honestly, there weren't women in the group. It was the six guys. Megan got a little bit of a pass because she was Austin's sister, but it wasn't as if she ever went to poker night or anything like that.

"That's what he said. Don't try to dig for details, I don't have any beyond her name and email address." Austin took another chip and scooped a generous helping of salsa with it.

I followed suit, letting the tangy condiment take over my senses. "Okay. We go see the property again this evening and then...?"

"Then I make an offer. You're right, I want it. The location matters more than anything else. But since I'm not going to use the buildings, I don't really want to pay for them."

Good luck. I didn't imagine the previous owners were going to care. But it probably didn't hurt to ask. "If they're firm on their asking price?"

He sighed. "I guess I'll pay it. I want the location. But I'm going to try to negotiate first. Can't hurt, can it?"

I shook my head and offered a smile. I wasn't sure how things were going to go with this youth center idea of his, but I was grateful I got to be a part of it from the ground up as more than just Austin's friend.

18

AUSTIN

I knocked on Scott's front door and then walked in. "Hey, guys!"

"Austin. Hey, man. You're the first one here." Scott waved me in to the kitchen. "Come on in and have a seat. Hungry?"

"A little. Am I early?" I twisted my watch around on my wrist. No. I was seven minutes later than our usual start time. "Did I miss a text?"

Scott shrugged. "Not that I know of. Stuff happens, though, right?"

I chuckled. "That it does. How's married life treating you?"

Scott's eyebrows lifted. "Not your smoothest segue, although I guess given what I've picked up from Whitney, it's not surprising that you're asking."

Heat crawled up my neck. He wasn't wrong. Now that Kayla and I were an official item, I could admit that my thoughts were drifting toward marriage more often. It was, obviously, too soon to say any of that out loud. It would be a week tomorrow. We hadn't even kissed yet. "You're dodging the question."

"Married life is amazing. Five stars, highly recommended." Scott chuckled. "You testing the waters?"

I shook my head. "Not yet. But I won't lie and say I don't want that."

"And Kayla?"

"How do you *know*? It's probably too early. We've tiptoed around it a little, but things are new. It's all shiny and fun, you know? Plus, at work we have to keep it a little quiet. Thankfully, we have a history of eating lunch together, so that's not a change."

"I have to say, when Whitney and I got together, it was a little strange. I mean she lived here because of Beckett. But it wasn't until we were married that I was home with her all day. It's really nice." Scott grabbed a bag of chips and opened them before setting them on the kitchen table. "I guess you've had that all along."

I guess I had. And he was right, it was nice to know I'd get to see Kayla at least for a few minutes every day. I hoped she looked forward to it as much as I did. I reached into the bag for a handful of chips.

"Hey, I'm late. Sorry!" Noah's voice carried into the kitchen.

"You're not alone. Almost everyone's late today." Scott leaned out the kitchen doorway. "Austin's here."

"Nice." Noah appeared in the doorway. "You ever talk to Jenna?"

"Yeah. It's tricky since I'm at school during her usual working hours, but we finally got the chance to connect at lunch yesterday. She seems excited about the project." I reached for more chips. "She sounded surprised that I'd gotten her name from you, though."

Noah frowned. "Huh. Wonder why?"

"I asked her just that. She said because the two of you haven't really been in touch for the last five years."

"Has it been that long?" Noah's eyebrows lifted. "I guess it has."

"Who's Jenna and why is Austin talking to her?" Scott was looking between us as we spoke. "Also, do we want to move into the living room and start? We can probably get a round or two in before everyone shows up."

"Yeah, that's fine." I grabbed the bag of chips. They were my favorite kind and I wasn't going to be able to stop eating them. I didn't buy them often for just that reason.

"Jenna's a girl I knew in high school. We kept in touch a little during college, but I guess we lost touch over the last few years." Noah shrugged like it was no big deal, but I caught a glimmer of something in his eyes.

Interesting.

"So, you were best friends? Like me and Kayla?"

Noah scoffed. "No. Friends, sure. Just pals. No biggie. You asked in the group chat about architects and I remembered that was the direction she was leaning, so I passed her info along. That's it."

I exchanged a look with Scott. Noah was spending a lot of time explaining how little their relationship had meant. And it was rapidly becoming a case of someone protesting just a bit too much.

"Uh-huh." Scott shook his head. "You stick to that story if that's what you want. But free tip? Tone down the denial when the other guys ask."

Red flooded Noah's face. "Did you hear Cody has a closing date on his townhouse?"

"Smooth subject change, bro. Seems to be the night for them." Scott picked up the deck of cards and started to shuffle.

I cleared my throat. "It's a nice place. I knew he was putting in an offer, but I hadn't heard it was accepted."

Noah nodded. "Last week, yeah. I think they were hoping to

hold out for someone to offer more than they're asking. You know what the market's like right now. But Cody didn't want to play, so he told his agent to let them know his offer was expiring, and I guess they'd had some tours but no other offers, so they took it."

"Nice." The market was definitely heating up, but expecting offers above asking when I felt like they were already priced near the top of the acceptable range teetered on the edge of ridiculous. "He offered full price?"

"He did. Said he didn't see the point in arguing when he could afford what they were asking, and he wanted the house." Noah reached for the two cards Scott had dealt him. "I'm not sure that's the best plan when it comes to buying a house, but maybe it is. Guess I need to figure out what I'm going to do."

"What do you mean?" Scott tossed his bet into the pile in the center of the table.

"Well. Cody's moving out. I could take over the rent on the whole apartment and stay put. Or I could look around for a house of my own. Or a condo like Tristan. He said there was one in his building coming on the market soon." Noah let out a blustery breath. "But I'm not sure what the right choice is."

I'd never really considered just how blessed I was to have my grandma's townhouse. This wasn't a decision I had to deal with. I guess maybe down the road, if either Megan or I got married, we'd have to decide who kept the townhouse and who found something of their own. And that was a no-brainer to me. I could afford to get another space, so it made sense that I'd move. Unless Megan ended up marrying someone who already had a place.

Someone like Cody.

I'd made a point of not thinking too hard about the conversation he and I'd had over burgers. I stood by my comment—I honestly didn't mind if he wanted to ask Megan out. Nor would I mind if something serious developed between them. But I didn't really want to dwell on it.

Megan didn't date a lot. Never had. So it was tricky to think of her being involved with someone.

"Yo. Austin. Where'd you go, man?" Noah nudged me with his elbow. "Are you in?"

"Sorry." I glanced at my cards. They weren't anything to write home about, but there were a few more cards yet to be dealt. Things could change. I tossed a couple of poker chips on the pile. "Sure, why not."

Scott flipped the next card.

I checked mine even though I knew that hadn't helped any.

"So? Thoughts?" Noah drummed his fingers on the table.

"Do you want to own something? Fiscally, I guess, it makes more sense than continuing to rent. Equity. Investment. Blah, blah." I grinned.

Scott laughed. "Yeah, those last words are the important ones for sure."

"Don't underestimate the importance of blah." Noah shook his head. "All right. I guess I'll let the leasing office know I'm moving out when our lease is over. Which means I should probably start looking around at what's available."

"Seems reasonable." Scott reached for his phone. "I'm going to text the others and see what's going on. It's Friday, right?"

I snickered. "It had better be. I'm not planning on teaching anyone anything tomorrow."

"What's the story with this learning center? How's that going?" Noah tipped back in his chair while we waited for Scott to finish texting.

"Good. I've got an offer on the property across the street from my school. The building's a complete teardown, but the location couldn't be better." I was still waiting to hear what the current owners thought about it. Commercial real estate apparently moved at a different pace than residential. "I'm hoping to hear something this coming week. But I don't know for sure. I'm fairly confident the original zoning will work for what I want to do there, so that's one headache averted. Tristan's double-checking, just to be sure."

"I'm surprised he needs any clients other than us." Scott chuckled and set down his phone before dealing another card. "No one's responding. Should we be worried?"

"Nah." Noah shook his head. "Cody's been working on a big project with Jackson. It's possible he's still there. Jackson's wife is a restaurant chef-owner, so I'm pretty sure he doesn't have someone at home hoping for him to hurry up and get there."

"Unless they have kids." How would it work to run a restaurant and balance a family? People did, most likely, but I couldn't wrap my head around it. I could see, easily, how two teachers would make that situation work though. Would Kayla want to keep working? Maybe she'd decide she wanted to stay home. Or homeschool? I'd be fine with that. It wasn't like we'd be trying to make things work on our salaries alone.

"True." Noah shrugged. "I'm not sure if he does."

"How do you work with someone and not know about their family?" Scott frowned and flipped the final card. "When I was at Robinson, I think I knew more about the family lives of people who sat near me than was probably reasonable or healthy."

I snickered. "I don't know a lot about the family or personal lives of teachers who aren't in the math department. And even then, we have one teacher—I'm pretty sure she's been teaching math since Isaac Newton was around—who isn't one for sharing."

"Maybe because everyone cracks jokes about how old she is?" Noah shook his head. "You think that might have something to do about it?"

I flinched. "Maybe. To be fair, I don't think we say them aloud."

"She has to know. That kind of thing is obvious." Scott pointed a finger at me. "You know better."

I sighed. I did know better. "Yeah, all right. I'll do better. Point being, I don't think it's super weird not to know all the ins and outs of your coworkers' lives."

"Not even 'coworker.' He's basically the second in command. And really, he's around more than Mr. Ballentine, so he might as well be in charge. How much did you know about Joe Robinson's personal life before he did the whole heart attack and matchmaking contest thing?"

Scott flashed a grin. "All right. That's a point. Nothing. He was a name on the building. An occasional nod in the hall or the elevator. He could have been married six times with twelve kids for all I knew."

"My *point* was that Cody might be working late. That was all I was trying to say." Noah looked at his cards again and shook his head. "I'm out."

"Me too." I wasn't going to try and bluff Scott. Chances were high he had a good hand, and I had a pair of threes. That wasn't going to win any contests. "Wes has been making himself scarce a lot these days. Anyone else notice that?"

"Not until you said something, no." Scott frowned and pulled the pile of poker chips toward himself. "He's still pretty serious about the dive shop thing, and now that he's free of Robinson, I guess he's been taking some classes."

"Classes?" I frowned. "Like dive classes?"

"Nah. Business classes, is my understanding. You'd have to talk to Cody. The two of them were discussing it at our place a couple weeks ago." Noah pushed back his chair and stood. "You have any soda in the fridge?"

"Oh, yeah, sure. Help yourself." Scott collected the cards and started shuffling.

"You want anything?" Noah pointed at me and then Scott.

"I'll take something without caffeine, if there's an option like that." I was officially old enough that I didn't need to risk it. I had enough trouble sleeping that I didn't want to add to the problem. Although, to be fair, my lack of sleep was less about age and more about Kayla.

"Should be. We keep root beer for Beckett as a treat. In fact, that sounds really good. I'll take one, too." Scott grinned. "Thanks, Noah."

"Sure thing." Noah disappeared into the kitchen.

"Are we playing again or do you want to call it?" I wasn't really in the mood for cards. And three wasn't nearly as enjoyable as our usual group. I'd be okay watching TV or just hanging. Or heading home early and calling it a night.

Noah brought the sodas and distributed them. "Let's not bother. I wouldn't mind an early night since I guess I'm going to start looking at real estate. Maybe I'll get online and poke around a little."

"I can hook you up with my agent, if you want?" Scott reached for his phone. "She's a friend of the family and we were pleased with how she helped us find this place."

Noah shrugged. "Sure. Shoot me her details. Never hurts to have someone on tap."

Scott poked at his phone before clicking it off. "Done."

Noah's phone chimed. "Thanks."

I popped the top of my soda and took a long drink. When would be too soon to excuse myself? It was a nice evening. Not too cold, for all it was just after Valentine's Day. Maybe I could swing by the bookstore and convince Kayla to go for a walk. We could grab ice cream or something.

"Earth to Austin." Scott grinned at me when I looked over. "Where'd you go?"

"Sorry. Just thinking." I definitely didn't want to share my thoughts. The guys would never let me hear the end of it. Even if it was only two of them.

"Uh-huh. Thinking about Kayla, I assume." Noah wiggled his eyebrows. "Fill us in."

"No. I mean yeah, I was, but there's nothing to fill in that you don't know. We went to the banquet for youth on Saturday, and she finally agreed that we could date exclusively."

"Finally?" Noah shot Scott a look. "Did you know they were dating non-exclusively?"

"I did not. When did that happen?"

I shook my head. "It didn't. We weren't. I just—there were some weird moments in there before I asked her to the dinner, because she'd been going out with Luke, and I guess she didn't think I was serious about us. I don't know. It's fixed now, though."

"So no more dates with the youth pastor?"

"No. Turns out, he wasn't feeling it, either. So that's good. At least she won't go down as the woman who left the guy heartbroken."

Noah snorted. "They went out what, twice? I don't think heartbreak can come after two dates."

"I don't know." Scott spun his soda in little circles. "I would've been pretty heartbroken if Whitney had dumped me after two dates."

"Aw." Noah patted over his heart. "Twu Wuv."

Scott grabbed a poker chip and tossed it at Noah, but he ducked.

"Children. Do I need to send you both to the principal?" I grinned and ducked when Scott threw a poker chip at me.

"Maybe it's time to go." Noah drained his soda in several long swallows and set the can down on the game table. "My new home isn't going to find itself."

"Probably not." I chugged the last of my drink as well, then stood. "I think I might stop by the bookstore."

"Talk about true love." Scott rolled his eyes, but they were glinting with humor. "Tell my wife I'm home alone, would you?"

"Maybe. Then again, maybe she secretly looks forward to this time away from you." I picked up both my can and Noah's. I could toss them in the recycle bin in the kitchen on my way to the front door.

"Next time you talk to Jenna, tell her I said hi." Noah grabbed the handle to the front door and tugged it open.

"Will do. See ya, Scott. Thanks for hosting." I stepped through the door and paused on the porch, turning to look back in where Scott stood. "Do you want to get back to rotating? Now that you've got a better handle on things with Beckett and all?"

Scott shrugged. "I can do whatever. If someone wants to host, just let me know."

That was fair. I didn't have a burning desire to host, but I didn't mind doing it if Scott was feeling overburdened. We did trade off on snacks—although this week, Tristan had been in charge of food, so that hadn't worked out super well. It wasn't like him not to let us know if he couldn't make it...what was up with him?

I pulled the door closed and jogged down the steps to the street. I was definitely going to drive over to the bookstore. If the girls didn't want to end their evening early, that was all right. I could grab a book and get ice cream on my own.

But it really would be so much better if Kayla would come.

19

KAYLA

The bells over the door jingled and I looked along with Megan and Whitney. My heart gave an extra little thud when I spotted Austin. My face heated and my mouth went dry. It had been like this ever since our walk by the river Saturday night.

Had it only been a week? Really?

"Hey, Austin. Poker's at my house. You lost?" Whitney's voice was full of teasing. She leaned back, presumably because she'd be hidden from Austin by bookshelves and patted a hand on her heart.

I gave a little shake of my head.

Megan just grinned.

"Half the guys didn't show. Noah, Scott, and I decided to call it early. So I came here, hoping maybe I could convince my girl to go for a walk. Maybe grab an ice cream?" His gaze locked with mine, and he lifted an eyebrow in invitation.

I stood, dusting my hands on my jeans. I wasn't dressed for a date. Not that it mattered. Austin had seen me in grubby, hanging-out clothes a lot. We'd been besties for years. So it shouldn't matter. Still, I was self-conscious. "I like ice cream."

Megan snickered. "I like ice cream. Can I come?"

"Pfft. Who'd run the store?" Austin glanced at the chair where Beckett was entranced by the picture book he had open in his lap. "I guess Beck could handle it."

Whitney chuckled. "He probably could. Other than not being able to count past ten—and it gets a little shaky after five. But he's cute, so maybe people would be okay with not getting change."

I grabbed my purse. "I guess I'll see you guys later."

"I guess you will." Megan rolled her eyes. "Enjoy your ice cream."

"We will. You could always pick some up on your way home. You know they're open late on Fridays." Austin held out his hand to me.

It was weird slipping my hand in his in front of the girls. His fingers closed around mine.

We left the bookstore hand in hand and stopped on the sidewalk in front.

He tipped his head to the side. "Do you want ice cream? Maybe go walk by the water? Or is it too cold?"

"Nah. It's not too cold." Today had been relatively nice, though once the sun set the chill had started creeping in. But I wasn't going to risk having Austin change his mind. If he wanted ice cream and a stroll in the park by the river, then that was what we'd do.

The ice cream shop was on the way toward the river. Unsurprisingly, there wasn't much business tonight, so we were in and out with our cones in a matter of minutes. There were a few people out walking, but definitely not anything like the crowds that would flock in the summer when people headed toward the river hoping for a breeze.

"I'm sorry your poker night fell through." I knew it was something he looked forward to every week. It wasn't about the cards. It was time with his friends. I got that. Especially since I'd started looking forward to my own Friday nights with the girls.

"I don't understand why none of them let us know they weren't going to make it. I don't want everything to fall apart, you know? I get that with Scott and Whitney married, and now we're dating, maybe the guys are worried that things are changing, but I don't see why they'd have to." Austin gave our hands a little swing. "If nothing else, if we get everyone else paired off, we can start doing stuff as couples."

"Whoa there. We're not matchmaking." I shook my head. "No one wants that."

Austin chuckled. "Maybe, maybe not."

I turned my head and studied him. "No. Put that idea out of your head. What if people had gotten ideas about pushing us together? How do you think that would've worked out?"

"A lot like this?" Austin stopped. We'd reached one of the benches by the water's edge. "You wouldn't have backed away just because our friends put us together, would you?"

I drew in a breath and looked out over the Potomac. Probably not. I'd been on my way to being in love with Austin for long enough that I probably would have jumped on any opportunity for him to see me as something other than his best friend.

"Exactly." Austin sat and tugged me down beside him. "Depending on how you look at it, Luke played matchmaker by making me realize how I felt and what I was about to lose."

"I guess we should write him a thank-you note." I burrowed up against Austin. He slid his arm around my shoulder and tucked me close.

"That seems excessive."

I chuckled and licked my cone. "This is nice."

"It is. Sometimes, at school, it's all I can do to keep from pulling you close for just a minute. I probably spend entirely too much time thinking about it."

My lips curved. "You know Lola and Darius?"

Austin snickered. "I do. And yeah, it'd be great to be able to indulge in PDA like they do. On the flip side, I'd just as soon they did a little less. The other day I had to stop and interrupt because Darius's hand was just a little too inappropriately placed."

"Seriously?" I tilted my head so I could see Austin's face. The two of them were the joke of the school. They were good kids, but they only had eyes—and hands and tongues, unfortunately —for each other.

Austin bobbed his head from side to side. "It was just too close for comfort. Lola, of course, got all defensive."

"She does that. I think because she knows better. I don't think she'd behave like she does if Darius wasn't pushing." I didn't have any basis for that. Lola and Darius had gotten together basically at freshman orientation, and they didn't seem in any hurry to change that. "I don't know. Maybe they'll end up one of the few high school couples who go on to have a long, happy life together."

"Stranger things have happened." Austin leaned closer until our noses touched. "I can't help but notice we aren't on school grounds right now."

My breath caught. "No. We're not."

Austin shifted. His lips brushed across mine. My eyes drifted closed. I lost myself in the kiss. It could have been five seconds or fifteen minutes. I had no idea. I just knew that I was with Austin and that he—finally—saw me as more than a friend.

Gradually, he eased back. "I've been wanting to do that for a while."

"I've been wanting you to do that for a while."

Austin's eyebrows drew together and he studied his ice cream a moment before looking at me. "How long?"

"What do you mean?"

He cleared his throat. "The way you said that sounded like you meant more than the week that I meant."

"Oh." I looked away. I wanted to hunch my shoulders. It shouldn't matter. We were together now, so it was okay. "Um. Maybe about a year. Little longer."

"A year." He let out a laughing breath. "You're pulling my leg."

"No."

He was quiet for so long, I turned to look at him.

"Why didn't you say something?"

I sighed. "I wanted you to notice me."

"Is that why you started hanging out with Megan? And pulling away from me?"

I nodded. I didn't know if he could see me in the twilight, but I didn't have any words.

"I'm sorry." Austin's voice was quiet. "I'm so sorry."

I twisted on the bench so I could face him, and cupped his cheek in my hand. "Don't be sorry. There's no reason for it. Even if this had never happened, you wouldn't owe me anything. I value your friendship. I value you. It's one of the reasons I never said anything. I didn't want to risk losing what we have. And I know there are people who get super annoyed by that in movies, but it's true. You're the most incredible friend I've ever had. If that friendship was all I ever got to have with you, I would have been incredibly blessed."

"Kayla." He covered my hand with his own. "I love you."

I leaned forward and kissed him. "I love you, too."

We sat in companionable silence for several more minutes as we finished our ice cream. I didn't want to leave. It seemed clear that Austin didn't either. But it was starting to get chilly, especially when the breeze kicked up off the water.

I shivered.

"We should get you home. You drove to the bookstore?" Austin stood and tugged me to my feet.

"Yeah. My car's in the garage." I pointed to the parking structure.

"Handy. I'm surprised you didn't try for street parking."

I chuckled. "I did. But it's Friday night. The spots were full and I didn't feel like spending an extra twenty minutes hoping, you know?"

"Yeah." He shifted and wrapped his arm around my shoulder, tucking me in close to his side. I appreciated it on many levels—it was warmer, to start. And it was Austin. "What are you up to tomorrow?"

"No plans." I slid my arm around his waist. "Just the usual. Clean the apartment. Play with the cats. Procrastinate grading."

He laughed. "Minus the cats, that sounds about like my plans. Plus, it's my week to hit the grocery store. Feel like hanging out? We can procrastinate on grading together."

It all sounded so settled. Almost like a married couple. And as much as I knew people on the outside would think we'd said "I love you" too fast, I suspected they'd be appalled by my thoughts already straying toward forever. But this was Austin. We'd been friends forever. In so many ways, he knew me almost better than I knew myself. "Yeah. I'd like that."

"Then it's a date. Text me when you're up and we'll hammer out the details?"

"Sounds like a plan." A good one, even.

It wasn't long before we made it to the parking garage and Austin was leaning on my car door, holding me close. We stood there wrapped up in each other long enough that I started to feel the chill seeping in again. A car honked as it drove past.

Austin stepped back.

"I could drive you to your car. Save you the walk?" I opened the car door and sat behind the wheel.

He shook his head. "Nah. Go home. Tell Ada and Charles that I'll see them tomorrow."

I grinned. I loved that he loved my cats. It had always been a plus in our relationship. So many people got offended when Charles decided to be aloof. Not Austin. He rolled with it. And then went out of his way to charm the guy. A lot like he'd charmed me. "Will do. Good night."

Austin closed my car door, knocked on the window once, and stepped out of the way.

With a sigh, I locked the doors before starting the engine and backing out of the space. When I shifted into Drive, Austin waved, then turned and strode toward the exit.

My apartment wasn't technically in Old Town. That was a good thing—I couldn't afford the price increase that came with the historic address—but it was close enough that I was home before long.

I tossed my purse on the couch, kicked off my shoes, and called to the cats. "I'm home, guys."

No one came trotting out to see me. I dug my phone out of my purse to check the time. It was a little early for them to have called it a night, but it wasn't unheard of. I headed into the kitchen for a snack.

I wasn't ready to sleep.

I wasn't sure I'd be able to.

Kissing Austin had been everything I imagined it would be.

I stared in the fridge. It was definitely good that Austin needed groceries tomorrow, because I did, too. If he hadn't mentioned it, I probably would've just made a delivery order. The prices were a little higher, but not enough that it wasn't worth the splurge now and then. But walking the aisles with Austin actually sounded fun.

I grabbed a bottle of juice out of the fridge and shut the door.

I spotted a swish of tail as I turned. "There you are."

I opened the bottle and took a drink as I crossed the kitchen and went back into the living room. Ada balanced primly on the back of the sofa. I ran my hand down the length of her body. "It wasn't just girls' night at the bookstore after all. Austin ended up coming by, so we went for a walk instead."

Ada looked interested—at least to me she did. It was probably wishful thinking. On the other hand, why else did people have pets if not to have someone to talk to at the end of the day? I filled her in as I settled on the couch and propped my feet on the coffee table. She jumped into my lap and butted her head against my chin.

"Careful. I don't want to spill the juice." I nuzzled the top of her head. "Where's Charles?"

Ada didn't say. But she didn't seem upset like she did when Charles managed to get himself trapped somewhere he couldn't escape. So for now, I'd leave it.

"What do you say we watch a little TV before bed? Maybe *The Martian*?" I shifted to grab the remote and queue up the movie. It was my go-to for relaxing entertainment these days. Neither Ada or Charles seemed to mind.

The best part? I'd seen it enough times that I could replay kissing Austin and not miss anything important.

20

AUSTIN

"Are you ready?" I'd dismissed my last class of the day five minutes early, packed up my things, and hurried to Kayla's classroom. The final bell had rung when I was halfway there and I was nearly run down by kids—all as excited as I was to start spring break.

"Just about." Kayla flashed a grin as she gathered a stack of papers and a pencil case, I knew she used to hold flash drives. "Can you check that all the computers are powered down?"

"Sure." I walked the rows in the lab, wiggling mice and listening for fans. I found one that had rebooted, not shut down, and got it sorted before continuing.

"Everything set?" Kayla flipped off the lights in her office and joined me in the lab.

"Yep. You've got your luggage in your car?"

"I do. I feel bad that there's no youth activity for the church this week. It seems decadent to be heading down to the Caymans with the gang when we'd talked about a service project."

I bit my lip. I understood what she was getting at, but at the same time, I couldn't regret not being in charge of teenagers for my week off. I was ready for a break. A real break. And some uninterrupted fun time with Kayla. Oh, sure, in the last seven weeks we'd found a rhythm of sorts. We spent nearly every weekend together—not always alone, which would have been a bad plan all around. So we did things with Scott and Whitney, or with Megan, or with the whole group. Sundays were church and lunch at the diner. That kind of thing. We also worked in two or three evenings during the week where we'd have dinner and hang out while we graded homework or prepped lessons.

It was comfortable.

And it was really the same kind of routine we'd been in before Kayla had pulled away because she had feelings for me.

Of course, now there was kissing.

I smiled.

"What?" Kayla looked over her shoulder then back at me. "Why are you grinning?"

"I'm trying to work up to agreeing with you, but I really don't." I shrugged. "Sorry?"

She chuckled. "No. It's fine. Luke is still going. Did you hear?"

"I didn't." I frowned slightly. I also hadn't realized she was still chatting with Luke. It didn't matter. It wouldn't. She could have friends of any gender she wanted. I trusted her. She loved me. "I'm surprised he didn't try to get a group of adults to join him."

"He did ask if I thought our group would want to come. I talked to Megan and Whitney about it—they thought everyone was looking forward to the beach enough that it wasn't worth raising. I put Luke in touch with Cody, though. Maybe some of the Ballentine guys are going. I don't know."

We reached the stairs and started down. I buried my frustration that she'd had all these conversations with people who weren't me. Of course, seeing as how it all related to Luke, I could kind of see why she might have hesitated. But only kind of. Because it wasn't like I cared if she had guy friends.

Oh, fine. I cared a little. And really just because it was Luke. Since he'd tried to date her and everything.

Which hadn't worked. And really, I owed him a thank-you of sorts because he'd basically been directly responsible for me and Kayla getting together.

Ugh.

I was annoying myself. "I hope he has a good time."

Kayla glanced at me, a little line forming between her eyebrows. "You're upset."

"No. Why would I be upset?" I hated how stiff I sounded, but it wasn't like I'd chosen it.

She sighed. "I didn't mention that he'd asked because I didn't want you to worry. Or be mad. Looks like I chose wrong."

"I'm not worried or mad." I wanted to leave it there, but the look she gave me made that impossible. "I guess I wish you'd felt comfortable talking to me about it. I don't want us to have secrets. Or parts of our life that we can't share."

"That makes sense. I'm sorry."

I would have liked to have taken her hand and squeezed it, but we were still on the school grounds and we'd agreed to keep our relationship quiet. Or as quiet as we could. We'd told our department chair, who assured us it was fine provided we remained professional at school. In fact, she'd seemed surprised that we were only just now dating. I smothered a chuckle. Apparently, most of the staff had assumed we'd been dating this whole time.

I pushed open the door that would take us out closest to staff parking, and let her go ahead of me. "It's okay. And we have a week at the beach to look forward to."

She tossed a grin over her shoulder.

"Mr. Campbell!"

I turned to see Trevor sprinting across the parking lot toward me. I stopped to wait.

"I'll see you at the airport?" Kayla cocked her head to the side.

"Yeah. I can't imagine this will take long. I'm right behind you." I sighed a little as she headed toward her car. I'd tried to convince her we could carpool to work and leave together, but she hadn't wanted to hear it. Sometimes it still felt like we took a step forward as a couple and then six in the wrong direction.

"Mr. Campbell!" Trevor stuttered to a stop, panting. He waved an envelope at me. "I got in."

"The MIT program?" I grinned and held up my hand for a high five. "Congrats. I'm not surprised though. Did you get a scholarship?"

Trevor shook his head. "No. That's why I wanted to catch you. Did you mean it? Can you really pay for it? I know teachers don't make bank."

Compared to some of the families that sent their kids to school here, I was well paid. But, generally speaking, he wasn't wrong. I was grateful that the whole billionaire thing wasn't super common knowledge. "I meant it. I'm happy to do it. When do they need the payment?"

"All the details are in here." Trevor thrust the envelope at me. "I figured maybe you could just bring it back after spring break?"

"I can do that." I took the envelope. "I'm proud of you, man."

"Really?" The incredulity in Trevor's voice nearly undid me.

"Really." I slapped the envelope against my leg. "I'll take a look tonight—tomorrow latest—and get it figured out."

"Thanks, Mr. Campbell." He grinned at me. "I gotta bounce. Since it's spring break, I picked up extra shifts at the Safeway. Me 'n the guys are talking about getting a limo for prom. But man, those ain't cheap."

I chuckled. "They're not. But they can be fun. I didn't realize you were seeing anyone."

Trevor snorted. "You're not old enough to talk like that, Mr. Campbell. But Ana Garcia and me hang sometimes. I bet she'll look fine in a nice dress at prom."

I wasn't going to comment on that. "Sounds like you've got it all figured."

"Not all, but I'm working on it. You and Miss Jones going to chaperone together? Talk about looking fine in a nice dress." Taylor wiggled his eyebrows.

I cleared my throat. "We haven't talked about it."

"Man. I hope you do. Better than fusty old Mr. Berry staring down his hawk nose like you done something wrong just for dancing." Trevor rolled his eyes then checked over his shoulder when a car honked. "That's my ride. Later, Mr. C."

I shook my head a little and tucked the envelope into my bag. Should I set up some sort of official scholarship fund for the students here? It'd be a simple enough thing to do. There would have to be some kind of application process, probably. I didn't know everyone.

And then there was the matter of keeping it anonymous on my end.

I could probably laugh off covering one summer camp for a talented student. But a scholarship program was going to invite questions.

I mulled it over as I walked to my car, got in, and started toward the airport where our plane was waiting. A quick glance at the time said I should be well within the arrival window we'd agreed on in our group text. I didn't want to miss it and end up making the pilot come back for me.

Thankfully, traffic wasn't awful. The Friday of spring break was usually a beast. But I'd mapped out backroads so I could avoid 95 and the Beltway altogether. The snippets of traffic reports I caught as I flipped radio stations made it clear that had been a wise decision. Everyone was leaving town, it seemed like. And if they weren't leaving, they were coming from far away to spend their spring break seeing the sights of DC. Maybe catch the tail end of the cherry blossoms.

I couldn't blame them. DC in the spring was fantastic.

But the white sand and turquoise water of the Caymans was so much better.

I found a parking spot at the airport, collected my bags, and headed inside. With a private plane, security was slightly less of a pain, if only because the line was shorter. Before long, I was approaching the lounge.

"Am I the last one here?" I scanned the group.

"Still waiting on Tristan. He said he's eight minutes out." Scott snagged Beckett as the little boy ran by, and pulled him into his lap. "The pilot's getting everything ready for us to board. No one minds stopping to pick up my folks on our way down?"

Everyone shook their head.

I didn't understand why Scott kept asking. We'd all agreed it was fine—a great idea, even. His parents knew all of us. We got along fine. And it'd be nice for Whitney and Scott to have backup with Beckett. Not that the rest of us didn't pitch in and help when we could, but I appreciated that Scott didn't just assume we all wanted to take on responsibility for him.

I plopped into a chair beside Kayla. She was chatting with Megan and Whitney about something. I didn't want to interrupt so I looked around the lounge.

Wes dragged his chair over. "Think you'll dive this trip?"

I scratched under my ear. I'd done the certification course at Christmas with the rest of the group. I liked it. But I wasn't as gung-ho as Wes. Obviously. Since he was in the process of starting his own dive shop. "I don't know. I guess I'll see what Kayla wants to do."

Wes shook his head. "You're sunk already, aren't you?"

I shrugged. He said it like it was a bad thing. I didn't agree. If I was sunk, I was happy there. "How are your classes going?"

"They're okay, I guess. I remember why I didn't take business classes in college, though. And I don't care what you say about math, accounting is evil."

I chuckled. "I never enjoyed accounting, either, if I'm honest. There are all kinds of math. You're not going to keep your own books?"

"I was thinking about it. Now? No. I'm hunting around for someone to handle it for me. But I still think I should know enough to be sure it's right, you know? And I have to do the day-to-day stuff like entering sales, ordering equipment. It's not like I can get away from it completely. But I'll want someone to come in and go over everything and handle payroll." Wes blew out a breath. "I didn't think it'd be this complicated, honestly."

I nodded. "That sounds like me and this learning center. It's all well and good to think 'oh hey, I want to do this thing' and it's a whole other mess to see what the actual steps are to follow through."

"You said it. Still. I think it'll be worth it." Wes drummed his fingers on his knee a moment. "Do you think I'm crazy?"

"For the dive shop?"

"Yeah."

Did I? "Not really. It's not something I'd want to do, but that doesn't mean you shouldn't. It's kind of like Megan and the bookstore. Retail anything has never been my dream, but I'm glad there are people who want to do it."

Wes snickered. "Makes sense. And I totally forgot Megan was doing the bookstore. I bet she has an accountant she can recommend. Maybe some payroll tips, if it comes to that."

"Pretty sure she just uses a program that does it all for her. Grandma might have had an accountant set it up for her initially, but at this point, I think it's all Megan." I glanced over where the ladies were still chatting. They'd scooted closer together and were laughing at something Whitney was saying. "I bet you can find time to talk to her about it on the trip."

"Yeah, maybe. Or I'll make a point of it when we're back. How is she taking a week off?"

"She has some part-time people she trusts who were willing to take the hours. But I think she's planning on heading home on Wednesday."

Wes frowned.

"You can always close up on vacation days, if that's what you're worried about."

"Nah. I'm going to need employees. Obviously. I can't do it all on my own." He sighed. "Maybe this is dumb."

"Don't be like that. Give it some time and see it through. You prayed about this, right? You feel like it's something God's good with you doing?"

Wes nodded.

"Then keep praying and take the steps." I bit my lip. It was good advice that I needed to take for myself. I was getting more and more stressed with the learning center. And now I was thinking of adding the scholarship fund—pretty sure I was going to add it, if I was honest. It definitely was in line with the way I felt called to use my money.

"They're ready for us to board." Scott stood, shifting Beckett to his hip.

I collected my bags and fell into step beside Kayla. "Ready to go?"

"Oh, yeah. Everything okay with Trevor?"

"Yep. He got into the MIT summer program. I told him I'd cover the cost if he didn't get a scholarship."

Kayla stopped and looked at me before leaning in and pressing her lips to mine. "I love you."

I didn't think I'd ever get over how those words made me feel inside—all warm and tingly. "I love you, too."

I followed her down the small jetway to the plane, more than ready to start a week of relaxation away from everything with the woman of my dreams.

21

KAYLA

Waking up in the house Austin and his friends had rented in the Caymans was one of my favorite parts of the trip so far. My bedroom looked out on the ocean and I could scoot up in bed and look out through floor-to-ceiling glass at the waves as they lapped on the sand. If I wanted, I could slide open the door, step out onto a small porch, down a few steps, and be there in the sand and surf. But for now, I was content to stay in bed. It was the ultimate contrast to my harried mornings getting up and ready for school.

I had a brief pang of longing for Ada and Charles.

They were being well loved. My next-door neighbor doted on them and was probably checking in on them more than the once a day I'd asked of her. Probably because it gave her a reason to get up and move around.

Still. I missed them.

A flash of bright color caught my eye. I shifted so I was sitting up a little more and watched as Austin and Cody, both in bright red swim trunks, made their way down to the water. Cody pushed Austin, who in turn splashed water on Cody.

I couldn't hear what they were saying, obviously, but their friendship made me smile.

Seeing Austin in swim trunks certainly contributed to that smile as well.

Mmm. And that was enough of that line of thinking.

I tossed the covers back and threw my legs over the side of the bed. If the boys were already outside splashing in the water, there would be coffee and some sort of fresh pastry in the kitchen.

Since this was a co-ed trip, I'd been sleeping in shorts and a T-shirt. I glanced down, shrugged, and started out into the hallway. No one had had a problem with my version of pajamas yet. I didn't anticipate it becoming one today.

I padded into the kitchen.

"Morning, sleepyhead." Whitney grinned at me over the top of her coffee cup. "I figured after three full days here you'd be a little more on the raring to go side of things today."

"That'll teach you. I only pretend to be a morning person for the sake of my job." I shot her a grin and moved to the coffee maker. "But if I'm holding people up, I can set an alarm."

"You know we don't have set plans." Whitney tipped her mug and took a long drink. She set it down on the table. "I guess I should go check on Scott and Beckett. They were getting ready to go build another sand castle. I should probably help. Wes said to tell anyone I saw that he's planning a dive this afternoon and everyone's welcome. Text him if you want to join."

I finished doctoring my coffee. "Will do."

I wasn't sure about diving. I'd gotten certified with everyone else at Christmas. But what I wanted to do was spend time with Austin, and he didn't seem super keen on diving. But I'd ask him when he got back from swimming with Cody.

I took Whitney's deserted spot at the table and unlocked my phone. I spent some time reading the day's assigned readings for my current through-the-Bible-in-a-year plan and praying. Finished, I switched over to my email. I didn't have any that seemed pressing, so I got up to get a refill on my coffee before opening up one of the social media apps that I rarely had time to worry about. I frowned at the number of notifications on the top menu. I hit the bell to drop the list down, and my frown deepened.

Why were so many people tagging me on the same article?

Unease churning in my gut, I tapped one of the notices and it took me to the post.

"Oh, no." I closed the app and opened a browser. After a deep breath, I put Austin's name in the search bar.

The top six results were all different articles with the same theme: billionaire teacher.

Austin was going to flip.

I clicked off my screen and sipped my coffee. What was I supposed to do? What was the right move?

We were on vacation. Austin wasn't super plugged in at the best of times. I imagined he'd turned his cell off and stuck it in his bag as soon as he'd gotten on the plane. And I doubted very much he'd bothered turning it back on yet.

Was it better to ignore it now and just deal with it when we got home? I wouldn't like that myself. I'd want to know now so I could plan. Maybe get over the initial horror of it before I was in a position to have to deal with it. Because he was going to have to deal with it as soon as we got back. Knowing the media in the DC area, that was a given.

I set my phone down and stared into my coffee.

All I could think of was the reminder to treat others the way I would want them to treat me.

No matter how much I didn't want to tell Austin, I was going to have to.

I drained my coffee and carried the mug over to the dishwasher so I could load it in. For all that the guys had buckets of money—and the house they'd rented reflected that in spades—they didn't go over the top and hire people to clean up after them on a daily basis. Instead, it was a lot like traveling with a group of college friends—everyone needed to clean their own messes and help out.

Did any of those articles explore the fact that Austin was still just a regular guy?

Maybe I should read them before I talked to him about it.

I glanced back at the table where my phone sat, taunting me. Fine. It was better to talk to Austin with all the information, anyway.

I sat back down, picked up my phone, and took a deep breath before tapping on the first article that came up.

My head was throbbing by the time I finished reading four of the reports. No one had a lot of information. It was all, "unnamed sources" and a few references to articles that had run without names when the guys had all made their money in the first place. There were several interviews with students and other staff at the school—those, at least, were positive. Or mostly. One student had taken the opportunity to slam Austin because the kid had earned a C minus in his algebra 2 class.

Knowing Austin, the kid had been given plenty of opportunities to change that outcome.

I rubbed little circles in my forehead as I prayed for the right approach and words to use when I brought this up to Austin.

"Hey." I must have jumped, because Austin started to laugh. He rubbed my shoulder. "I didn't mean to startle you. I thought for sure you heard me come in."

I shook my head and managed a weak smile.

"You all right?" His concern was evident as he searched my face. "You don't have to get out of bed, you know? There's no harm in lazing around. We're on vacation."

"Just a headache. It'll go away." I glanced around. "Where's Cody?"

"Cody?" Austin looked puzzled. "How'd you know I was hanging out with Cody?"

"My bedroom looks out on the beach." I grinned. "I might have watched the two of you playing in the surf a little this morning before coffee."

Austin chuckled and leaned close. He pressed his lips to mine. "You should have come out."

"Did you miss the coffee part of that?"

"I forgot about your addiction." He shook his head. "A good swim would wake you up even better."

"Maybe. I don't see myself finding that out." I should tell him. Now was the perfect time. There was no one else around. And still, I choked. "Whitney mentioned Wes was putting a dive together for this afternoon. Did you want to go?"

"Do you?" He took my hand and lifted it, then brushed a kiss across my knuckles. "I want to spend the day with you. So I'm game for whatever."

I melted. "I wouldn't mind just hanging here. We could bike into town for a bit and shop and then maybe just park by the pool? Even if everyone saddles us with dinner because we're keeping close."

"You know they will, too." Austin shrugged. "But that sounds nice. We can figure out the food when we're in town."

"If we volunteer, they can't complain about what we make, either." I squeezed his hand. "Have you checked your email at all?"

"Nah. It's vacation. I turned my phone off on the plane and haven't missed it." He nodded to where my phone sat on the table. "I see your extra appendage is sticking close."

"Hey. I'm not that bad. It's not like I'm on my phone during the workday." Mostly that was because it was a pretty serious writeup if I got caught. Our administration was absolutely not okay with teachers using their phones. Even during our lunch or planning time was frowned on, though they couldn't technically do as much when students weren't around.

"True." He tipped his head to the side. "Why did you ask?"

I sighed. "There's something you should see."

His eyebrows lifted.

I unlocked my phone, navigated back to the article, and slid it over to him. "Read this."

I licked my lips as he looked down at the screen. I didn't want to read over his shoulder or anything like that. And I'd already seen it anyway. But it was awkward sitting here while he read.

What was he thinking?

His lips thinned. It was the only reaction I could pick out. Austin used a single finger to slide the screen up.

When he reached the end of the article, he pushed my phone away, leaned back in his seat, and cleared his throat. "Well."

I winced. "Yeah."

"How did they find out?" He rubbed the back of his neck. "Trevor? Was it because of that? I don't...the summer program isn't that much. Any teacher could afford to cover it unless they were a bad money manager."

"I don't know. I can't see Trevor going to the press. What would be his reason?" I hated to think it was Trevor. That kid had such potential, and Austin was trying to feed that potential. If Trevor had thrown that away, it was going to be even harder on Austin than dealing with the fallout of these articles. Whatever that was going to be.

Austin shrugged. "Some people like to see their name in the paper."

"His name's not there." I regretted the words as they were

coming out of my mouth. Now wasn't the time to defend anyone. Austin needed my empathy and support. And it wasn't as if I knew for certain Trevor wasn't behind the whole thing. I just didn't want him to be.

Austin's look bordered on a glare.

"Sorry." I rubbed his leg. "Maybe it'll all blow over before we get back? Maybe the fact that we're out of town will help?"

He shook his head. "I should go get my phone. I imagine I've got messages looking for a comment."

"You don't have to do that." I bit my lip. "I debated not telling you. I think you should enjoy your vacation. Should I not have told you?"

"No." He took a deep breath and blew it out slowly. "No. I needed to know. I would've been seriously torqued if you hadn't told me and I found out later that you knew while we were here."

I managed a slight smile. At least I understood that much. "What if you took a day? Just today? We can let it simmer, maybe talk to the others and see what they think."

He sighed. "That's not a bad idea. Tristan probably has an idea of the right way to handle it. Maybe Scott, too, for that matter. Both of them have had to deal with more publicity than the rest of us."

"I think that's smart." I waited, trying to figure out what to say. "Are you all right?"

He scoffed. "No. I'm really not. I've got about ten thousand 'what ifs' running through my head. How do I keep teaching math when this cat's out of the bag?"

I opened my mouth to deny that it'd be a problem and then had to bite back the words. Sunny optimism had its place, but right now was not it. Because he was right, it was going to make things sticky. Especially if the news *didn't* die down quickly.

Austin pushed his chair back and stood. He squeezed my

hand before letting go. "I'm going to go take a shower. Why don't you get in touch with Whitney and let her know we've got dinner handled? We can head into town in an hour or so?"

"Sure. I'll be ready when you are." I grabbed his hand to keep him from running off. "Hey. I love you."

His smile was tight and didn't really reach his eyes. "Love you, too."

I wanted to tell him it was going to be all right in the long run, but I could tell he wasn't in a place to hear it.

So I let him go.

22

AUSTIN

I closed the door to my bedroom and threw myself onto my bed. This was a disaster. I worked so hard to keep my personal life—all aspects of it—separate from school. I just wanted to teach math. To have a chance to share the beauty of math with kids and see the occasional student—kids like Trevor—come to life.

Was I going to be able to do that still?

It depended on how quickly the news blew over.

When we'd first made all the money, there'd been a little coverage. Mostly Tristan had been the point man on that, and he'd managed to keep the vultures away from the rest of us. Still, I'd gotten a few people coming around, asking for handouts, but in the overall scheme of things? I'd been the one who'd had the least publicity.

Looked like that was over now.

I blew out a breath and dragged myself off my bed. I'd showered outside after playing in the ocean, but I wanted a real shower, not one designed to keep sand out of the house. If nothing else, it was good thinking time.

And that was what I did. I stood under the strong, hot spray of water until my fingers started to shrivel and the water was more warm than hot. Then I got out, dried off, and got dressed. It was time to face the day.

Time to face facts.

I was done wallowing. Now, I'd make a plan.

Who had put the reporters on my scent? That was the worst part. The not knowing. I was so careful to avoid saying anything at school. I didn't dress any differently than I ever had. I didn't drive a flashy car. So how had someone found out?

The learning center?

I bit my lip. That was a possibility. It wasn't as if I'd been silent about that. Nor had Kayla been. It wouldn't take much to find out what the property I'd bought was listed for—that was all public record. And the fact that demolition should be starting this week while I was away was another clue.

I sighed. That was probably the answer. Which made it all my own fault. In some ways, that was good. I'd hate to think that Trevor or another student was responsible for siccing the press on me. So now, the question became: what was I going to do about it?

"Oof." I nearly rammed into Scott's dad as I turned the corner heading toward the stairs. "Sorry, Mr. Wright."

Scott's dad tipped his head to the side. "I think it's about time you called me Eric like everyone else does. Don't you think?"

I grinned. "I'll try. I'm not sure how well it'll stick."

Eric laughed. "Fair enough. Renee wants you boys to all call her by name, too. In her mind, she's adopted you all and is standing in as a second mother."

"Couldn't ask for someone better." It was true. I loved my parents, but Scott's folks were also amazing. "Are you busy right now?"

"Not with anything that can't wait. What's up?"

I gestured to the stairs. "Could I chat with you about a few things? I've been meaning to ask about setting aside some time."

"Sure." Eric turned and started down the stairs. "Kitchen okay? I wouldn't say no to a snack."

"Snacks are good." I followed behind Scott's dad. Hopefully Kayla wouldn't mind putting off our trip into town for a bit. In fact, I'd love it if she'd join in the conversation. She always had good ideas and insights. It was one of the things I loved about her. Always had.

Kayla wasn't in the kitchen yet. I took it as a good sign. If she was spending extra time getting ready, maybe she understood I needed a minute—or twenty—to adjust my attitude. I probably owed her an apology for my response to the news. What was that thing about not shooting the messenger?

Eric brought a container of fresh fruit over to the table, along with two bowls and forks. "Island living. I definitely could get used to this."

"Florida isn't tropical enough for you?" I waited until he'd scooped a bowl of fruit before getting my own.

"Oh, I love our place there, don't get me wrong, but I wouldn't be sad about living here, either." He speared a pink, juicy cube of something. "Although I say that and then start thinking about how long it takes and how expensive it can be to import things to an island and maybe I'm better off just visiting."

I chuckled. That was my thought. I could admit that I'd browsed real estate listings when we were here in December, but more from the idea of owning a vacation home than actually relocating. And even then, I didn't want every vacation to be in the same place. I could see Wes splitting his time—that made sense if he was truly going to do the dive shop thing. But the rest of us? I didn't think any of us were ready for a permanent relocation.

"What's on your mind?" Eric was working his way steadily through the fruit.

I blew out a breath. "Couple of things. First, has Scott mentioned the learning center I'm setting up?"

Eric grinned, nodding. "He has. I think it's a fantastic idea. I love that you're keeping it close to your school, too. You know what those kids need. It's so easy, sometimes, to look at the affluence of Old Town and forget that there are people seriously hurting right next door."

"It can be, for sure." I poked my fork into some of the fruit but didn't eat it. "I maybe should have talked to you about doing it all under the charitable umbrella. Seems that something leaked to the press and now there are articles about me that hit all the papers this week."

Eric frowned. "We can still move it over. That's easy enough. Long term, that's probably the better solution, but it won't help with the publicity now. Is it going to be a problem?"

I ran a hand through my hair. "I don't know. I don't see how it wouldn't be, you know? Like you said, there are a ton of families around the school who have needs—big needs—and on paper it looks like I have the money to magically fix them."

"Except, of course, that it wouldn't really fix them."

I'd thought having all this money would be an easy way to impact lives right out of the gate. Then, after dabbling and ending up making things worse, I'd realized that handouts don't actually fix things. At least not always. There were systemic issues at play that money couldn't fix. I sighed.

"But you can still help. You just need to set it up so it really is helping, not creating new problems."

"And that's why I need you." I toyed with the fruit on my fork. "And maybe Mrs. Wright."

Eric fixed me with a look.

"I mean Renee."

He grinned. "Better. She's pretty content to manage things once I get them set up. What are you thinking?"

"Well, the learning center, to start. There are salaries and overhead and all that to figure out. I don't want to charge kids to use the resources. At the same time, I wonder if having a nominal fee for the families who can afford it would make them value it more? Some kind of sliding scale, maybe, that made it clear that learning was absolutely the point. Not after-school babysitting. And it's not a place for the gangs to gather, either."

Eric's eyebrows lifted. "I don't guess I realized that was a problem in your area."

"Oh, yeah. We've got some pretty significant issues with gangs at our school. The whole area struggles some, but they're talking about metal detectors at the doors again for us." I shrugged. I wasn't opposed. But I also didn't necessarily think they were going to fix everything. Again, we ran into systemic problems that the highly visible bandages weren't always able to conquer. Even if they made people feel better about trying.

"Huh. All right. You definitely want this to be a place that's safe. Is the easiest way to do that to employ security on top of the tutors?"

I frowned. I didn't want security running around. That said, Eric was probably right that it was the best solution. "Probably. See? This is good. Will you help me hash out all of the staffing that I need? I've got a good handle on the mission and the building, you know? But I start getting bogged down when I get to the rest."

Eric grinned. "Happy to. And I'll chat with Renee about the best way to handle fees if we end up thinking they're needed. Is that it?"

I shook my head. "No. But it goes hand in hand. I want to set up some kind of scholarship fund for the kids at my school. Something they can apply to get summer camps covered. Maybe even a portion of college tuition? I want it to be merit-based, though, in addition to need."

"Okay. And it's only open to kids who go to your school? You don't want to open it to anyone?"

I rubbed the back of my neck. "Is that wrong?"

"No. Just asking."

"Okay." Guilt tugged at my heart. Should I have a scholarship fund for anyone to apply to? I still wanted to be involved in screening applicants—it seemed like opening it up at a larger level would make that impossible. Maybe if I ended up wanting to go that route, I'd figure a second scholarship out and tie it to my alma mater. Chances were high they'd be happy to have some sort of endowment from me. "Maybe down the road we'll expand."

"Sounds like a plan." Eric knocked on the table and stood. He carried his bowl over to the sink, rinsed it, and put it in the dishwasher. "Let me noodle on things a bit and I'll shoot you an email with some suggestions. We can talk about it more this week, too."

"That works." I took a bite of the fruit. "Thanks."

"My pleasure."

Kayla came into the kitchen. She was wearing a sundress and a big floppy brimmed hat. "Hey. I'm late. Sorry."

"There's no late in the islands." Eric grinned. "You're a picture. I take it the two of you aren't going on the dive trip either?"

"Nope." Kayla patted the little purse, which had a skinny strap crossed from her left shoulder to right hip. "We're biking into town to do some shopping. We're going to check out the market and handle dinner. You can spread the word on that, if you see anyone. I texted Whitney and Megan though, so hopefully people are already finding out."

"Excellent. Can't wait to see what you come up with." Eric waved as he headed out of the kitchen.

I finished the last piece of fruit and stood, carrying my bowl over to the sink. When it was loaded in the dishwasher, I turned to Kayla and held out my arms. "He's not wrong. You are a picture."

She stepped close and slid her arms around my waist. "You feeling better?"

"I am. I'm sorry I didn't react well."

She chuckled. "I think you're allowed to need a moment when your secret identity gets splashed on the front page."

"Secret identity, huh? Like a superhero?" I flexed a bicep. "I am...MathMan!"

Kayla chortled. "I'm not sure anyone actually wants him as a superhero, but we can go with it."

"Yeah, yeah. No one appreciates the amazingness of math."

"I do." She glared at me.

"Except you." I leaned in to kiss her nose. She shifted so our mouths met. It was a minute or two before we came up for air. I cleared my throat. "I guess we ought to head into town?"

"I guess we should." She bumped my hip with hers. "Don't worry about the papers, okay? What's the worst that can happen?"

My stomach sank. I wasn't someone who believed in manifesting or tempting fate or anything like that. I believed God was sovereign and that He watched over me, and cared for me, and would help me to walk in His will.

At the same time?

I was really good at coming up with worst case scenarios. And I *really* didn't want to find out which one was the most likely to occur.

23

KAYLA

I stretched my arms up over my head as my eyes gradually opened.

Gosh, it was good to be home.

I was grateful Austin had convinced everyone to leave on Friday so we had the weekend to get settled and ready for a new week. I'd gotten caught up on my grading and a little ahead on my lesson plans while we were on the island, so it wasn't that I had a ton of work to do. But it was still wonderful to be back in my own space.

I'd texted my neighbor that I was back.

Ada and Charles were both giving me the cat version of the silent treatment. They'd get over it. They always did. They'd get over it faster with a little incentive.

With that in mind, I dragged myself out of bed and headed to the kitchen. I kept a few cans of tuna in my pantry for when I needed to bribe the creatures. This seemed like a good reason.

I was opening the can when my phone rang. I frowned at the display before tapping to accept the call.

"Hi, Luke. What's up?"

"Is he really a billionaire?"

I closed my eyes and let my shoulders sag. Ada jumped up on the counter and butted my hand with her head. It would have made me laugh under different circumstances. Now, it did get me to finish opening the can, but any joy I'd had about luring back my cats' affection had fled. "He is. Why?"

"Figures." Luke scoffed. "I never had a chance, did I?"

"Actually, you did." Sort of. There was the whole "I'm in love with my best friend" thing. But I could have gotten over that. Probably. "You realize his money has nothing to do with me, right?"

"No. I don't realize that at all. Why would I?"

"Because the times we went out, I thought we got to be friends and so you know I'm not like that? And let's not forget, buster, that you weren't rushing to fall in love with me, either. Why don't you tell me what the problem really is? Because I don't think it's Austin's money or the fact that you and I mutually agreed we weren't suited." I wanted to be angry, but I just couldn't get there. This wasn't like Luke. At all. And although I didn't want to date him, I still counted him as a friend.

"I..." He sighed. "I'm sorry. I shouldn't have called."

"Yes. You should have. Spill the beans." I glanced around the kitchen. Ada and Charles were at their bowls daintily nibbling tuna. I probably had coffee. "Do you want to come by? I don't have a lot on hand, but I can manage coffee. You could grab donuts from somewhere."

"I don't think coming over is a good idea. Do you ever run?"

"Other than when I'm chased?" Running wasn't my idea of a good time.

Luke laughed. "Walk?"

"Walking I do."

"Meet me on the path to Mount Vernon? We can walk by the river. I'll fill you in."

I glanced down at my pajamas and ran through a quick

inventory of what I'd need to do before I could leave, plus travel time. "Sure. I probably need an hour."

"That's fine. Thanks, Kayla."

"No problem." I ended the call and drummed my fingers on the counter. Then I picked up the phone and called Austin.

"Unh."

I laughed. "Morning, sunshine."

"It's Saturday. Why are you up so early?"

"Cats." I ran a hand down Ada's back. She arched into my touch and I smiled. She was always quickest to forgive. Charles would need another day. "Even if I had to bribe them into loving me again."

"Aw."

There was rustling on the other end of the call and I pictured Austin sitting up in bed. Then I dragged my thoughts away from that, because I now had entirely too much firsthand experience with him shirtless. Dwelling on Austin shirtless in bed was not the way to keep my thoughts pure.

"What does this have to do with waking me up?"

"Luke called. Something's up with him. He asked me to go walking on the Mount Vernon trail with him this morning. I wanted to...I don't know...let you know, I guess." I frowned. Maybe I shouldn't have? It wasn't as if I couldn't have friends. Male friends, even. But it seemed like if the position had been reversed, I would have preferred a heads-up.

"Mm. Have fun with that." There was a pause. "If he says it's okay, will you fill me in? I have a feeling this is about me, right?"

Was it? I didn't see why it would be. On the flip side, he'd started the whole call out asking about Austin's money. So maybe it was. "Dunno. It's possible. But yeah, of course, I'll keep you posted. Thanks for not being weird about it."

Austin laughed. "You can have friends. I trust you. Also? I love you."

"I love you, too. Go back to sleep."

"Gonna try. Bye."

The call ended. I shook my head and set the phone down before heading to my room to shower and dress. I wasn't sure how far Luke expected to walk on the trail. Surely not all the way to Mount Vernon and back? Did I need to bring a water bottle?

I spent a few extra minutes rubbing Ada. I hadn't planned to leave the house today to, hopefully at least, remind the cats that I was back. But friends were worth a little extra effort. If I needed to bribe the babies with tuna again tomorrow, then that was what I'd do.

"I'll be back. Promise. Maybe even before lunch." I hadn't really eaten breakfast. Maybe I'd drive through Starbucks and get coffee and a scone on my way.

Not too much later, I pulled into a parking spot at the trail entrance Luke had suggested. He was already there, sitting on the trunk of his car.

I'd eaten the scone, but there was still plenty of my latte in the cup, so I grabbed it before closing the car door and locking it.

"Hey."

Luke looked up from his phone and managed a tight smile. "Hey. You ready?"

"Sure. We're not going all the way to George's house, right?"

Luke chuckled. "Probably not. Although it's a good run down and back."

I gave a mock shudder. "I don't think I knew you ran. Long distances, even."

"I'm doing the Marine Corps Marathon this year."

I winced. He was one of those people. "Good luck?"

He laughed again. "Thanks. I'm actually starting to look forward to it."

"Better you than me." I sipped my coffee and fell into step beside him on the asphalt trail that ran along the Potomac River's edge. Should I prompt him? As much as it was a beautiful spring morning, and the river was lovely, this really wasn't what I wanted to be doing today. "How was your trip to Mexico?"

He glanced over at me, his eyebrows lifting. "How'd you know about that?"

"You mentioned it. Did you not think I listened when you talked?"

He shrugged. "I guess I didn't figure you cared."

"Well, I do. Not a good trip, I take it."

"No, it was great. Jason and Karin and their daughter are really amazing people. They're only recently back down there after an extended sabbatical. The town loves having them, though. That's obvious. And they're doing such important work. We got quite a bit done. It was...refreshing."

I considered the pause that came before his last word. "Does that mean you don't feel like you get things done here?"

"Your students must love you."

Okay. That was an odd segue. I sipped again. "I guess. Until they fail an assignment."

He smiled. "You're insightful. And no. I don't really feel like I get anything done here. Every time I try to do something that isn't exactly the same as what the previous youth pastor did, I either get shot down completely or grudgingly approved."

"Approved is still good, though, right?"

He shook his head and looked out at the river. We walked in silence a little before he continued speaking. "Grudgingly means it's destined to fail. Or get canceled later. At a minimum, there's so much resistance that I can't get volunteers and I can't get people to commit to coming, which makes it hard to plan and...well, you get the point."

I did. I'd faced a tiny bit of that when I'd first gotten hired at the high school. The previous computer teacher had retired and he'd been someone the kids, parents, and other faculty all adored. He'd basically been a fixture at the school. One of those teachers who left a legacy. I was definitely not what a lot of the parents expected as his replacement. But with public school, there was less they could do about it. If they wanted their kids to have computer classes, then they'd had to figure out a way to work with me.

Luke didn't seem to have that luxury.

"I'm sorry. How can I help?" I didn't do a lot with the youth group—didn't really have the time to commit to much—but I could do something.

He looked at me and smiled. "I love that you ask. But at this point, nothing. I'm handing in my resignation on Monday."

I stopped.

It took Luke a few steps to notice. Then he paused and turned back, a quizzical look on his face. "What?"

"You're quitting?" That was going to be frustrating for the kids. There were parents who helped out, sure, but Luke was in charge. Without him, it'd go back to barely controlled chaos in the youth group room on Sunday morning and no activities beyond that. I'd heard the rumblings and complaints from the handful of students who attended our church. They'd been so pleased when Luke came aboard.

He nodded once. Decisively. "I am. I'll stay until they find a replacement. Or for up to a year."

"What will you do?"

He started walking again.

I jogged a few steps until I was, once again, at his side.

"I'm not sure, actually. Jason had some questions that I couldn't answer when I was in Mexico. They were challenging. And eye-opening."

When he didn't elaborate, I jabbed my elbow into his side. "Are you going to share?"

"I don't think so." He glanced over and offered a tight smile. "Sorry. I thought I would, you know? But now? I think maybe it's better if I keep it close. At least for a while."

I nodded. Not because I understood, but so he knew I heard him.

"That's why I wanted to talk to you, though. I think I need to say thank you. Because if you hadn't agreed to go out with me, and if you hadn't given me a shot, I'm not sure I ever would have realized that being here—being a youth pastor—wasn't what God wanted me to do."

"Ookay. I'm not sure how I had anything to do with it, but... you're welcome?" I drained the last of my coffee and started looking ahead for one of the trashcans on the path so I could ditch the cup.

Luke slid his hands in his pockets. "I told you, didn't I, that Pastor Chaz has been pushing me to marry? It's why I asked you out in the first place. But in Mexico, some of Jason's questions— and the time he and I spent praying together—confirmed what I knew deep down but hadn't wanted to acknowledge. Marriage isn't something God has for me."

I spotted a trash can and angled so I could toss in my cup as we passed. It gave me a little time to try and decide how I was supposed to respond. Except I still wasn't sure. "I don't really know what to say. I'm glad, I guess, that you're more confident in God's plan for you. Though I'm not sure what that has to do with you not being a youth pastor anymore."

He offered a tight smile. "Several of the parents think it's inappropriate for a young, unmarried man to work with the youth."

I frowned. "That's...why would that matter?"

"I guess they're worried I'll try to date a senior? I don't know.

I've always been careful to avoid any situations that could be misconstrued, but it doesn't seem to be enough." He shrugged. "It's why I don't think the pastor will mind that I go. In fact, I wouldn't be surprised if he had someone already lined up. Just in case."

I couldn't see that. It wasn't how I pictured Pastor Chaz at all. But then, I really only knew him from his sermons on Sunday morning. As much as I went to church, I wasn't what anyone would consider involved.

Luke stopped. "We can start back, if you want."

"Okay." I turned around and we started back down the path toward the cars. We hadn't gone far. "I should come over here more often. It's a nice walk."

"I like to run all the way down and back on Mondays. Sometimes I'll go more than once when I have a lot on my mind. It's a good trail. And the breeze off the water helps it stay cool...well... cooler, in the summer."

"Luke. Why did you bring up Austin when you called?" I was still trying to make sense of this whole morning. Yes, I considered Luke a friend of sorts. But we weren't besties by any stretch. He didn't owe me advance notice of his decision to leave. Nor did he owe me the inside scoop on his future plans. In fact, he didn't owe me anything.

"Pastor Chaz seemed to think I was the one who talked to the reporters. I'm semi-friendly with the guy who wrote one of the first articles—he's a runner, too, so we've bumped into each other here and there. I guess the pastor was concerned it was my version of revenge for us not working out. But I promise you, I didn't know."

I chuckled. "I know you wouldn't do something like that. I'd love to know who did, that's for sure, but it never occurred to me that it would be you. Austin and I have been best friends for a long time. Long before he made the money. I've loved him for a long time, too. Again, that predates the money. You were my attempt to move on."

His laugh held no mirth. "How'd that work out for you?"

"Pretty well, actually. Not the moving on part, but it lit a fire under Austin and made him realize it was worth risking our friendship to see what else might be there." I sighed. I just hoped the leak about his money wouldn't push him into doing something dumb like trying to break things off to keep me out of the public eye.

Oh, he could try, but I wasn't having any of it.

"Glad I could help."

I winced at the sarcasm in his tone. "Do I need to apologize again?"

He shook his head. "No. It's for the best. And the two of you seem happy together. I'm glad. Truly."

"Thanks." We were approaching the parking lot. "For what it's worth, I think you've been an asset to the church, and I'll be sorry to see you go."

"I appreciate that." Luke stopped. "Are you good to get back to your car? I think I'm going to go ahead and run for a bit."

"Sure. Have fun?" I didn't really get it, but whatever worked for him.

"I will. See you around. I guess."

"Yeah."

I watched him turn and start back down the path at a good clip before shaking my head. I wasn't convinced that I'd needed to meet him in person for this conversation. Or that we'd even needed to have the conversation in the first place. I sifted through our talk and sighed.

The only thing I could find that was interesting—and it was a stretch—was Pastor Chaz asking if Luke had gone to the press about Austin's money. That implied, at least to me, that the pastor knew about the money. And that he didn't think very highly of Luke.

Neither of which helped when it came to figuring out where the story on Austin came from.

Austin had put the whole mess in Tristan's hands. Tristan had contacts to handle PR. I guess the two of them had spent a little time coordinating while we'd been on vacation.

Austin had told me not to worry about it. And then promptly excluded me from any conversations.

I was trying not to worry. I was also trying not to be annoyed.

I wasn't doing well with either one.

I got back in my car and headed toward home. At least with Ada and Charles I knew what I needed to do to put things right.

24

AUSTIN

First day back after spring break was always hard. No one—not the students, not the teachers—wanted to be here. I'd gotten to school early, not because I was excited and looking forward to the day, but to try and avoid any unpleasantness that might come because of the articles.

So far, the news wasn't dying down.

I'd had entirely too many voicemails from reporters on my cell phone when I turned it back on. I hadn't called anyone back. Tristan assured me his PR people would take care of it, but so far, I wasn't seeing any evidence of that. At this point, I only answered calls from my contacts. But that didn't keep the thing from ringing constantly.

Given the fact that I'd had two people shouting my name as I ran from my car to the school, getting here early hadn't done much.

At least they hadn't followed me inside. I imagined they knew they'd get booted back out. Schools these days didn't tolerate random people on the property. I was counting on that to keep today fairly normal.

The subtle sounds of the school waking up started to filter

into my classroom and drew my attention back to the lesson plans I was playing with. I wanted to do something different. Shake things up somehow.

The footsteps in the hall got closer and I smiled slightly. It had to be Kayla. No one walked quite like her.

I was looking out the doorway when she stepped into view with a big grin and two enormous takeout coffee cups.

"Morning. Ready to get back at it? Shape young minds and get them to appreciate the beauty of learning?" Kayla stepped into the classroom and set one of the coffees on my desk. Then she leaned close and pressed a kiss to my lips. It wasn't quick or perfunctory. I found myself leaning in and my hand reaching up to cup her face.

"Well, hello."

She laughed and perched on the edge of my desk. "Hello, yourself. You're bright and early."

I shrugged. "I was trying to beat the press."

"Uh-huh. How'd that work for you?"

I tilted my head to the side and studied her. "I take it that means the throng has grown, not shrunk?"

"I counted news vans from two local stations and a clump of what had to be print reporters." She reached out and rubbed my arm. "Sorry."

I blew out a breath. "I guess I'll be putting in long days until it dies down. Or Tristan gets it figured out."

"Austin. You can't just live at school." Her eyebrows drew together.

"I don't know what else to do. So far, at least, they haven't sniffed out my home address. Or they're scared of parking enforcement." I tried a smile, but it felt wrong. "What am I supposed to do, Kayla?"

She glanced at the clock above my door. "Right now? Get set for first period. Buses are going to get here any minute. Maybe—

hopefully—you can have a normal day. That's what I'm praying for."

"Me, too."

She slipped off my desk, cradling her coffee in her hands. "I love you. You know that, right?"

"I do. Back at you."

She flashed a grin and disappeared into the hallway. I heard her greeting several students as she made her way toward her classroom.

I straightened my desk and took a drink of the coffee while I prayed—again—for a normal day.

By lunch, I was just praying to make it through the day. Every class so far, at least three students had tried to ask about the articles. Two separate kids had waited after class to ask for money. That was the worst. There was actual need there. And I could help. But I needed to do it the right way.

I closed my classroom door and dug my cellphone out of my desk. Kayla was probably waiting for me in her office, but she'd understand. For now, I needed to talk to Mr. Wright—Eric—and see how he and Renee were coming with the scholarship fund setup.

I found Eric's contact and hit Call.

He answered right away. "Eric Wright."

"Hi. It's Austin Campbell. Is this a good time?"

"Sure. Aren't you at school?"

I managed a weak laugh and sank onto the edge of my desk. "Lunch break. But it's already been a day. If I thought the administration could magically produce a sub, I'd be tempted to go home and hide for the rest of it."

"Sorry. That sounds rough."

"Yeah. Rough sums it up." I cleared my throat and gave a quick rundown of the morning. "I know I need to talk to Tristan about getting the media off my case, but do you have any suggestions of what to do about the money requests? I'd like to give them something more than, 'I'll get back to you.'"

Eric was quiet a moment. "I don't think we want to rush into anything. Work fast, definitely, but not rush. If you see the difference?"

I sighed. I did. I didn't like it—everything in me wanted this to just all be over—but I understood that came from fear and stress more than anything. "Yeah. I do."

"Good. So what I suggest is this: let me set up an application and get it online. Then, you have something to refer people to and it gives them something tangible and productive to do while we sort out the rest of it. In fact, it'd be good if you could work an announcement of the application process into whatever media Tristan is up to."

"That would be amazing." The turmoil churning in my gut eased. It wasn't what I'd call peace—not quite yet—but it was definitely working toward it. "I'll have Tristan get in touch with you directly?"

"I'll give him a call. He and I have worked together enough with other things that it shouldn't be an issue. That lets you get back to work where you can hopefully focus on the important stuff."

I laughed. "That would be nice. I'm not sure how likely it is."

"Chin up. We're praying for you."

I blew out a breath. "Thank you. I appreciate it."

"It's our pleasure. You tell Kayla hi from us, okay? And make sure we're invited to the wedding."

My mouth went dry. I wanted to marry Kayla, no question, but hearing it so matter of fact took me by surprise. "Sure. Will do."

Eric chuckled. "I'll text you a link when we're set. Bye."

The call ended. I frowned at my phone a moment before shooting a quick text to Tristan just letting him know that Eric would be getting in touch and the two of them were authorized to collaborate. I didn't care about the formalities of it, but Tristan often did. Probably had to do with the whole being a lawyer thing. Either way, a text should soothe him until I signed whatever he was going to end up needing me to sign.

I strode to the windows and looked out. From the second story of the school, the parking lot looked peaceful. But if I angled myself enough, I could see the news vans clumped near the front of the building.

Why wouldn't they just go away?

I shook my head. Lunch with Kayla was exactly what I needed now. I grabbed my insulated bag and started down the hall toward her office, trying to hurry past any of the classrooms with open doors.

Kids still turned to look. They nudged one another and whispered when they saw me. I earned more than one annoyed glare from someone lecturing as I passed.

This really needed to blow over. Fast.

Kayla had her office door shut. There were no kids in the lab, at least, which made it a little better. I knocked on her office door and waited for her to call out.

"Enter."

I poked my head in. "Hi. I needed to call Scott's dad. Sorry I'm late."

"You're fine. Come in and close that behind you." She gestured to the door and then took another bite of her sandwich.

I did as she instructed and studied her as I sat. "You've had a rough morning, too."

"I don't really want to talk about it."

I winced. "Does it help at all if I say I'm sorry?"

She shrugged and continued to eat.

I frowned and unzipped my lunch bag. Was she angry at me?

I didn't do this. I mean, okay, I guess I did, since I was the one with all the money, but it wasn't like I'd gone out of my way to get attention and disrupt her life.

I looked down into the bag at my food, then flipped the lid closed and zipped it back up. "I'm suddenly not very hungry."

Kayla set her sandwich down and pinched the bridge of her nose. "I'm sorry. I'm sorry. I just never expected this would be so..."

I waited, but she didn't finish the sentence. I wasn't sure, actually, what word went there. There were a ton of options. Leaving it blank worked, too. "Yeah. Tell me about it."

"Would it be different—better, somehow—if we knew where the leak came from?" Kayla picked up the sandwich and took another bite. "I've been trying to decide and can't."

"I want to say yes, but I don't really believe it. It's not like that would change anything. Say it's a student, what then? It's not as if I'd want disciplinary action taken."

"I would."

My eyebrows lifted at her tone. "Kayla. They're kids. You know it was probably they heard something and told a friend. The friend told a friend, who told someone else, and somewhere along the way, a parent heard and realized this was a great scoop."

She stuffed the rest of her sandwich into her mouth and shrugged.

"You really want someone to get in trouble because they talked to a friend?"

Kayla held up a finger as she chewed. She took a long drink from her water bottle. "Maybe not. But I'd be fine with the parent—or teacher, did you consider that?—who went to the press getting reprimanded."

I wasn't sure there was any reprimand to make. People were allowed to talk about what they knew. Or guessed. If they happened to do that with a reporter, well, that was allowed, too. But I was also pretty sure mentioning freedom of speech to Kayla right now was a bad plan, so I opened my lunch bag back up and pulled out the soda I'd packed.

She scowled at me. "You don't want them to pay?"

"Not really? It's not as if they published lies. They just revealed information I'd rather not have out there. But now it's out there and I have to deal with it. We both do." The article this morning had made a big deal out of the relationship between Kayla and me. Was that what had her so angry? "Unless you want to step away. Get off the circus train, so to speak. I wouldn't blame you."

"Is that what you want?" She crossed her arms.

"No." I reached across her desk and left my hand there, palm up, until she loosened and put her hand in mine. I squeezed her hand. "I love you. Nothing that's happened changes that. But I also understand that you're a private person and there's nothing wrong with that. I'd like to go back to being a private person, but I don't see it happening."

"Ever?" Her wide eyes betrayed the panic that she'd mostly kept out of her voice.

I wanted to tell her that I absolutely believed that when this bombshell died off, the two of us could go back to relative obscurity. But I didn't want to lie. "Not really. I'm building the learning center. That's going to be news around here for a while—at least until it opens. Maybe longer. I'm setting up the scholarship fund. Which, again, is news. Maybe I wish I could have done it all on the down low, but now that it's out in the open? I don't see it disappearing. At least not locally. Not for a while. And probably never completely. I'd love to be wrong though."

She looked away. "They're calling me a gold digger."

"What? That's insane." It definitely explained her anger, though. "I didn't see that. Which article did I miss?"

"Not the press. The kids. You're this hero in their eyes because you're doing all these good things, but because our relationship is new, they assume I'm only in it because I found out about the money. Even though we've eaten lunch together forever."

"That's...horrible." And it was from students, so it wasn't like I could offer to beat someone up. Not that I was that guy in the first place. I could probably defend myself, but I didn't want to be the one taking the first swing. "What did you do?"

"I ignored it. It's not like they're raising their hands and asking out loud. It's the muffled cough over words thing. Or the oh-so-subtly visible doodle. You know how kids are."

I nodded. I did. "Is there any way for me to help?"

She shrugged.

And here was the dilemma. Because I had ideas—lots of them. But would they make things worse instead of better? I didn't know. And I really didn't want to mess things up for her any more than I already had. "Well. *I* know you're not a gold digger. You're my best friend. You have been my best friend for years. That's not new. I love you. And that's not new, either. It just took me a while to get up the nerve to tell you."

Kayla looked up and met my gaze, a smile slowly blooming on her face. "I love you, too. That's not going to change because people are obnoxious."

I chuckled. "That's the spirit."

"You should get back to your classroom. The bell's going to ring in about five. I made the mistake of being in the hall when the kids were. It's worse. So much worse."

I winced. I couldn't imagine worse, but I'd take her word for it. I stood and crooked my finger at her.

She tipped her head to the side before pushing back her chair and standing.

I closed the distance between us and pulled her into my arms. "We're going to get through this. Together. Okay?"

"Yeah. Okay."

And then I broke my long-standing rule against kissing Kayla at school. Because she needed it.

And so did I.

25

KAYLA

"I'm so glad it's Friday." I sank into one of the overstuffed chairs in the bookstore and let my head drop back so I could stare at the ceiling.

"Rough week?" Megan was shelving a box of books nearby. Sympathy laced her tone, but she was also a lot more cheerful than usual.

"It was. For me at least. Sounds like that's not the case here?"

She looked over at me and grinned. "I know it's hard for you and Austin. I do. And I empathize, truly. But I'll tell you what, those articles have been amazing for the bookstore."

I snickered. "Glad to help."

"Hey. It's not like I'm rejoicing in your pain, but aren't you glad there's a small silver lining somewhere?" Megan picked up the box and shifted it to her other side so she could reach more of the shelf.

Was I? "Truth? Not yet. Maybe eventually."

"It's that bad?" Megan set down the stack of books and turned her full attention on me. "Austin hasn't said anything, so I really thought it was just general annoyance."

I shook my head. That was just like Austin. He tended to

downplay anything with his sister—and with me. I guess he figured being the strong, silent type was the right choice. It was a little annoying, even though I know it was well intentioned. "I had a meeting with the principal today after school. She's, I believe the word she used is 'displeased' with the current state of things. And if it continues, she's going to have no choice but to place the two of us on administrative leave for the remainder of the year."

Saying the words renewed the panic that had been trying to crawl up my throat since I left the meeting. I could only assume she'd had the same conversation with Austin, separately, because I hadn't been able to get in touch with him.

"She can't do that. Can she?" Megan picked up a book and angrily shoved it onto the shelf.

"Pretty sure she can. She's not one to say something like that without having first checked that she can follow through. When it comes to disciplining students, I always appreciated that about her. Now?" I bit my lip. "I can't afford to be put on leave. And I mean, I know Austin would help if I asked him and blah blah, but that's not what I want either."

"I could use help around here."

I lifted my eyebrows. "Really? I thought the whole reason you were able to do this full time is because you were, basically, a one-woman show. With a few part-time hours covered here and there by basically volunteers."

"Well, okay, yes. But if things keep going like they have this week that could change." Megan shrugged and went back to shelving books.

I didn't want to think about things continuing to go the way they had this week. Not that I wanted Megan not to have success. It was great that the bookstore was thriving. Too bad that was because my life—and her brother's life—was imploding. "I'll keep it in mind."

"Uh-huh." Megan shook her head. "Let's change the subject. Austin said you talked to Luke? How was his trip to Mexico?"

I pushed aside my confusion that Austin would mention my meetup with Luke. Did it bother Austin that much that he asked Megan about it? Was there some other way it would have naturally cropped up in conversation? "He said it went well. He has a history with the Garcias, I guess, so it was nice for them to have some time together."

Megan nodded. "I bet they got more done than they would have with teenagers around."

I managed a small chuckle. It was possible. But I hadn't gotten that impression. Of course, we hadn't really talked as much about his trip as we did his decision to leave the church. And that hadn't been announced publicly yet, so it wasn't my news to share. "Maybe so. Then again, I stand by the idea that kids can learn a lot about following Jesus by getting out of their comfort zone and sharing. Which they can also do locally. I get that, too."

"I wonder if they'll try to do some local missions this summer. I bet the homeless ministry downtown could use some manual labor assistance somewhere." Megan put the last book in her stack on the shelf and broke down the box.

"They probably could." And if Luke was going to stay through the summer, I'd suggest it. He'd told me he was willing to stay until they found a replacement, but I didn't see Pastor Chaz taking him up on that. Not based on some of the other things Luke had told me about their relationship. Should I reach out to him and see how turning in his resignation had gone?

Megan stood, picked up the flattened box, and gestured toward the back room. "I'm going to get another box to shelve. Back in a minute. If someone comes in—"

"I know the drill." I turned my attention to the main door. Whitney was running late—Beckett had apparently had a rough day and she wanted to get him settled rather than saddling Scott with a whiny toddler and making him miss poker night. Austin was going to try and swing by the bookstore when all was said and done.

That part I remembered.

The bells over the door jangled and a tall—like seriously tall —woman stepped into the store. She looked around.

I stood and stepped into her line of sight. "Hi. Can I help you?"

"Maybe? I'm looking for...hang on, I have it here." She pulled her phone out of her pocket and glanced down at the screen. "Megan Campbell or Kayla Jones or Whitney Wright."

"I'm Kayla." I tilted my head to the side and studied her more closely. She didn't look like a process server. Or a reporter. And those were the two types of people I absolutely didn't want to interact with...well...ever. But maybe looks were deceiving.

She grinned and put her phone away before holding out her hand. "Oh, good. I'm Jenna White."

"The architect." I shook her hand and gestured toward the sitting area. "Come on in and have a seat."

"Thanks. I mentioned in one conversation with Austin that I was having trouble finding a hangout group, you know? He mentioned how the three of you tended to get together on Friday nights at the bookstore and suggested I might be welcome." She hesitated next to one of the chairs. "Is that okay?"

I resumed my seat. "Sure. More the merrier. Megan's getting a box out of the back. She had a shipment in today and wants to get them on the shelves as soon as she can. Whitney's running late because her son had a rough day."

Jenna lowered herself to a chair. She perched on the edge a moment before scooting back and getting more settled. "Megan runs the bookstore?"

"Yeah. It's been in their family a while." I shifted to get more comfortable. "What do you like best about being an architect?"

Her eyebrows lifted. "Um. That's a question."

I chuckled. "Maybe so. It's not a line of work I ever explored. I don't even know what you really do all day other than what I see in movies."

"They're not all wrong. I guess I like turning someone's vision into a concrete structure. I like it even more when I can put some of my own vision into things—sort of blend the two together." Jenna lifted a shoulder. "And then there's the fun of working out all the rest of the plan—making sure everything is structurally sound, where does the HVAC go, that kind of thing. I like it all."

"Nice. It's good to do something you're passionate about. Megan has that."

"I have what?" Megan set a big box down on the floor and dusted off her hands. "Hi. Can I help you?"

"This is Jenna. She's the architect Austin hired. She knew Noah. When was that? High school?" I scooted over as Megan perched on the arm of my chair.

"Did I know that? About Noah?" Megan tapped a finger on her lips. "Maybe. It sounds familiar, but what do I know? It's nice to meet you. What brings you out this way?"

"Thanks. Just looking around on a Friday night, you know?" Jenna gave the one-shouldered shrug that seemed to be her default.

"No boyfriend?" Megan shook her head. "It's a sad world when someone who looks like you is dateless on a Friday night."

Jenna laughed.

I cringed and jabbed Megan with my elbow. "Sorry. She doesn't get out much. We're considering a social skills class for her, but it might be too late."

"Hey!"

"No, it's fine." Jenna was still chuckling. "I'm glad Austin suggested I come by. Do you mind if I worm my way into your friend group? As much as I love architecture, I don't fit super well with big groups of architects."

"It's fine by me." I smiled.

Megan nodded. "More the merrier. Especially since we never know if Whitney's going to make it. Married with a kid makes it hard sometimes."

"This is a fact." Jenna looked around the bookstore. "Can I help you shelve books?"

Megan's eyebrows winged up. "You *want* to shelve books? Why?"

"Lifelong dream." Jenna held up her hand. "Promise. I toyed with library science as a degree instead of architecture."

"Sure. Have at it." Megan sliced open the box and folded back the flaps. "I don't do anything fancy. Just alphabetical by author in each genre. I haven't sorted this box yet though, so generally I make stacks by genre before heading into the shelves to put them out."

"Even better." Jenna stood and lifted the box into the center of the seating area. She set it down on the floor then lowered herself next to it, sitting cross legged. She peered at me. "You'll help, right?"

"Sure. Why not?" I slid out of my chair to the floor and reached into the box for a book. "Piles by genre?"

Megan sat on the floor beside me and nodded. "Yeah. Should only be romance and sci-fi in there. Ought to be easy enough to tell them apart."

Jenna laughed. It seemed to be a natural thing for her to do. "Let's hope."

"So. Give us the scoop on Noah. He's one of the quieter ones. Keeps to himself. Always polite." Megan set a book on the romance pile. "So basically, he's either amazing or a secret serial killer."

"Oh no. Nope. I'm not dishing on Noah. Everyone deserves to let their past stay in the past. I will say I'm not surprised that he's quiet and polite. His parents were big on that." Jenna pulled out a handful of smaller paperbacks and sorted through them quickly.

The bells over the door jangled again.

"It's just me!" Whitney called out. Footsteps announced her arrival. "Why's everyone on the floor?"

"We're helping Megan sort books." I gestured to the growing piles. "This is Jenna, Noah's architect friend."

"Right. Austin's hired you for the learning center. How's that going?" Whitney sat in a chair.

"Good. The demo's nearly done, which is great. They were fast. And I emailed Austin plans this evening, so hopefully he'll get a chance to go over the changes this weekend and maybe we'll be closer to something final. Either way, we can get started on site prep starting Monday, but I'd love to get the ball rolling on the rest." Jenna reached for more books.

I stood, then bent down and picked up part of the stack of the romance novels. "I'm going to start sticking these on the shelf."

I wandered through the bookcases until I came to the right spot. I could still hear snippets of the girls' conversation, but I didn't try too hard to listen in. Jenna seemed nice. And professional. There was no reason for me to be irritated that she seemed to know so much more about the learning center progress than me. If I asked Austin for all the little details, he'd tell me.

I slid books onto the shelves.

The bright, glossy smiles of the couples on the covers made my heart ache.

Austin loved me. Right now was just a really hard time. For both of us.

We'd get through it.

And when we got to the other side, we'd be stronger for it.

I repeated the words to myself a few times. They were true.

They had to be.

26

AUSTIN

"That was some news, huh?" I glanced over to the passenger seat where Kayla sat. I'd picked her up for church this morning—something I'd been doing more frequently since we started dating officially. I liked the extra time it gave us together. Alone. And it meant we didn't have to take two cars to lunch—and we could choose to go somewhere different than the rest of the group, too, if we wanted.

Today, that was exactly what I'd wanted. She'd seemed on board.

"Hey." I reached over and squeezed her hand. "You okay?"

"Yeah. Sorry." She flashed a quick smile. "Just thinking. You mean Luke's resignation?"

I nodded. That was the news I'd meant. The pastor had mentioned it briefly during the announcements this morning. Most of the congregation had seemed surprised. The way she asked, I gathered she'd already known. "He didn't give notice? Just quit?"

She shook her head. "He was willing to stay until they found a replacement."

"Oh." That didn't make the pastor come off well. "That seems shortsighted."

"Right? Do you think it's common?"

"Is what common? Not letting someone work out their notice?"

She nodded.

"Maybe in an office setting. I don't know much about how churches usually operate." In fact, I'd never really been at a church where there was pastoral turnover. The old youth pastor leaving and Luke coming on had been my first exposure to the process, and even then, I couldn't really use it as a yardstick.

"What about schools?"

I swallowed. "Are you thinking of quitting?"

"I don't know." She turned in her seat to look at me. I was grateful we were nearly back to her apartment. We could talk about it over the grilled cheese she'd offered, and hopefully I could convince her to see that leaving the school wasn't the right choice. At all.

"Is this because the principal talked to us on Friday?"

"Yeah." She blew out a breath. "I wondered if she talked to you."

I sighed. "I should have said something. I guess I was still processing. Nothing quite like a subtle threat that your job is in danger because of something completely out of your control, right?"

"Something like that."

I turned into her parking lot and found a visitor spot. I wanted to comfort her, but wasn't sure how. I truly believed this would all, eventually, settle down. Go away? No. But get to a level that was something we could deal with or ignore? Yes.

It didn't seem like that would be reassuring to her. At all.

We walked in silence into her building and up to her apartment. She unlocked the door and the jingling of the bells on the cats' collars made me smile.

"You put bells on?"

Kayla shrugged, but a grin tugged at the corners of her lips. "It seemed like a good idea at the time."

"Uh-huh." I squatted down and scratched Ada behind the ears. "And what do you think about that, girl? You like your bell?"

She meowed at me.

I chuckled and scooped her up to carry and scritch as we made our way into the kitchen.

"You're still okay with grilled cheese?" Kayla stood with a loaf of bread in her hands.

"Yeah. It's a classic for a reason. Can I help?"

She shook her head. "It's easy. Two?"

"Please." Ada wiggled out of my arms and I let her leap to the floor. She padded off, probably to brag to Charles about all the scritches. Or not. I couldn't say what cats talked about amongst themselves. I settled on one of the stools at her kitchen counter. "Are you really worried about your job?"

"Are you really not?" She looked up from buttering bread. "She was serious. You know that, right?"

I did believe the principal was serious. But also... "Tristan sent a statement out to all the press outlets that have covered the story. I really think it's going to calm things down."

Kayla scoffed and reached for a pan.

"I'm not big news, Kayla. I'm just not. There's going to be something else local any minute now that will take the attention off me. And now, with Tristan's statement and the announcement of the learning center and scholarship? They've been fed. I don't have anything more to say that they could possibly want to hear."

"Do they know that?" Kayla turned on the stove and sighed.

"Because that's the thing. You know that and I know that, but the press? They're going to dig around and keep looking, because 'billionaire teacher' is a great human-interest story. It sells ad space."

I watched as she put the sandwiches together and set them in the pan. She had a point. But I still believed they'd let it go, to a tolerable degree. Maybe it was just wishful thinking. "Say you're right. You'd what, quit and then...?"

"I don't know. Are they going to follow me around? I'm only interesting because of you."

My stomach sank. I'd offered her an out before and she'd said no. She'd said she wanted to stay. Had that changed? "I guess you can remove me from the equation if that's what you need to do."

She closed her eyes. When she opened them again and met my gaze, she shook her head. "I'm sorry. I don't want that. I know this is hard on you, too. I don't know why I keep taking it out on you."

"Easy target conveniently located?" I offered a weak smile.

Kayla flipped the sandwiches in the pan, then came around to where I was sitting and wrapped me in her arms. "Probably. I'm sorry."

"Hey." I rubbed her back and rested my forehead on hers, savoring her closeness for a moment. "Don't worry about it. This is hard. We'll get through it. And if either—or both—of us end up losing our jobs, I happen to know about a new learning center that's hopefully opening in September. I think they'd be more than happy to hire both of us."

She eased back and returned to the stove. "September?"

"That's the earliest, but yeah. If everything with the county goes as scheduled, then we should be able to open not long after school starts." I leaned forward and rested my elbows on the counter. "I should introduce you to Jenna. I think you'd like her, and I get the sense that she doesn't have many close woman friends."

"As it happens, I have met Jenna and I do like her." Kayla grinned and slid the sandwiches out of the pan onto plates. "She came by the bookstore Friday night and ended up staying."

"Cool. How'd Megan take to her?"

She tipped her head to the side and put the plates down on the counter in front of me, then came around and joined me at the bar. "Don't you talk to your sister at all?"

I shrugged. Megan and I might live together, but we didn't actually interact very often. We weren't exactly ships passing in the night, but we definitely tried to respect the other's space. "I was grading most of yesterday. Then you and I went out last night. Church this morning, and now I'm here. I'll probably get around to asking her myself later, but you also probably know. And you're right here."

Kayla shook her head and muttered something that sounded suspiciously like, "Men."

I reached for her hand. "Let's pray."

"Always a good idea." Kayla squeezed my hand.

"Heavenly Father, thank You for this food. Bless the hands that prepared it and may it nourish our bodies. Please be with us in this situation with the media and give Kayla and me guidance so we know how to respond in a way that glorifies You. As always, I ask that You show me the way You want me to use the money. Let me be a good steward over the bounty that You've given. In Jesus's name, Amen."

"Amen." Kayla released my hand and blew out a breath. She picked up one half of her sandwich and bit in. The cheese strung out as she lowered the sandwich back to her plate.

I followed suit. "Mmm. This hits the spot. Thank you."

"Easy peasy." She shrugged away my compliment, but her

pink cheeks betrayed her enjoyment of it. "I guess I never thought about the hard parts of having billions."

I snickered. "I don't think anyone does. Not unless they happen to also have them. For me, the parable of the talents is almost always at the front of my brain, and I'm always worried I'm going to end up like the wicked servant who has his talent taken away and given to someone else."

"What do you mean? You're not hoarding your money in fear."

"Haven't I been? I look at how quickly Scott got his parents involved with setting up and managing not only his tithe but an expansive use of his money to build God's kingdom. I've lost track of the number of missionaries and other charities Scott has mentioned that he's supporting. And he's always offering to let us go in together and have his mom manage the philanthropic portion of our own wealth." I couldn't explain why I'd never taken him up on that. Well, I sort of could. The idea for the learning center had always been in the back of my mind.

"Well, you're doing it now. The learning center is going to be amazing. And I think the scholarship fund is a fantastic addition to the enterprise. Was that Tristan's idea?"

"It was." I was reasonably sure it was an accident—something that had happened because of rushed PR and bad proofreading—but it was a good one. When the statement came out, the announcement made it sound as if the learning center would be the organization behind the scholarships and grants. Even if it wasn't what I'd originally thought was best, it made sense. In fact, it was one of those "duh" moments. Even Eric agreed it was the ideal setup. "The application link is up now, and active, but I'm not tied to any specific award dates. So I can look at things as they come in and take my time evaluating them. If they're time sensitive, I might go ahead and act on them immediately, but otherwise my plan is to wait until after the center opens."

Kayla nodded.

I focused my attention on the sandwiches on my plate. Grilled cheese was always better hot, when the bread crunched and the cheese was all melty.

She didn't speak again until she was finished with her food. "I don't like admitting that I'm dreading tomorrow."

I frowned. I couldn't say I was raring to go back to school myself. And it was definitely an unusual feeling. "I haven't quite worked my way to dreading yet, but I hear you. I was hoping things would cool down as the week wore on. They just didn't, though. I keep thinking we need a political or celebrity scandal to get everyone's attention off us."

Kayla gave a short laugh. "Where are those scandals when you need them?"

"Maybe this week will be better. They've had the weekend away. My statement is out and circulating. You and I have been ignoring it at school, despite the pressure to comment or entertain questions." I shrugged. There was nothing more to do. "Did I tell you Tristan suggested I hire security?"

"Like a bodyguard?" Kayla's eyebrows lifted. "Have you been getting threats?"

"No threats. But yes, like a bodyguard. Apparently, Tristan's receptionist doubles as his security detail. Which explains why she's always around." I shrugged. "I'm really not on board with that idea if I can avoid it. Is that naive?"

"I mean, maybe? There's certainly a lot that can go wrong when you've got a ton of money. Kidnapping, blackmail, whatever. At the same time, I don't blame you for not wanting someone standing in your shadow constantly." Kayla stood, picked up her plate, and looked at mine. "Are you finished?"

I shoved the last bite into my mouth and nodded. I hadn't

really considered Tristan's suggestion seriously. It just wasn't something that made sense to me. How would I teach with a bodyguard hulking around?

And okay, sure, it wasn't as if the bodyguard couldn't find a way to blend in with the students. Maybe. But still. I shook my head. Not someplace I was going unless I had to.

"Tristan also suggested a security system for the house. We had something simple, but I do think I'll go ahead and upgrade that."

"Makes sense." Kayla opened her freezer. "I have ice cream if you want a little dessert?"

"Sure. There's always room for ice cream." I turned around and looked at Kayla's apartment. "You don't have any cameras or anything, do you?"

"No." Kayla brought the ice cream tub, bowls, and a scoop over to the counter. "The building's pretty safe. I've never worried about anything, living here."

Neither had I in my place. Should I push? I didn't want to make her nervous or have her worried about living in her home. Kayla was a strong, independent woman. It was something I loved about her. "If you ever decide you want a system—or to move—let me know and I'll help with the cost."

"I can handle my own finances." She frowned at me. "I'm not looking for handouts."

"I know that." I scrubbed a hand over my face. "I'm offering to help, that's all."

"Okay. Then I guess I appreciate it. Even if it's unnecessary." She put a bowl of ice cream in front of me. "I'm not with you because of your money."

"I know that." I looked up and waited until she met my gaze. "I do."

She nodded once. "Good."

I scooped a bite of rocky road and let the chocolate and

marshmallow soothe. I wanted to tell her that not being with me for my money didn't mean I couldn't still spend it on her. But that was unlikely to go over very well right now. So I'd leave it alone. We were in a good place.

Or a good-ish one.

It would be better if we could get back to the place where I was just another anonymous teacher, but that wasn't super likely. So we'd figure out a way to move forward from here.

Together.

27

KAYLA

"How are you doing?"

I glanced over as Austin fell into step beside me on my way out of the building. It was the end of a long day—school days seemed to be getting longer and longer right now—and I just wanted to go home to my cats. "Okay, I guess. You?"

Austin shook his head. "Just left a meeting with the principal. She told me my contract wouldn't be renewed after this year. I am, and I quote, too distracting of a presence on school grounds."

"Oh." I stopped and closed my eyes, gathering myself a moment, before I turned to look at him. "I'm sorry."

"Thanks. I guess it's not unexpected. Not with how things have been going. But I'm disappointed." He paused and cleared his throat. "She suggested I take the rest of the week to consider making long-term sub plans and letting someone else finish out the year."

"Suggested?" Anger stirred in my heart. "Or requested."

He shrugged. "Same difference, really. It doesn't feel like me working out the rest of the year is an option actually on the table. So I guess I'll be putting some long-term sub plans together. I hope they get someone who actually knows math."

I chuckled. "I'm pretty sure the one lady who was doing the long-term sub thing finally found a full-time drama position."

"I don't know why someone would take a math job—even a temp one—if they hated math."

I nudged him with my elbow. "A lot of people like paying bills and eating."

"Yeah, all right. But come on. There are other sub options." He scowled and kicked at a loose rock on the sidewalk. "I don't want to quit. I love my job."

I rubbed his arm, hoping to soothe. "You're going to love the learning center even more. And this leaves you free to be more involved in the day-to-day construction stuff. That's a good thing, right?"

"You know what's a good thing? Not leaving my advanced seniors in a lurch at the end of the year. Or maybe staying on top of the freshmen in my algebra class whose parents have convinced them they don't actually need to know this in real life, so they're barely skating by. Because I guess it doesn't matter that it's a state graduation requirement." Austin shoved his hands in his pockets. "I'm tempted to ask Tristan if I can sue the papers for ruining my career, but I know I can't."

"No. You were good enough not to bring up the whole free speech thing to me when I was ranting, so I'll return the favor."

His laugh was bitter.

I nudged him again. "Hey. This isn't like you. What else did she say?"

"Isn't that enough? I spent my whole life working toward this. And I realize that 'high school math teacher' isn't something tons of kids dream about being, but I did. I do. And now it's just gone." He snapped his fingers. "Now what?"

"Now we work on making a new dream. Maybe one we can

work on together." The principal hadn't told me my contract was unrenewed, but she had suggested that distancing myself from Austin—publicly—would probably be a better choice for career longevity. Like I was going to do that. Which meant I'd been leaving school with some heavy thinking and praying of my own to do. But talking to Austin made the answer a lot clearer.

"Together?" He tipped his head to the side and studied my face.

"Always." I leaned forward and pressed my lips to his. "I love you, Austin. I've loved you for a long time—much longer than we've been officially a couple. With you is the only place I want to be. So, if your learning center can use a kick-butt computer science teacher? I'm your girl."

For the first time in our conversation, Austin's smile was genuine. He slipped his arms around me and tugged me closer. "You're the only one I want by my side. You're going to marry me, aren't you?"

My heart thundered in my chest and I struggled to keep my voice calm. "You haven't asked me."

"I'm asking you now. Will you? Marry me?"

A thousand emotions swirled through me at once. "Of course I will."

His lips descended on mine and the annoyances of the day slipped away as I got lost in him.

An ear-splitting whistle, followed by several catcalls made me jolt.

"Yeah, Mr. Campbell! Woo!"

"Nice, Miss Jones! You go."

My face heated and I stepped back. I cleared my throat. "Well."

Austin laughed and held my hand despite my efforts to tug away. "Nope. You said yes."

"I did." I tugged again, but didn't put much oomph behind it. "I do have to mention that there's no ring."

"I'll fix that. Promise." Austin drew an X over his heart. "In fact, what are you doing tonight? Want to go over to Tyson's and scout the mall? We can grab dinner and make it a whole thing?"

I bit my lip. Tonight was Luke's last night at youth. I'd been planning to go and...be moral support, I guess. He hadn't asked. He probably didn't need me. He certainly didn't know that was in my plan, so it wasn't like he'd miss me.

"Yeah. Let's do that. You want to follow me home so I can change? Then we can go in your car." I'd need to feed the cats, too. They were going to be annoyed with me for leaving so soon after getting home, but they'd deal. For all the things people tended to say about cats, mine liked their routine, which included after-school cuddling.

"Sounds like a plan." Austin pulled me close for a quick kiss. "I'll see you there in a few?"

I nodded, grinning.

Holy smokes! I was trying to wrap my mind around the fact that I was engaged. Officially. To Austin.

In my car, I double-checked that my phone was connected to the Bluetooth and tapped Megan's contact.

"Hey. What's up?"

The fact that she answered assured me that the bookstore wasn't super busy, but I went ahead and confirmed anyway. "Got a minute?"

"Yeah. We're dead right now. Usually are, this time of day, although with schools starting to get out, I think we'll pick up in another thirty or so. Hey, what kind of summer programs should I have? I want to find ways to get more people in with kids out of school."

I fought a laugh. "I will try to concentrate on that in just a minute. First, I need to tell you something."

"Okay. Hit me. But also, please think about summer programs that would appeal to teens. I know story hour can get the moms and tots in, which is fine—it's good—but I need to grab the whole age spectrum."

"Okay." I blew out a breath. Maybe calling was a bad idea. Maybe Austin and I should just swing by after we got a ring and had dinner and we could show her. "Teens like prizes. You could do a raffle of some sort. Although, you don't necessarily want to tie it to purchases, because teens can't always spend like their parents. What if you worked with the library? You could offer a gift card for the bookstore as prizes for summer reading."

"Hmm. That's an idea." I heard the bells on the door jangle. "Oh. Gotta go. Text me or something. Okay? Bye."

I shook my head and switched back to the radio. So much for talking to Megan about the fact that I was poised to be her sister-in-law.

Oh well, we had time.

And now that I thought about it, I liked the idea of springing it on her when I had a ring.

I pulled into my parking spot and cut the engine. I grabbed my things and pushed open the car door. I saw Austin pulling into a visitor spot nearby and gave him a quick wave as I headed inside.

Charles and Ada greeted me at the door. Their bells jingled cheerily as they followed me to the bedroom. I changed out of the skirt and blouse I'd worn to school and into dark jeans and a nice shirt. Maybe I should have stuck with dressier, but I was ready to be in comfortable clothes. Most afternoons, I got home and changed straight into pajamas.

Most afternoons, I hadn't just gotten engaged.

I grinned and scooped up Ada, who was doing her best to make life challenging by winding through my legs. "Austin asked me to marry him. What do you think about that?"

Ada didn't answer, but I liked to think she approved.

We'd obviously live in Austin's townhouse after we got married. Wouldn't we? The cats would like it there—more room to scamper. More places to hide.

Would Megan mind? Would she want to live in my apartment? I'd renewed my lease in January and they had pretty stiff terms for breaking it.

When would we get married?

There were a lot of questions to answer, and maybe I shouldn't be worried about them right now. Maybe I was supposed to be basking in the glow of my shiny new ring for a few days—weeks?—before getting caught up in the next steps.

Except what I was most excited about was starting my life with Austin.

It felt like I'd been waiting on that most of my life.

I slid back into my flats and headed toward the kitchen. "I'll get your dinner out for you. I know it's early, but you don't have to eat this minute. You can wait until you're hungry."

I glanced at Charles and chuckled. "You're always hungry. But I'm feeding you, so don't expect a second dinner when I get back. Got it?"

He meowed innocently. I didn't buy it.

I scooped kibble into their bowls, checked their water, and, satisfied, ran my hands over both of their furry backs.

"Be good, okay? I'll be back in a bit. With a new sparkly for you to admire." I grinned as I hooked my purse over my shoulder. I locked the door behind me and hurried down to the parking area.

Austin was waiting in the lobby.

My mouth watered at the sight of him leaning, like he didn't have a care in the world, against the wall by the door.

He pushed off and pulled his hands out of his pockets as I

approached. "Ready? I was going to come up, but then figured I might miss you if you took the elevator."

"I'm ready." And, unaccountably, nervous. But he didn't need to know that.

"Did you call Megan?" He took my hand as we passed through the doors and out into the parking lot. The spring air carried hints of the river on its breeze.

"I did." He knew me too well. "But she was on a tear and I couldn't get a word in. Then someone came in so she hung up."

Austin laughed. "Maybe we'll stop by after we're done."

"My thoughts, exactly." I squeezed his hand before letting go to climb in to the passenger side of his car when he opened it for me.

He shut the car door, then rounded the hood to his side and slid behind the wheel. "Dinner first?"

"It's a little early?" Even considering the time it would take to get over to Tyson's, I wasn't going to be hungry for a while yet. And I really wanted our engagement to be ring-official.

He chuckled. "All right. Ring first. Food second. And in that case, maybe we'll head back over to Old Town and celebrate at Gadsby's."

"That sounds perfect." And it did. What could be more celebrational than fancy peanut soup at a restaurant that had served George Washington?

"Then that's the plan." He backed the car out of the parking space and started out of my apartment complex. He kept glancing over as he made the turns that would get us to the Beltway.

"What?"

He laughed and shook his head. "I just wondered if you knew what you wanted for your ring. I'm fine with whatever. And obviously price doesn't matter, so I'm not worried about that. But I don't even know where I'd begin if I was going on my own to pick something out for you. I don't think I would have gone with a diamond, for all it's tradition."

Hmm. I wouldn't mind a diamond. They were, like he'd said, traditional. But... "This might be a cliché. And if you hate the idea, it's okay to tell me."

Austin shook his head. "I really don't care as long as you love it and it's on your left hand's ring finger."

"I always loved Princess Diana's sapphire. There's something about it that just seems so much friendlier than a diamond. I wouldn't mind finding something along those lines. It could even be a different stone. It doesn't have to be a sapphire. Although, I do love blue." It sounded silly when I said it aloud, but I couldn't take the words back. I didn't even want to, honestly. Maybe, when we were walking along a row of sparkling glass-topped cases, I'd change my mind.

"Okay."

I glanced over at him. That was it? Just "okay" like I hadn't essentially asked for some of the crown jewels? "We should look at wedding bands while we're there."

He grinned. "Sure. Although I was thinking that I'd be happy with one of the cool silicone ones."

I snickered. "No. I'm not walking around with Diana's sapphire while you sport something I picked up for thirty bucks online."

"Maybe I want a *Star Wars* one. Those cost more."

I shook my head, laughter bubbling up in my chest. "No. Come on."

"What? It could be fun. We can get matching ones for days you don't want to wear a fancy ring. Yours can have Leia and say 'I love you' and mine will have Han and say 'I know.' It's perfect."

I looked at Austin's smirk and tried to decide if he was serious. "Why don't we hold that in reserve for our fifth anniversary. That's silicone, right?"

"Pretty sure it's wood." He winked at me.

"Why would you know that?" Seriously. Who even knew there were traditional gifts these days? It wasn't something my parents had ever bothered with. Or mentioned. I think I only knew because I'd stumbled down a Wikipedia rabbit hole one night and, one thing led to another, and I was reading through the traditional anniversary gifts.

But I hadn't committed them to memory.

Apparently, Austin had.

"Dunno. I like random facts. That just happens to be one I have in my reservoir."

"Well, we're still getting you a real wedding band. I'm not exchanging a *Star Wars* band with you in church." I paused. Was it too soon to start talking about the wedding? Nah. Just because we kicked around ideas didn't mean we had to stick with them. "We're getting married at church, right?"

"I was hoping, yeah. I'm not into the Elvis impersonator idea. But it also doesn't have to be a big, fancy thing. Unless that's what you want?" He looked at me, one eyebrow lifting. "What do you want?"

I sighed. That was a question. I wasn't completely sure how to answer it. Like most little girls, I'd certainly spent time thinking through and dreaming about my wedding. But that was all abstract. Now? With the prospect of marrying Austin becoming a reality? I didn't know what I wanted.

"That's a long pause." Austin took my hand and drove with the other. "You having second thoughts already?"

"No!" I shot him a concerned look and rolled my eyes when I saw the smirk on his face. "No. I just don't know. It seems like the bigger the wedding, the longer we have to wait."

"We can wait. If that's what you want."

"Maybe we can find a way to some middle ground. I do want a church wedding. And a white dress. And a party with my friends. But I don't want one of these massive affairs for hundreds that cost more than teachers make in a year. Even though you could afford it."

"Then that's what we'll do. We'll find middle ground."

I smiled. Middle ground sounded good. "We have time. Ring first. Then dinner. Then, maybe a late night stop at the bookstore to share our news."

28

AUSTIN

"Congratulations!" Scott and the rest of the guys cheered in unison as I stepped into Scott's living room for poker night.

"Thanks, guys." I accepted a bottle of root beer from Cody. "It's been a week of ups and downs for sure. But getting engaged to Kayla is the best, brightest spot."

"Nice. What's Megan think?" Cody stood beside me, his elbow bumping into mine. "She squealed, right?"

"She did." After a minute. And that hadn't gone by Kayla. She'd spent the whole ride back to her apartment obsessing and overthinking and generally filling the car with words that I'd struggled to process. I'd been a little disappointed by those two beats before the squeal myself.

"When's the big day?" Cody slapped my shoulder. "Man, we're falling like bowling pins."

"I think the phrase is 'dropping like flies,' Cody." Tristan shook his head and reached for the bag of chips in the center of the game table. "Even with the wrong words, it's a fair assessment."

"What? There's two of the six of us. That's only a third.

Hardly a startling majority." I shook my head. Dropping like flies. Whatever. "Do the math before you make statements like that."

"Pft. I'm not doing any more math today." Noah rubbed the middle of his forehead. "We have a new initiative that they're considering. Mr. Ballentine and Mr. Trent are both determined to double-check all the numbers before launch. And I got tasked with the spreadsheet and manual check of all the costs."

"Spreadsheets are fun. What's your problem with them?" Cody frowned. "I was on the phone all day talking to potential vendors for the gala in November. Not sure why I ended up in charge of that, but I'd rather have the spreadsheet. Wanna trade?"

Noah laughed and shook his head. "No. Suddenly, my job seems much better. Thanks."

"Yeah, sure. Happy to help." Cody shrugged. "When are we gonna have poker at my place? I'm set up now."

"Next week is all you." Tristan pointed.

I laughed. Tristan was always happy to hand off hosting. "Nice, Tristan. Way to share."

"Hey. Cody wants to host, I'm not saying no. I had to actually run the vacuum after our last game night because it was too much to leave for the next time my cleaning service came." Tristan crunched chips.

I gestured toward the crumbs that fell from Tristan's shirt as he ate. "I don't think you can blame us for that. Not all the way. You need a plate?"

"I'm good." Tristan brushed the crumbs onto the floor.

Scott winced. "Guess I'm cleaning up later tonight, too."

"Are we playing, or what?" Cody pulled out a chair at the table and sat. He reached for the deck of cards and started to shuffle.

"Yeah, yeah." Noah dropped into the seat beside Cody. "Hey, Aus, what were the downs?"

"What?" I paused in the middle of pulling out my chair and tried to figure out why Noah was asking.

"You said it was a week of ups and downs. Engaged is obviously the up. What's the down?" Noah reached for a handful of chips.

"I, uh, am officially out of a job at the end of the school year." Possibly sooner. I didn't want to go there, though. I was still mulling the principal's offer. I was going to call it an offer not an ultimatum, because it wasn't as if she'd ordered me to leave the school grounds. She just made it very clear that was her preference.

"Can they do that?" Noah looked between me and Tristan. "Can they just let him go because of the media?"

Tristan frowned at me. "I'm surprised, possibly a little offended, that you didn't tell me about this when it happened. When did it happen?"

"Wednesday. And there was no point in calling you, because she's perfectly within her rights to do it. My contract was up for renewal; she's declining to do so. I can look around at other jobs available in the county, see about a transfer." I shrugged, hoping it came across as nonchalant. What they didn't need to know was how unlikely it was going to be for any other school to want me, either. There was the media coverage, to start out. And then there was the fact that I definitely wasn't going to ask for—because I wasn't going to get it—a recommendation or reference from my current administrator.

"But?"

I sighed. Tristan always heard more than anyone said. More than people wanted him to hear. "It's just not happening. After the media storm, no one is going to hire me and bring reporters and all that publicity to their campus."

"I thought there was no such thing as bad PR?" Cody picked up his cards and looked at them.

"I guess it depends on the industry. If you're a teacher, pretty much any media coverage that doesn't involve a one-time mention of having won a grant or some other award is definitely negative." I looked at my cards and focused on not frowning. "It's fine. Really. I'll just be full time at the learning center. It's not as if there won't be plenty to do there, and since I own it, no one can fire me because of some media coverage."

I wasn't wrong. There would be plenty to do. Just because I'd intended to hire a center director to handle it didn't mean I couldn't do it instead. Maybe I'd find I enjoyed it.

If I was lucky, I'd have the opportunity to help out with math tutoring. Then, at least, I wouldn't be completely out of the teaching arena. I'd still be helping kids see the beauty in math. Or at least pass their classes.

"You all right?" Cody's voice was quiet, surfing under the chatter of the other guys.

"Yeah. Just thinking. My principal suggested that I might want to go ahead and let a long-term sub take over for the remainder of the year."

"She what? That's not right, man." Cody scowled. "I don't think it's right that she can fire you in the first place over this."

"She didn't fire me." I was going to adamantly correct anyone who said otherwise on that score. Because just no. "She just didn't renew my contract. And yeah, maybe that's splitting hairs, but not to me."

"Sorry. You're right. What are you going to do?"

I shrugged. "Not sure yet. But maybe she's got a point. The kids are distracted. The parents are frustrated. I was really hoping the circus would die down some by now, but it hasn't. And Kayla pointed out it would give me more time to focus on the learning center. So there's that."

"More time for wedding planning, too." Cody grinned. "Maybe, since Kayla will still be teaching, you could just take that whole task on."

"Har har." I rolled my eyes and tossed chips into the pile as the betting came around the table.

"You never did mention your date." When I frowned at him across the table, Scott added, "Wedding date?"

"Oh. Come on, we've been engaged three days. Can't we have a few minutes to let it settle and, I don't know, bask?" I would put Kayla on the plane to...well...not Vegas, but somewhere and elope in a heartbeat if she was up for that. But she wanted a church wedding, and I could get behind that, too. "Probably in the winter? I don't know how long it takes to coordinate a typical wedding."

"Don't look at me." Scott grinned and flipped over another card in the middle of the table. "How Whitney pulled off our wedding as quickly as she did still amazes me. Of course, Whitney amazes me, so I shouldn't be surprised."

All the guys groaned and various mutters about newlyweds whispered in the air. I might normally have participated in ribbing Scott, but since I was looking to join the ranks of the married guys sooner rather than later, I'd sit this one out.

Conversation shifted to other topics as we played another three hands of poker. Then, before it got too late, we were all wrapping up and heading for our cars.

I checked the time on my phone. The bookstore had closed thirty minutes ago. There was very little point in stopping by to see if Kayla was still there. She'd said she was ready for an early night tonight—she probably hadn't even stayed until closing.

Had Jenna swung by again?

I'd meant to give Noah a jab or two about her, just to see what there was to see. Which might be nothing. He certainly acted like it wasn't anything. But that was why I was suspicious.

And I didn't feel like it was something I could bring up with Jenna herself. She worked for me—not even as an employee, just someone I hired to do a job. It would be extremely unprofessional for me to ask.

I should see if Kayla could find out.

I got into my car and sat behind the wheel a moment before going ahead and texting Kayla about the idea. Then I started the car.

My phone rang and I grinned at Kayla's face on the screen. I connected the call through the Bluetooth.

"Hi. I wasn't sure if you'd still be up."

She laughed. "I'm up. I just didn't want to be out late. I doubt very much I'll get to bed before eleven, though."

I debated asking about coming over. But she was allowed to have some quiet time at home on her own. She used that to recharge. We both did. It was important to remember and respect that going forward. "So? What do you think? Can you nudge information out of Jenna and see what the deal is with her and Noah?"

"You should talk to Megan. Your sister's already hot on that trail. But if tonight was any indication, there's nothing there and never has been. They went to prom together, but I get the feeling that was more of a mutual backup plan than anything else."

I nodded. "That sounds like something Noah would do. He has backup plans for everything, seems like."

"Is he still going on about six months' worth of non-perishable food as a minimum?"

I laughed. "I think he's starting to push for a year, given the state of things. But yeah, he's a planner, for sure."

"I think the term is 'prepper.'"

"Nah. He's not that far gone yet. Is he?" I would have said I'd know better than Kayla. Noah didn't do a lot of interaction when the whole gang was around. He liked to hover on the edge and talk to one or two people at a time. I was always surprised he worked for a lobbying organization, where networking and schmoozing were part of the deal.

"Maybe not. But you should definitely talk to Megan and see if she gets a different feeling. How was poker?"

"Good. I broke even, so I'll take it."

She chuckled. "Yeah. I'm super worried about you losing a whole two dollars."

"You never know. It could be the difference between feast or famine someday. The guys were definitely curious about our wedding date, though. Did you get a chance to talk to your folks and see what their calendar looked like?" I didn't want to push, but I wouldn't mind getting it set. I pulled into my parking space, switched the phone off of the car stereo system, and cut the engine.

"How do you feel about July?"

"This July or next July? Because I have different feelings depending on what you choose."

Kayla laughed, loud and long. When she had her breath back, she said, "This July. As in a little over two months from today."

"Then I feel very amenable. Can you have what you want on that timeframe?" I got out of my car and locked it, then looked around. I didn't spot anyone hanging nearby, ready to ambush me on the way to my townhouse. There'd been a few reporters who tried when the media frenzy first started, but permit-only parking that was vigorously enforced seemed to have helped. I started toward the front door.

"Yeah. I don't want huge. Just nice. The church is open the first and the eighth—do you have a preference?"

I slid the key into the lock and pushed open the front door. Inside, I closed and relocked it behind me. "The first. That's sooner."

"We're on the same page there. And, hey, bonus, some years we'll get a four-day weekend out of our anniversary because of the fourth. All right, I'll get us on the calendar. What do you think about having the reception at Gadsby's? I happened to notice that's an option. They have that big back patio area, and no one could do better with the food."

"Sold. Do you want me to get in touch with them and arrange that?" I suddenly didn't feel like I was pulling my weight. "I want to help."

I kicked off my shoes and scooted them out of the middle of the floor so Megan wouldn't trip on them when she got home. I should probably talk to her about living arrangements tonight, too. If Kayla and I were...wait. "Do you want to live here, after? Or we could buy something else in the area if you'd rather. Something that was just ours right from the start."

"I love your townhouse, but I don't want to displace Megan. I know she enjoys being able to walk to work. I'd also been thinking I could offer her my apartment until the lease runs out. It's a longer drive, so she might not want it. I don't really have a problem with her staying put either. I just don't know if she'd want to live with newlyweds."

My face heated. I wasn't sure about my sister living with us either. "I'll talk to her tonight. If she wants to stay here, do you mind us finding our own place? Or we can live in your apartment until we find something or the lease is up. I'm fine with whatever means we're together."

"Why don't you see what Megan wants and we'll go from there?"

I nodded even though Kayla couldn't see me and headed into the kitchen. "All right. I guess I'll let you go. I love you, sleep well."

"I love you, too. Night."

I tapped my phone and ended the call before tucking my

phone in my pocket. It was good to have a date. Kayla had never answered me about who was going to get in touch with Gadsby's. I'd follow up with her in the morning.

My life had changed a lot this week. I was grateful that for now, at least, the good changes were outpacing the bad.

29

KAYLA

"Shotgun!" Megan raced to my car when we hit the parking lot after church.

"What are you, twelve?" Whitney shook her head and glanced at me. "Is shotgun still a thing when you're thirty?"

I shrugged. "Driver still picks tunes, so I don't know why not."

"Seriously?" Whitney laughed. "All right, well I guess I'm in the back seat listening to Taylor Swift."

"Tell me you mind." Because really, who didn't love Taylor? She had fans from twelve to sixty. Maybe older. She was timeless.

"I mind the back seat." Whitney scowled at my car. "After the first stop, we're alternating."

"What? No fair. I called it." Megan crossed her arms.

"Children. Don't make me get your father involved." I rolled my eyes and hit the unlock button on my key fob. "Alternating is fair. You know it, too, Megan."

"Fine." Megan's expression morphed into a scowl. "Spoil sport."

I didn't know if she meant me or Whitney, and I wasn't going to explore it further to find out. Mostly because I didn't care. "Are we done with the drama now? Because I have to say, as the bride, that I expect the rest of today to be all about me finding my perfect wedding dress."

Whitney grinned and looked over the roof of the car at Megan. "Aw, look. She's already a bridezilla."

Megan started to laugh.

"I am not." I pulled open the car door and got behind the wheel. "If the two of you are done with comedy hour, you can get in the car. I'm seriously rethinking my bridesmaid choices."

"Oh, yeah?" Megan got in and pulled the passenger car door closed. She reached for her seatbelt. "Who else would you ask?"

She had a point. There was no one else I'd consider asking. I had a handful of casual acquaintances at school or from the few times I tried out women's ministry things at church, but no one I considered a friend. Certainly not a good enough one to ask to be a bridesmaid.

"Look how quiet she is." Whitney pulled the back door closed. "I'm in. Let's roll. Where to first?"

"Food first." I started the car. "What do we want to eat? My treat. So, keep that teacher's salary in mind." I started backing out of my space in the church parking lot. Chances were high they'd choose something either in Tyson's or on the way there. We'd decided to keep the bridal boutique in Old Town as our last stop. One, because it was back home and that meant we could get to it another day if we ran out of time. And two? Because the word "boutique" suggested to me that it was more than I wanted to spend on a dress.

Mom and Dad had given me a decent budget. And Austin had said to get what I wanted and he'd make up the difference. But I didn't really want to do that. It was a dress I'd wear one time. Why would I spend thousands and thousands on it?

So. The mall and the, hopefully, cheaper chain stores.

"Friday's? I haven't been there in ages. Are they any good?" Whitney had shifted to the middle seat in the back so she could lean forward and be part of the conversation.

Megan nodded. "They're still okay. That works for me."

"Friday's it is." I hadn't been there in a long time, either, but if they had some kind of fried chicken salad, I'd be fine. Or a burger. Burgers were always good.

"Did Austin tell you about the principal basically telling him to quit his job before the school year is over?" Megan glanced over at me, eyebrows raised.

"No way! Why would she do that?" Whitney made a rude noise. "That's ridiculous."

"She did. I don't know if he's going to do it or not. I hope not. At the same time, I wouldn't blame him if he did." I sighed. I didn't relish the idea of going into work every day and not being able to see Austin. He was an ingrained part of my routine. Sure, we'd be married in basically two months, but that didn't mean I wanted to see less of him. "I'm trying to decide if I'm going to stay myself."

"Really? You'd leave? I thought you loved teaching." Megan shifted in her seat.

I navigated the Beltway on-ramp and merged before replying. "I do love it. I absolutely feel like it's what God called me to do. But that doesn't mean I have to stay in a public school. There are all kinds of places to be a teacher."

"Like a certain learning center opening soon?" Whitney patted my shoulder. "Then you and Austin would be together twenty-four seven. I have to say, I'm a fan of that myself."

"You like hanging out with Austin?" Megan teased.

"You're a laugh riot today, aren't you?" In the rearview mirror, I caught a glimpse of Whitney sticking her tongue out.

"I'm jealous. My two besties are going to be old married

ladies and I haven't been on a date in forever." Megan sighed and sank down in her seat some.

"What about that guy—oh, what's his name? He comes into the bookstore every time I'm there at least. Has about ten million questions for you." Whitney rubbed her hands together. "Ahh, why can't I come up with his name?"

"Not Reuben?" I snickered. "Tell me that's not who you mean. You went out with Reuben?"

Megan groaned. "Look, we had coffee. He seemed nice and a little desperate and I tried saying no, but he kept asking, so I thought it might get him to stop."

"Uh-huh. Did it?" I checked my mirrors and changed lanes to get around the slowpoke who thought the speed limit signs *meant* something on the Beltway.

"No. Ugh. I finally ended up telling him very bluntly that I wasn't interested. Wouldn't ever be interested. And if he kept asking, I'd be filing a report of harassment with the cops. I'm not sure that's actually a thing, but it did finally get him off my case." Megan covered her face.

"Sorry. I didn't realize he'd gotten like that. I wouldn't have teased." Whitney squeezed Megan's arm. "Do you have security cameras at the store?"

"I do now." Megan shrugged. "I knew I needed them before that. Reuben just pushed me over the edge."

Our conversation lulled, then drifted through various inconsequential topics as we made our way around the Beltway to Tyson's. I never really minded all the driving that living in this area demanded. Even if I got stuck in traffic. There were people who hated it—and I could understand that—but there was so much to see and do, I figured it made up for it.

I signaled and got into the right lane as we neared the exits for Tyson's Corner. "Someone might have to remind me where Friday's is though."

"I'll get it on my GPS. Hang on." Whitney rustled in the back seat and after a moment, her phone started telling me to prepare to exit.

"Perfect, thanks." I eased into the exit lane.

Megan held her hand out, and Whitney put her phone into it.

"Even better. Now I won't miss a turn." I followed the GPS directions to the restaurant. I might have remembered how to get here, but it definitely wouldn't have been as smooth.

We parked and went in. The place was hopping, so we ended up taking a high-top table in the bar area. In some ways that worked out better—I was pretty sure our food got to us faster than I saw it hitting tables.

When we'd finished—and narrowly avoided splitting a dessert—we headed back out to the car.

"I'll let you sit up front again since it's such a short drive to the mall." Whitney reached for the back door handle.

"I thought we were alternating." Megan crossed her arms. "You're just trying to get the front seat for the drive back to Old Town."

"Yes. Yes, I am. Deal with it." Whitney opened the door as soon as I unlocked them and sat in the back.

Megan sighed. "Unfair."

"Get a grip, Megan." I shook my head and got behind the wheel. We had to wait a minute for Megan to finish pouting, then she got in. "Are we ready now?"

Megan nodded.

"Yep." Whitney spoke from the backseat. "Do you know what style you're looking for?"

I chewed my lip as I backed out of the spot and pointed the car toward the mall area. This, at least, I knew how to do without someone chiming in my ear about the next turn. "In theory? I think fairly simple. Maybe A-line? I know I don't want a mermaid because I'm not Morticia Addams."

Whitney snickered. "That's something I'll never get out of my head now. Thanks."

"I like mermaid dresses. They're fun." Megan pointed at me. "You have to try one on. Just to see."

I groaned. "Maybe."

Even if I tried it on—even if it was the most amazing thing ever—I absolutely wouldn't be buying it. Because seriously, no. I didn't get them.

"I don't want strapless. Maybe a halter style, but honestly? I think I want sleeves. It feels more modest? I don't know if that's the right word. I don't have any hate for someone who loves strapless—there's nothing wrong—it's just not for me." Other than occasionally for sleepwear, I didn't tend to wear tank tops even in the summer, when the heat and humidity around here definitely called for them. Pretty much the only time my arms were bare was if I was in a swimsuit.

"That's a good start." Whitney rubbed her hands together. "I have a good feeling about this."

It was good someone did.

I turned into one of the parking garages at the mall and started the slow and ridiculous process of circling higher and higher looking for a spot.

"There's one." Megan pointed. "On the right. Just past the yellow Mini Cooper."

"I see it. Thanks." I accelerated a little and hit my turn signal. It was the automotive equivalent of calling dibs. It probably worked half the time.

Thankfully today was one of the winning days.

Once we'd parked, we made our way from the car into the mall and, after one wrong turn, found the bridal shop.

"Hi. I'm Kayla Jones. I have an appointment."

The woman at the desk glanced at her book, and then stood. "Follow me. Jerica is going to be the consultant working with you today. I'll get you set up and then let her know you're here."

Megan jabbed me in the ribs with her elbow.

I laughed.

Whitney broke off from the group and stopped in front of a gauzy, navy-blue dress that hit just below the mannequin's knees. "Have you thought about bridesmaid dresses at all? Because this is gorgeous."

I went back to where Whitney stood and reached out to feel the fabric. It was silky and soft. The drape was good as well and the style would flatter both Megan and Whitney. "I hadn't. But you're right. This is perfect. Megan—" I turned and waved her over. "—do you like this?"

"Yeah. That's fabulous. What are your colors?" Megan reached out to stroke the skirt of the dress.

"July first, right? So I was thinking blue and white. I don't want too much red, but I'll throw a little in. Just not over the top Americana, you know? So this would work. Do they have your sizes?" I grinned. That was a big checkmark on my list that I hadn't even dared to hope we'd get to today. Megan's and Whitney's tastes weren't exactly the most similar things in the world.

"Here's me." Whitney pulled a dress off the rack.

Megan flipped a few more hangers out of the way before taking off a dress. "This should work for me."

The woman from the desk stood watching us with an amused, if impatient, smile.

"Sorry."

She waved it off. "Don't be. We just got that in this week. I'm sure it's going to be a big hit. It's eye-catching and, despite the fact that everyone says it and very few mean it, I really do think it could be worn again."

I laughed. I had four bridesmaid dresses that had been

touted as rewearable. I'd yet to find an occasion that they fit. But I agreed that these navy dresses would work for a nice night out.

"Why don't you ladies try those on while I get Jerica. I believe when you made the appointment you said simple and A-line."

I nodded.

"Jerica should have already pulled a few options that fit. She'll be right out."

The woman left, tugging the curtain that separated the large-ish dressing area from the rest of the store and the other try on sections.

I pointed to the smaller changing area. "Go try them on. I don't care who goes first, but let's be sure you like it on your body, not just the hanger."

"Me, first." Whitney grinned and hurried into the little area.

"You really like it?" I glanced at Megan, who was holding the dress out at arm's length. "I don't mind if we need to look for something else. Honestly, even if it's a different style but the same color, I'm fine."

"I love this. I don't know if it'll look as good on me as it's going to on Whitney, but that's okay. We'll give it a whirl." Megan flashed a grin.

Whitney came back out and did a little spin. "What do you think?"

"I love it. It's like it was made for you. Is it comfortable?" I walked around Whitney, taking it in from every angle.

"Very. Go try yours on, Megan." Whitney made a shooing motion.

Megan scoffed but disappeared into the changing space. It didn't take her long to return in the dress.

She was right, it wasn't as amazing on her as on Whitney, but it was still lovely.

"I like that. A lot. What do you think?" I gestured for Megan to turn.

"Good grief." Megan spun in a fast circle. "I like it. It's soft and comfortable. Or as comfortable as a dress is going to be."

Whitney chuckled, then lifted her eyebrows. "So? It's up to you, obviously."

"I love it. If you're happy, I'm happy." I shook my head as Megan headed quickly back into the changing room. "I guess she's also excited to get out of it."

"Yeah, well. Not everyone loves playing dress-up." Whitney smoothed the skirt of the dress. "You're sure? I don't want you to feel pushed."

"I don't. I love it."

"Okay." Whitney grinned.

Megan came out with the dress back on the hanger, and Whitney hurried in to change.

I nudged Megan's arm. "You okay?"

"Yeah. I am. Promise." She looked around. "Austin brought up living arrangements on Friday."

I nodded. "He told me he was going to."

"You're really okay with him moving into your apartment? Or you guys finding your own place? I just...the townhouse was Grandma's, and I know Austin owns it now, but it makes me feel like she's still here instead of in Florida. Plus, I can walk to the bookstore."

"Totally get it. It's fine." I patted her arm. I liked having it settled, one way or the other. Besides that? I didn't care. There was room in my apartment for Austin. Maybe I'd have to do a little rearranging, but that was still doable.

The curtain separating our space from the store slid open and another woman appeared with her arms full of white satin. "Hi. Thanks for your patience. I'm Jerica. Let me go hang these up in the changing room, and I'll be right back."

I opened my mouth to warn her that Whitney was in there changing, but she stepped out before I had to. She scooted past Jerica with a smile and made her way to a hook on the wall where she hung her navy dress.

Megan's eyebrows lifted and she took her dress over and hung it as well.

The two of them sat in the comfy looking chairs facing a circular raised platform.

"Okay. Again, thanks for waiting. The bride is Kayla, who is..."

"Me." I lifted my hand.

"Lovely." Jerica's eyes sparkled. "Who do you have with you?"

"My bridesmaids. Megan and Whitney." I pointed them out as I said their names. After a little more conversation, Jerica herded me into the changing room.

My eyes bugged ever so slightly at the miles of satin and tulle hanging on hooks in the room.

"Simple and A-line, yes?" Jerica eyed me a moment before nodding. "That could work. We'll start there, at least."

As I watched her begin to unzip the first dress, I swallowed. This was real. I was getting married. To Austin.

I grinned.

This was going to be fun.

30

AUSTIN

"Mr. Campbell. A word, please?"

I sighed and fixed a bright smile on my face as I turned back to Principal Sanders. "How can I help you?"

She gestured for me to follow her.

I checked the time on my phone. Unfortunately for me, there was still plenty before the first bell. I prayed silently as I made my way into the office, past the secretaries, and down the short hallway that led to the principal's office. Even though I wasn't a student, it felt as though I was heading toward doom.

"Have a seat." She gestured to a chair and then closed the door to her office. She made her way around her desk and sat, then tented her fingers in front of her. "I've had a few conversations with the superintendent. He and I both believe that placing you on administrative leave until the end of your contract term is the wisest, most appropriate action."

"But—"

"No. I'm sorry. Your presence here has become a nuisance. Reporters continue to attempt to sneak onto the grounds, taking security away from their job. Last week, one of the tenth graders pulled a knife in the locker room and nearly stabbed a rival for his girlfriend's attention. Thankfully, Mr. Betters was able to intervene, but it's not the PE teacher's job to handle knife fights." She sighed. "And that doesn't even touch on the number of parent complaints I've received from parents whose students have been approached and offered money for videos of you teaching. Or answering personal questions."

Which explained the number of personal questions I'd been asked all week. Chances were high the kids had gotten together and decided to split the money. Then one could film and the other could draw my attention away. Because they knew—or they ought to know—that I wasn't allowing them to use their phones openly in my class. That was a long-standing rule.

I also didn't answer personal questions.

They'd been finding that out.

"I'd like to point out that I haven't indulged this. Those kids have gotten nowhere."

She nodded. "Yes. I've had frustrated parents calling about that, as well, as they'd appreciate the extra money that you could provide very easily."

I sighed. "There are only six weeks left in the year."

"Yes. Exactly. Only four of those, typically, will be actual instruction. We all know the final two weeks of school are usually much lighter when it comes to school work. So a long-term sub versed in mathematics should be perfectly capable of running your classes for the remainder of the term." She held up her hand when I opened my mouth to speak. "I don't think you understand that your option has been removed. I'm placing you on administrative leave. Your contract is not renewed. The sub should be here in another five minutes or so, I expect you to get him set up and then leave the premises and I don't anticipate seeing you again except in the papers."

I wasn't one for violence, usually, but the thin almost-smirk she gave me pushed me closer than I'd ever been.

I didn't trust myself to speak, so I nodded once and stood.

"Don't make this harder than it has to be, Mr. Campbell. I know what belongs to the school and what doesn't." She stood as well.

"If you think I'd take anything from these kids—any single thing—you don't know me at all. Which, I guess if we look at the situation, we can see is the case. So you know, I'd be within my rights to take the two classroom sets of graphing calculators I purchased with my own money. But I won't. Because my kids deserve access to them. And you declined the purchase request every year I worked here." It seemed like a good enough exit line, so I turned and marched from the office.

One of the secretaries called out a greeting. I managed to smile and give a brief wave, but didn't stop to chat like I normally would have. She'd find out why soon enough. It was better not coming from me, anyway. Let the rumor mill spin things however they needed to.

I was out.

Anger churned in my gut, but I forced myself to breathe as I climbed the stairs to my classroom. Maybe I'd have a few minutes to take a last look and collect my few personal belongings. I didn't actually have many. School wasn't the place for that. I was all about the math. And I wanted my students focused on the math, too.

But of course, because that was how today was going, the long-term sub was already sitting at my desk when I got there.

He stood and extended his hand. "Hi. I'm Don Fellows. I guess I'm filling in until the end of the year. Math, right?"

I nodded as I shook his hand. "That's what they tell me. You're comfortable with calculus, I hope?"

"Calc?" Don's eyes widened. "Well, it's been a few years. I'll just stay a few chapters ahead, I guess."

Great. Fantastic. I gave a tight smile and reached into my bag for the composition notebook I used to make notes about lesson plans. Should I just tear out the relevant pages? No. It wasn't like I'd be doing this again. I handed it to him. "Here are the lesson plans. The binder clip is at this week. I have a few ideas sketched out for each class for next week, as well, but they need some refinement. I guess you'll figure it out."

"Can I reach out with questions?"

I wanted to say no. It wasn't the right response. No matter how wrong this seemed right now, none of it was Don's fault. And yet, I also didn't want him getting in trouble. "It's fine with me, but you should probably talk to Principal Sanders first. Since I'm guessing she'll say no, I'll let Ms. Henderson know you might need help. She's great. Three doors down on the left."

"Anything I need to know other than this?" Don lifted the lesson plan book.

It was all I could do not to laugh. Yeah, bud, there was a lot more you should know. You could start with calculus and go from there. He'd figure it out. If he didn't? Most of my students were decent kids.

They probably wouldn't eat him alive.

"Most likely. But you won't know until you know. If Sanders okays it, feel free to reach out. Otherwise, definitely get Jess to lend a hand." I looked around the classroom one last time, then reached for the bottom left drawer of my desk. I had a few little things there—emergency granola bar, a Koosh ball for thinking time, that sort of stuff. It all fit in my bag. "Good luck."

I left my classroom and headed to Kayla's. I didn't want her finding out through the grapevine.

I knocked on her classroom door. Unlike my room, the lab already had a handful of students sitting at computers, working furiously to get homework done. Kayla was leaning over a student's shoulder, pointing at her monitor.

She glanced up, grinned, and held up a finger.

I stayed just outside the door. This wouldn't take long, and I didn't want to do anything that risked Sanders' wrath.

"Hey." Kayla leaned against the door jamb. "What brings you this way? I thought you had a big pop quiz to prep."

Right. I should maybe have mentioned that to Don. On the flip side, the kids would be happy to have dodged that bullet. "Sanders put me on administrative leave until my contract ends."

"She what?" Kayla hissed the words and glanced over her shoulder at the lab.

I followed her gaze. No one was looking at us. I shrugged. "I guess she got the okay from the superintendent. So I'm out."

"Austin." She rubbed my arm. "Are you okay? Of course you're not okay. That's me being stupid. I'm so sorry. What can I do? Should I quit? I will."

"No. Don't hose your students. If you want to come to the learning center full time in the fall, you can let her know you're not coming back next year, but I'm not pressuring you either way. I want you to do what makes sense for you. What makes you happy." I glanced over her shoulder. All the students were busy on their machines, so I leaned in and brushed my lips over hers. "This is okay. I can focus on the wedding and the center. In fact, do you have anything wedding-wise you need me to do? I've got free time."

She leaned back and studied my face. She must have seen what she was looking for, because she nodded once. "I'll text you a list. You're sure?"

"Yeah. Of course." I cleared my throat. "I meant to tell you—Megan wants—"

"To stay in the townhouse. She told me yesterday."

I winced. "Sorry."

"It's fine." Kayla smiled. "And I'm fine with that. Did you want to plan on my apartment until December and then we can readdress? Or I can break the lease, it's not that big a deal."

"Your apartment is fine. That'll make it easier for Charles and Ada to get used to me being around more."

"Please. They love you." Kayla squeezed my forearm. "So do I."

"I love you, too. I should probably go. You've got students and I'm betting Sanders is watching my car, waiting for it to leave." I tried a smile, but it felt flat.

"Dinner tonight? Maybe Mia's?"

Lasagna might just make up for a really bad day. I nodded. "Sounds good. Six?"

"Sure. I'll see you there."

"Text me that list. I'm serious." I pointed at her, winked, and started to turn. "Bye." I tossed the words over my shoulder and headed toward the stairs. I'd make a point of going out the main entrance so Sanders could see. I wouldn't want her to think I was lurking in the halls, waiting to accost some unsuspecting student with a derivative.

I laughed at myself as I pushed through the main doors.

"Hey, Mr. C, you're heading the wrong way. Class is that way." Trevor pointed back into the school.

"Yeah." I stopped and pressed my lips together. What was the right thing to do here? I blew out a breath. He'd find out soon enough. "I'm out—too distracting."

"No way."

I nodded. "Way."

He chortled. "No one says that, Mr. C."

"I just did." I held out my hand. "You're going to be okay, Trevor. Keep your head down and focus on that MIT summer program, okay? Do me proud."

"You know it." Trevor eyed my hand a moment before shaking it, then offering me a fist.

I bumped it. "Later."

If nothing else, that exchange made it clear to me that it hadn't been Trevor who started the whole mess. That, at least, was good to know.

I got to my car, put my things in the passenger seat, and started the engine. Where to? Home?

Or...

I backed out of my spot and pointed my car back to Old Town.

Monday mornings weren't a particularly busy time for shopping. And I was about three hours too early for Megan to be opening the bookstore. I should have thought about her changed hours before heading this way.

Still, I snagged a street parking spot and walked over to the café on the corner of the bookstore's block. They were doing a bustling business.

I waited in line and eyed the indoor seating. There was a little table in the corner that would be perfect, if I could snag it.

No one had claimed it when I reached the counter. Looked like most people were getting breakfast to go. Made sense. Most people had jobs.

There was a little clutch of anxiety in my chest at that thought.

I had a job. I was now, officially, the director of the Alexandria City Learning Center. Or whatever snazzier title I came up with. Or, more likely, Kayla came up with. It definitely needed something better than that.

I placed my order for here and pointed to where I planned to sit. The woman at the register told me someone would bring it right over. I dropped the change from my twenty into the tip jar.

Maybe it was too much, but at this point I had it to spare, so why not.

I sat in on the padded bench seat that ran the whole length of the wall and drew the small round table closer. I liked the corner spot. It was cozy and out of the way. And I wouldn't bother anyone if I made a few phone calls.

I was getting ready to text Kayla a reminder to shoot me a list when my phone buzzed. I grinned when I saw that it was exactly what I needed.

She'd even put them in her preferred priority.

All right, I'd start at the top and work my way down. The first was reaching out to Gadsby's Tavern about the reception. I doubted they were open yet, but if I recalled correctly there was an online form.

I brought up their website in my phone's browser and started looking around, glancing up when one of the café employees set a plate with a breakfast bagel sandwich and a huge mug of coffee, with whipped cream, on the table.

Aha. There was the form. I set the phone aside and reached for the coffee.

I'd had two refills on the coffee and made inroads on four of the items on Kayla's list when a shadow fell across the table.

I glanced up.

Megan was frowning at me, one hand holding a large coffee in a to-go cup. "Austin? Why aren't you at school?"

"Funny story."

She shook her head. "I doubt it's going to leave me rolling in the aisle. Come on. You can help me open and give me the scoop."

"All right." I checked that I had all my things as I scooted out from behind the table and fell into step by my sister.

Outside on the sidewalk, Megan planted her free hand on her hip. "Did they fire you?"

I started walking toward the bookstore. "Depends, I guess, on how you look at it. They kind of already had by not renewing my contract. But today they put me on admin leave."

Megan growled.

"Easy there, tiger. It's okay." Megan's head jerked around, and she scowled at me. I lifted my hands. "It is. Promise. I won't lie and say I'm not angry, but once I got past the initial shock, I'm not surprised. They asked me to leave. I didn't. So they took matters into their own hands. The media's been worse than I realized. I can't blame her."

I would like to, but if everything Sanders had mentioned was actually happening? Yeah, I didn't blame her. And the other teachers—besides Kayla, at least—were probably elated.

Megan unlocked the bookstore's front door and gestured for me to go in.

I took a few steps into the store and waited while she flipped on lights and relocked the door behind us.

"I don't like it." Megan frowned. "What did Kayla say?"

"She asked if she should quit, too."

Megan chuckled. "Good girl. And you said?"

"No. Work out the rest of the year and then do what seems right."

"Seriously?" Megan's hands were back on her hips. "It'd serve the principal right to have Kayla walk out, too."

"But it would be bad for the students. They're innocent here." Mostly. Maybe not whoever started this whole mess. Although, depending on how I looked at it, maybe I was the one who'd started it when I participated in Scott's crazy scheme. "I'm okay. I'm focusing on the learning center and wedding planning. This is going to be good. You need to let it go, all right?"

Megan sighed. "That's really what you want?"

I nodded.

"Fine." She shook her head and started toward the back

office. "Maybe you can help me with the bookkeeping now that you have all this free time."

"I thought you hired that out." I followed her and dumped my bag on one of the chairs in the office space.

"I did. I do. But you're cheaper labor."

"Nope. Accounting isn't my thing. It's a specialized skill that does not magically appear just because someone likes math. I can try and look, but you're better off leaving it to the professionals."

"Spoilsport." She dropped into the chair behind the desk, pouting for a moment before straightening and booting the computer.

I enjoyed watching her. She was a pretty good deal for a little sister. We had our moments, but overall, I was grateful Mom and Dad had rescued her from the cabbage patch. And it was absolutely some sort of garden delivery, because thirty or not, I preferred not to think of my parents as having kids the more traditional way.

"What are you staring at, weirdo?"

I snorted. "You. Weirdo. I was thinking you're pretty cool for a little sister."

"Yeah, well, you're not bad for a stinky older brother." She sighed and leaned forward, propping her chin on her fists. "You really don't think Kayla minds me keeping the townhouse?"

"Really don't. She said as much this morning. Stop worrying and give me an assignment. I happen to be excellent at shelving books."

Megan chuckled. "We did a lot of it on Friday, but check the stockroom. If there's a box, it needs shelving. Don't feel like you have to stick around all day."

"I don't mind."

"Yeah, I might." Megan grinned and shooed me away.

I left my bag in her office and went to the stockroom. There were several book boxes waiting, so I grabbed one and headed back out into the shelves. I might not know exactly what life was going to look like going forward, but at least I had people who loved me to make it go more smoothly.

31

KAYLA

The bell rang and I let out a big sigh.

My students whooped and hurried for the door.

I couldn't blame them. School was, officially, over for the year.

I watched as the last student escaped—I knew they definitely classified it that way—and started down the rows of computers making sure they were all shut down properly. It wouldn't do to leave the lab a mess.

I still had a few teacher work days this week. There were final grades to submit and faculty meetings to attend. And then I, too, would be free.

I'd been praying about what to do a lot. So had Austin. I warmed through, thinking of the time we'd spent together holding hands, praying about the future—our future. It was a good thing there were only two more weeks to our wedding.

I couldn't wait.

I got the feeling Austin couldn't, either.

I bent down to pick up some dropped paper and a pencil. Probably spilled out of someone's backpack when they dashed from the room. I chuckled.

A throat cleared.

I turned, eyebrows lifting when I saw Principal Sanders. "Good afternoon."

"Miss Jones." Her lips were pinched. Her whole face looked pinched. I wondered, again, what it was that made her so unhappy.

"How can I help you?"

"I received your resignation this morning. I have to say, I'm disappointed."

I moved to the next computer on the row. "I imagined you would be. And I am sorry. But I think it's the best decision."

"Best for whom?"

I powered down the final computer, walked to the trash can to deposit the scraps of paper, and gestured toward my office. "Would you like to come in and sit down?"

"No. I don't have a lot of time. It's a busy day, as you can imagine."

"All right. Then I guess I'd say best for everyone. I'll be working across the street at the learning center that Austin is building. I imagine you've seen the equipment. They're making great progress and are on schedule to be able to open mid-September. The center will have more flexibility to meet students where they are, rather than teaching to an imaginary median. Better for the students. More fulfilling to me."

"I see. I didn't realize Mr. Campbell was recruiting from the staff here."

"I don't believe he is." I pointed to the ring on my left hand. "We're getting married in a couple of weeks. Overall, this move just made more sense. I'm sure you'll be able to find a wonderful replacement. You have the whole summer to interview."

"You ought to know that isn't necessarily enough time." Principal Sanders crossed her arms. "You really ought to have given more notice."

"I didn't want to risk being put on administrative leave instead of working out the rest of the year." I couldn't stop the words. I should have. I knew it even as I was saying them.

Her lips thinned. "That was a very unique case."

"And still." I glanced up at the large clock on the wall then back at the principal. "Was there anything else?"

"No. Please get your final grades submitted and then you're free to go. There's no need for you to attend the final faculty meeting." She turned on her heel and stomped from the room.

My shoulders sagged. I shouldn't be surprised. Especially not after my dig about Austin. But I'd thought, just maybe, I'd be allowed to participate in the farewell party that we had every year for departing teachers.

So much for that.

A tentative tap on the door made me stiffen. I didn't want to deal with anything else. I forced a smile and looked over. My eyebrows drew together when I saw Lucy hovering in the doorway. "Lucy?"

"Miss Jones? Can I talk to you a minute?"

"Sure." Maybe her father had relented and she was going to be able to focus more on math than computers. That would be a best-case scenario.

She slowly made her way over to where I stood and stopped. She twisted her fingers together. "Um. I wanted to apologize."

"For what?"

Lucy swallowed and looked away. "I think I'm the reason Mr. Campbell got fired. And you."

My eyebrows lifted. "Neither of us got fired, honey. And really, I don't see how..."

She nodded. "I didn't go to the press. But my dad...he was so angry that you said I shouldn't do computers and Mr. Campbell had sent some information about actuaries home. I didn't know he heard me telling Mom what I overheard that day when you and Mr. Campbell were having lunch. I just thought it was cool that he had all that money and still chose to teach. But Dad—"

My heart broke as Lucy began to cry. I wanted to be angry—it had cost us so much—but I couldn't. I reached out and touched her arm. "It's okay, Lucy. It really is. In a lot of ways, I think it's working out for the best. Mr. Campbell can focus on his learning center and I'll still get to work with him every day over there. Don't take this on."

"Are you sure?" Lucy swiped at her cheeks.

"I'm sure. And you did a great job on your project. I'm pretty sure you're going to have a solid A-minus when everything's said and done. That should make your Dad happy. But Lucy? Don't let him dictate your whole life, okay?"

She nodded. "I'll try. I've been reading about actuaries and it sounds so cool. Mom said she'd help me persuade my Dad."

"Good. That's really good. I hope you'll come across the street to the learning center and see us some next year. At least to say hi?"

Lucy nodded. "I will. Thanks, Miss Jones. I really am sorry."

"You're welcome. And it's okay. Like I said, I think when all is said and done, this is for the best."

Lucy offered a slight smile before she turned and left the room.

I sighed.

It was good. It was fine.

I went back to my office and closed the door.

I sat at my desk and logged into the portal where we submitted our grades. I had all my final grades ready to go—it was just a matter of inputting them. So I'd do it now and be finished. If I took all my things with me when I left today, I could just be done.

A clean break before starting a new life in every way.

I was in the middle of putting in the last class worth of

grades when my phone rang. I glanced at the screen, expecting to see Austin's face. Luke?

I tapped to accept the call. "Hi, Luke."

"Hi. Um...it's okay that I called, right?"

"Sure. How are you? I miss seeing you around church."

He laughed. The sound was freer than I remembered it being before. "I didn't figure I could still attend after resigning. It just seemed like a bad idea. I've been back at Grace and enjoying Pastor Brown's sermons again."

"He's great." I'd tried out Grace several times. I'd go in a heartbeat if the church wasn't such a long drive on Sunday mornings. There was just no way I was going to commute like that. People did. Luke was a case in point. "I'm glad you're not sour about church. I'm disappointed with how Pastor Chaz handled things."

"I think he's under a lot of pressure. I'm not sure we pray for our pastors as much as we ought to." Luke cleared his throat. "I mostly was calling to say congratulations. I heard you're marrying Austin soon."

"July first, yeah. Thank you." Why was this awkward? Luke and I had barely dated. And we weren't amazing friends, or anything like that, so I hadn't thought to invite him to the wedding. "Would you like to come?"

"What? Oh, to the wedding?" He chuckled. "I'd love that, actually, but I'll be gone. That's the other reason I was calling. I got a job in Colorado. I'll be helping one of the Christian organizations out there to start up a nationwide ministry for singles."

I grinned. "That's amazing. That actually sounds perfect for you."

"It is. God is good. Even when it feels like He isn't, you know?"

I laughed. "Yeah. I know. I'm happy for you, and I'll be praying that God has His hand on the ministry. It's definitely needed. If I didn't have my little friend group, I don't know what I'd do. The churches around here…"

"Exactly. Seems like that's the case everywhere. Once you're out of the college class, you might get lucky and find a group for adult singles, but it's more likely you'll just have to integrate into classes designed for couples. Which isn't always bad. But sometimes the questions get old."

I hadn't run into a ton of it, but then again, I had a tight friend group and didn't really go beyond that. I wasn't in a small group or Sunday school class. I didn't go to women's ministry things. And I guess, if I sat and analyzed it, the reason might well be fear that it would happen just like Luke described. "I don't know if I consciously realized just how needed what you're doing is."

"If you'd asked me a year ago, I wouldn't have, either. Now that I'm recognizing that God has said no to a wife and family for me? That I'm content with that answer? It put me in a bit of a spin. There's a lot of work for the church to do here. I'm excited to be part of that."

"I'm happy for you, Luke. If you end up doing a newsletter or something like that, sign me up. I'd like to be in the know so I can share."

"Yeah? Thanks. I'll do that." He blew out a breath. "I guess that's it. Congratulations, again, on your upcoming marriage. I know God will bless the two of you."

"Thanks. I'll be praying for you, Luke."

"Back atcha. Bye."

I ended the call and stared at my monitor for a moment. It was good. This was something that Luke would be amazing at. I was glad he landed on his feet—that God came through. God always did.

I finished entering my grades, checked that they were officially submitted, and powered down the machine. I gathered up my personal items and, after a final look around, turned off the lights as I left my classroom.

I stopped by the front office to check out. The secretaries didn't seem surprised—word traveled fast when Sanders was unhappy—but they all wished me well.

I got in the car and called Austin.

"Hey, babe. You're late. You done?"

"One hundred percent. Sanders is ticked. So I finished my grades and all the end of the year stuff. She's fine with me not coming in again. I feel like I burned a bridge." I didn't like that. I didn't want to have ruined my chance of teaching in public school again. Even if I didn't currently have plans to do it, it wasn't good to lock the door.

"I'm sorry. Should I not have offered you a job at the center?"

I laughed and the worry about teaching in public school lifted. "What? No. I'm excited about that. About working with you."

"You're not going to get tired of being around me twenty-four seven?" Laughter tinted his words, but I also caught the tiniest hint of concern.

"Austin?"

"Yeah?"

"Not even the smallest bit."

His breath whooshed out.

"I love you."

Austin's voice was thick with emotion. "I love you, too. Dinner?"

"Definitely."

"I'll meet you at the apartment."

My eyebrows lifted. I was fine with that, but I'd also imagined he meant dinner out. I had food and could throw something together...but, gosh, that wasn't what I wanted right now.

"What if we met somewhere? I wouldn't mind sitting at a table and having someone serve me."

"That's exactly what I had in mind. Just in a more comfortable setting. With cats."

I chuckled. "Best of both worlds. I'll see you at home."

I ended the call and started the car, then pointed myself toward home.

Home.

The definition was shifting and I hadn't realized it until now. It was less about a place and more—so much more—about Austin.

That was something only God could have done. And He had. Because He was good.

Always.

EPILOGUE

Cody

I was supposed to be paying attention to the mini-sermon Pastor Chaz was giving—I knew that—but I couldn't stop my gaze from drifting to Megan. The navy-blue dress she wore made her look like a fairy from one of the books she sold.

Of course, her gaze wasn't drifting around. She was focused with laser-like precision on the pastor. And on her brother.

Austin and Kayla stood hand in hand, gazing into each other's eyes. If I didn't love both of them, I'd probably gag. It was like something out of a chick flick. And okay, sure, it was good that they got here. They'd been best friends for so long, I think we all saw it as inevitable. Well, all of us but them. Austin could be clueless sometimes.

I looked at Megan again.

Talk about clueless.

When Austin came with me to look at the house I now lived in, I'd sort of hinted around that I was interested in his sister. I'd half expected him to go all Hulk smash about the idea, but he hadn't. He'd basically given his blessing.

And I'd been too chicken to do anything more about it.

"Do you have the rings?"

At Pastor Chaz's words, Austin turned to me with his hand out. I blinked back into focus and reached into my pocket for the slim platinum band he'd given me before this all started. Where was it?

I swallowed the panic rising in my throat and reached into the other pocket.

Austin's head tipped to the side and his eyebrows drew together.

My fingers touched metal. *Thank You, Jesus*. I gave him a toothy grin when I put the ring into his hand.

Austin shook his head slightly and turned back to Kayla. "With this ring..."

I shifted my gaze back to Megan. She was looking at me, laughter dancing in her eyes. Something of how I felt about her must have shown, because she sobered and studied me intently for five glorious heartbeats.

Then she turned her attention back to her brother and his new wife.

I wasn't jealous. Exactly.

When Pastor Chaz introduced Austin and Kayla as husband and wife, I waited, palms sweaty, for them to start back up the aisle. When they reached the halfway point, I stepped forward to offer my elbow to Megan.

She looked at me—almost as if she was seeing me differently —then slipped her hand through my arm.

We walked down the steps of the platform and started up the aisle, and I realized I would trade everything I had for this moment to go on forever.

Maybe it could.

If I could work up the nerve to ask my best friend's little sister on a date.

Click to read more about Cody and Megan in The Billion-aire's Secret Crush.

ACKNOWLEDGMENTS

Getting to the end of a book draft is always a big deal to me. It never seems to be the easy, downhill slide I want it to be. For this book? I owe a huge debt of gratitude to my family — more than usual — because we ended up deciding to move right as I was sprinting toward the looming date with my editor. And so, my husband and boys were responsible for the lion's share of clearing clutter to get the house ready to put on the market. And they knocked it out of the park.

I have to say, though, if you have a big book deadline, maybe don't also start the moving process at the same time. Zero stars. Do not recommend.

I'm also so grateful to my writer friends. Writing without a group of writers is a lot like trapeze without a net. These ladies keep me grounded and help me stay out of my head and they make me laugh and I love that we can share not just our writing lives, but our real lives, too. Valerie, Jess, Lynnette, Stephanie,Hannah, Kendra, and Mandi — Love you, ladies.

I'd be remiss if I didn't mention Lesley Ann McDaniel, editor extraordinaire. I wish you all could read the notes she puts in my margins as she fixes all my various errors—she's hilarious. If we didn't live on opposite coasts, I would want to sit and have coffee with her whenever possible. If there are problems still within, they are all me, not her. Because sometimes I don't listen.

Readers - y'all astound me. I was so nervous about writing billionaires, but so far, you've seemed to embrace my take on them with vigor. And I'm so grateful beyond words.

More than anyone, however, I am grateful to Jesus. He gives me stories and words and sometimes, when it's all done, I sit back and look at what's there on the page and am amazed at His goodness, because it's not me.

WANT A FREE BOOK?

If you enjoyed this book and would like to read another of my books for free, you can get a free e-book simply by signing up for my newsletter on my website.

OTHER BOOKS BY ELIZABETH MADDREY

Billionaire Next Door

The Billionaire's Nanny

The Billionaire's Best Friend

The Billionaire's Secret Crush

The Billionaire's Backup

The Billionaire's Teacher

The Billionaire's Wife

Postcards, A Novel

So You Want to Be a Billionaire

So You Want a Second Chance

So You Love to Hate Your Boss

So You Love Your Best Friend's Sister

So You Have My Secret Baby

So You Need a Fake Relationship

So You Forgot You Love Me

Hope Ranch Series

Hope for Christmas

Hope for Tomorrow

Hope for Love

Hope for Freedom

Hope for Family

Hope at Last

Peacock Hill Romance Series

A Heart Restored

A Heart Reclaimed

A Heart Realigned

A Heart Redirected

A Heart Rearranged

A Heart Reconsidered

Arcadia Valley Romance – Baxter Family Bakery Series

Loaves & Wishes

Muffins & Moonbeams

Cookies & Candlelight

Donuts & Daydreams

The 'Operation Romance' Series

Operation Mistletoe

Operation Valentine

Operation Fireworks

Operation Back-to-School

Prefer to read a box set? Find the whole series here.

The 'Taste of Romance' Series

A Splash of Substance

A Pinch of Promise

A Dash of Daring

A Handful of Hope

A Tidbit of Trust

Prefer to read a box set? Get the series in two parts! Box 1 and Box 2.

The 'Grant Us Grace' Series

Wisdom to Know

Courage to Change

Serenity to Accept

Pathway to Peace

Joint Venture

Prefer to read a box set? Grab the whole series here.

The 'Remnants' Series:

Faith Departed

Hope Deferred

Love Defined

Stand alone novellas

Kinsale Kisses: An Irish Romance

Luna Rosa (part of A Tuscan Legacy)

For the most recent listing of all my books, please visit my website.

ABOUT THE AUTHOR

USA Today bestselling author Elizabeth Maddrey is a semi-reformed computer geek and homeschooling mother of two who lives in the suburbs of Washington D.C. When she isn't writing, Elizabeth is a voracious consumer of books. She loves to write about Christians who struggle through their lives, dealing with sin and receiving God's grace on their way to their own romantic happily ever after.

facebook.com/ElizabethMaddrey

instagram.com/ElizabethMaddrey

amazon.com/Elizabeth-Maddrey/e/B00A11QGME

bookbub.com/authors/elizabeth-maddrey